Whiskey Man

A Deep South Book

ALSO BY HOWELL RAINES

My Soul Is Rested

Whiskey Man

Howell Raines

The University of Alabama Press

Tuscaloosa and London

Library of Congress Cataloging-in-Publication Data

Raines, Howell.
Whiskey man / Howell Raines.
p. cm.—
"A Deep South book."
ISBN 0-8173-1067-3 (alk. paper)
1. Young men—Fiction. 2. Depressions—Fiction. 3. Alabama—Fiction.
I. Title. II. Series.
PS3568.A414 W48 2000
813'.54—dc21   00-059981

British Library Cataloguing-in-Publication Data available

This book is dedicated to
Richebourg Gaillard McWilliams
and to Susan Woodley Raines.

Whiskey Man

I got to Milo one day ahead of Franklin D. Roosevelt. Of course, he was just passing through. I was coming home from Tuscaloosa, where the state of Alabama has its university and its asylum for the white insane. You might say FDR stole my thunder, at least as far as Ozro Jenkins was concerned. The minute I rolled into Milo, riding in no high style in the wagon of a farmer I had bummed for a ride up from Jasper, Ozro popped out of the constable's shack like the seed from a squeezed plum.

"Brantley, hey, Brant, wait till you hear what's happened," he yelled, as if I had been away overnight. As I climbed down from the wagon, he came heavily toward me across the dusty expanse of the Y. Heavily. Ozro stood five and a half feet tall and weighed two hundred and eighty-nine pounds on the cotton scales over at Fever Springs, and nothing moved in Milo that he didn't make it his business to know about, unless, of course, Bluenose Trogdon happened to be doing the moving. Ozro had every pound in motion as he shuffled toward me, making his best speed. The farmer handed down my suitcase and I turned to take Ozro's charge.

"I'm telling you, Brant, it's the biggest thing ever hit Pover County."

I caught one of his hands and shook it.

"College was fine, Ozro. Nice of you to ask."

"Roosevelt's coming, right here to Milo."

"I just knew he would."

"You don't believe me, go ask your old man."

"I missed you, too, Ozro, each and every day."

"Aw, hell, Brant, as the duly e-lected constable of the unincorporated municipality of Milo, I do hereby welcome you home." He hitched his pants, preparatory to walking. "Now come on."

Ozro stumped off, leaving me no choice but to settle for his scant greeting and follow. I had expected a bigger welcome from Ozro of all people. I had been long enough gone, and it was no easy trip getting up to Milo from Tuscaloosa. After leaving the train in Jasper, you had to catch a ride with someone unfortunate enough to be heading back into the hills. Even then you needed dry weather to get over the roads and maybe a little luck, too, to get across the old Sipsey bridge, where you could look down through the gaps in the floorboards and see the river so far below it looked like a green ribbon going among the boulders. Everything worth a damn either stopped at Jasper, like the good roads and steady bridges and electric lights, or went around us, like the main north-south train lines. The Tennessee and Georgia line from Memphis to Atlanta did run through Milo, but the T&G hardly counted, since it couldn't carry you south to the places where things get done for you or to you in Alabama.

Ozro and I climbed steps under a sign that said GOOD NEIGHBOR MERCANTILE, B. B. LASTER, PROP. and entered the long dim store. The prop., who was selling something to a small boy at the rear of the store, saw us enter, pulled the crank on the National Cash Register, making bells ring, and gave me my welcome.

" 'For this my son was dead, and is alive again; he was lost and is found. And they began to be merry,' " said B. B. Laster. "Luke, the fifteenth chapter, verse twenty-four."

That was a trick my father had, quoting scripture to fit the occasion every time he rang up a sale. Back when I was a kid, the farmers and Saturday loafers used to line up a dozen at a time, making nickle and penny purchases, trying to run Poppa dry. He was famous as an unstumpable Bible man. The little boy headed for the door, passing us as we went down the long corridor of shelves toward the back counter where my father waited.

"So I'm the prodigal son," I said.

"No, what you are is the first Laster ever to finish college," he said. "Ever to go for that matter."

It was true. Before me, no Laster had ever left home unless the government made him. They had made my father go to France, where he fought the War but did not, I'll wager, consort with low women.

"Tell him," Ozro demanded. "Tell him right now, B. B."

"Ozro," my father said patiently, "in case you didn't notice, this here is my son that I have not seen for two years."

He just stood there beaming at me, his eyes shiny. I had not been fair to him, staying gone so long. I had even stayed on two months after graduation, writing Poppa that I had been chosen to do some special research for one of my professors. This was not exactly the truth, but then, what is, exactly? I handed him my diploma. He put it in the safe, said it was a valuable family document.

"God bless you, son," he said suddenly. "For being home, for doing good down there and being home."

"Now, y'all got that over, you tell him about tomorrow, B. B.," Ozro butted in.

It was just as well. I didn't know what else to say to Poppa.

"What's got Ozro topping cotton, son, is that Roosevelt's coming through here on the T&G line on his way down to his place in Warm Springs. The other day Ozro got a letter from Congressman Will Bankhead's office saying the train might stop over here a minute or two. Mr. Will and Senator John Bankhead aim to get aboard the train up at the Tennessee line."

"Oh, they gwine stop it all right." Ozro stomped over to the drink box and got a strawberry soda. "That 'might' is just some of that roundabout Washington talk."

3

"The letter said they *might* stop *if* they had time," my father cautioned.

"That's not so roundabout," I said. "I wouldn't stand between the tracks to welcome them, Ozro."

"B. B., tell this pup of yourn that if that train don't stop and if I don't make me a little speech and then if Mr. Roosevelt don't make him a little speech, maybe say 'Thank you, Constable Jenkins, you got yourself a fine town here and I'm counting on your support' and like that, if that don't happen just like I'm telling it, there ain't no dogs in Georgia. Tell his young ass that, by God."

Ozro turned the soda up and sucked it dry in one long pull.

"That's just what Franklin D. Roosevelt needs," I said, "the support of a fat hillbilly constable who condones the poaching of the King's deer and no telling what else."

The poaching of the King's deer was an old private joke between Ozro and me, but when I mentioned it, he just scowled and went over to rack his empty.

"Or maybe he just wants to see if he can work a little deal of some kind with Bluenose," I said. "That's probably the only reason he's coming through, just to get Bluenose to ask his customers to vote for Roosevelt. That ought to just about carry north Alabama for him."

"Don't make no Bluenose Trogdon jokes to me," Ozro snapped. "You wouldn't think it was so funny if you had to put up with that crazy son of a bitch the way I do."

"That's about enough cussing in my store," Poppa said.

"Well, I'm sorry, B. B., but there ain't no other way to put it. The son of a bitch has gone crazy as a bess-bug, roaring around drunk all the time, not paying a bit of mind to what folks think."

"Sounds about the same to me," I said. "You don't exactly expect a whiskey man to be a sterling example to the community."

"I don't know nothing about no whiskey. I just know a wild man when I see one."

4

"Well, I reckon I'll see for myself tomorrow."

"I reckon you won't. One thing you nor Franklin D. Roosevelt nor nobody else won't see tomorrow is Bluenose Trogdon."

"Why's that?"

"Never you mind. You just hush up before you talk yourself out of a chance to shake the hand of Franklin D. Roosevelt."

"I'm not interested," I said. "I'm a Hoover man myself."

"A *Hoover* man!" Ozro's good spirits revived immediately. "Well, son, if you are, you're the onliest one in Pover County that Palos and Altos engineer ain't starved some sense into. I got to make my rounds with that one. B. B. Laster, the biggest Democrat in seven states, done raised hisself a Hoover man."

My father laughed. "Walk Ozro out, son, and see if you can stop him from spreading scandal on the family. I'll be on to the house directly after closing time."

I picked up my suitcase and followed Ozro down the steps. We stood blinking in the afternoon sun slanting at us from above Bealey Hibbert's store across the road.

"No fooling, Brant, it's good to have you home," Ozro said. "You was just kidding about Hoover, wasn't you?"

"Sure I was. But you tell me what Hoover's done to us that your fine brother Democrats in Montgomery didn't do fifty years ago."

Ozro looked flustered. "I ain't saying we ever got justice from Montgomery, but if it wasn't for folks like me and your daddy and Judge Coxwell over in Fever Springs, we wouldn't nevera had what little we have got out of Montgomery. You think we got it rough here, just take a ride on up the road to Winston County, in case you've forgot what it looks like. If them bastards up there would ever quit going Republican, we'd all be a heap better off. They're a plague on this whole section."

"Sure they are, Ozro." I clapped him on the shoulder. "I'd just as soon be a Democrat as anything else. I don't study politics these days." Which was true enough at that moment. But in my

5

time at the University, I had studied politics enough to know that when it comes to who gets what, there are no accidents. If we got a touch more than Winston County, it was only because we had gone a little less deep into the same historical mistake that all the hill country made. That was the way I liked to think of it—our Historical Mistake.

"Well, now you ain't going to miss the e-vent, are you, Brant? You coming down to the tracks tomorrow?"

"I wouldn't miss it. It's not every day you get to see Ozro Jenkins *and* Franklin D. Roosevelt. I'm betting you wind up secretary of agriculture after he gets a look at that belly."

"There's somebody else going to be there you'll be wanting to see more than Franklin D. Roosevelt," Ozro said.

"Who would that be?"

"How many other folks you know just got back to Milo from college?"

"Oh, Blake."

"Oh, Blake! Boy, this is Ozro Jenkins you're talking to, not some professor you can fool into thinking you got good sense. I was over to the post office this morning, and Miss Sarahgrace done told me and everybody else y'all coming back to get married."

"You ought to know better than to believe a Republican," I said.

Ozro laughed. Folks used to say Sarahgrace Gilliland, a spinster lady, must have converted Republican because she held on to her post-mistress job after Hoover was elected.

"She'll be changing back come November," Ozro said. "Meantime, I reckon she's the only Republican I would believe."

"You better not believe that," I said. "Maybe Blake wants to marry somebody else. Maybe I do."

"Maybe she does," Ozro said, "which is why you better marry her while you got the chance. Girl like that, I reckon she's had a power of folks want to marry her."

A power. It was an apt term on Ozro's part, if not in that application. Power was what Blake had all right, and what I had had over her once, a power that was almost magical. Mine had slipped, but I feared she still had the power to pull me back into a torment I had escaped only by the hardest and then barely. Even now, after more than two years, wanting her was a current in my life against which I swam steadily. It was not something I wanted to talk over with Ozro Jenkins. I set my suitcase down and stretched, giving myself time to come up with something else to talk—and think—about.

"Ozro, what makes you so sure Bluenose won't show up tomorrow? He's not in trouble with the Revenue agents, is he?"

"No, I couldn't be that lucky. I just caught him sober one day and got his solemn promise that he wouldn't come down to the tracks. Bluenose's got more than his share of faults, but going back on his word to me ain't one of them. I cain't afford no hoorah when Roosevelt stops."

"I'm just not believing Bluenose has gone all that bad until I see it for myself."

"Listen, you take a piece of advice from the round man. So, make that two pieces. One, you marry Blake King if she'll have you. Two, stand yourself clear of Bluenose Trogdon."

"Ozro, that's the main reason I went to college. Just to learn enough so I could start ignoring your advice."

Ozro snorted and started off toward his shack, then stopped and turned back to face me. He crossed his arms and they rested atop his belly as if on a table top.

"Here's some more for you to ignore," he said. "Don't be making that poaching joke in front of your poppa no more unless you want to get figured out in a hurry. B. B. Laster may be a Baptist, but he ain't dumb in no other way."

CHAPTER TWO

What's all this crowd, the Brantley Laster Homecoming Committee?"

The voice came from behind me, familiar and ironic. I turned around, looked down at her.

"Well, there you are," I said, caught in the rise of memories. She was squinting up into the sun, one hand lifted to shield her eyes. I felt caught in some kind of poured-in-glass memory scene; I saw each detail of her with a magnified, suspended clarity—the first smile in so long a time breaking over me, the clean fine lines of her face, the way her uplifted arm stretched her dress across her body.

"I guess you two own that platform." The hand came away from her forehead. She extended it toward me to be helped up.

"It takes Ozro's permission to get up here," I said. "I wouldn't want to break any rules."

"I don't remember that about you." She was still smiling, as if our memories were something to talk about.

"What in hell's the matter with you?" said Ozro, who came rushing from the other end of the platform as soon as he saw Blake standing there. He took her hand and pulled her up.

"He says he didn't want to break any of your rules, Ozro," Blake said, standing between us now.

"Just struck plumb crazy by the sight of you, if you ask me. Didn't I tell you she'd be here, boy?"

Whiskey Man

"Why don't you go and agitate the crowd some more?" I told him.

Ozro grinned, stomped off to the other end of the railroad loading dock he had commandeered as the speaker's stand, and busied himself trying to chase away the folks who had ganged up around the shed because he kept saying what an important place it was.

"So you came down here to see me." Blake was smiling at me again, giving me her look.

"I came to see Franklin D. Roosevelt," I said. "You just happened to be here, like bad weather."

"You aren't going to make this very easy, are you?" She did not sound surprised or disturbed. She said this and then stood there looking at me, her head tilted, lips parted a little.

"Make what easy, Blake?"

"The fact that I came back to Milo to see you. That's the only reason I *would* come back to this place."

"Don't start that shit," I said.

"Don't be one. Give it a chance."

"For what? You don't think you can come back and make everything all right, just like that, do you?"

"That's what I think," she said. "I want to talk to you about it."

"This isn't a good place."

I indicated the crowd with a sweep of my arm and then turned back toward the tracks. Up and down, as far as you could see, people lined both sides. Farmers, their drudged-out wives, children, old people propped up in kitchen chairs, all waited patiently in the rising heat, waited in defeated silence for one brief look at this man with the strange name and the promises. I want to tell the truth. I had had it pretty easy compared to the people lining those tracks. At the University, I had never lived like the rich boys, but Poppa somehow kept a little money coming all the time I was there. So even though I knew what was happening,

9

being in college had been a kind of insulation, and it was a shock to see for myself that our people, who were used to being poor, had crossed over into another thing.

But I want to tell the whole truth. I was not at that moment worrying so hard about the Depression. For now, Blake stood there beside me, stood there foreign and fierce in her—well, there was no other word—in her beauty. I was stuck in the memory of that, how all the time we were growing up, inseparable in the truest way, I could never believe my luck in having someone like her love me. It was a good thing not to have believed in, my luck, for it did not last.

"Where?" she said.

"Where is what?" I had lost the thread of our conversation.

"A good place to talk, of course."

Ozro came hustling back toward us from the other end of the platform.

"Hey, Blake, you want to hear the speech Brant wants me to make for Roosevelt?"

"No, Ozro."

"I don't know any places," I told her.

"Aw, come on, Blake," Ozro insisted. "I want you to read this little old speech Brant says I got to use instead of this good-un I wrote last night."

"Use Brant's," she said, never taking her eyes off me. "I want to talk to you about what you're doing, your plans. We've been out of touch a long time."

"Didn't they teach you about repeating the mistakes of history over there at Agnes Scott?"

"Didn't they educate any of the hillbilly out of you at Alabama?"

"Tuscaloosa's not Atlanta," I said.

"Aren't you getting tired of this?" Blake had sensed, probably before I knew it myself, that I was going to give in to her, that I was only spewing a little venom from my giant supply.

"All right," I said. "We'll go for a walk tonight. About eight."

"A walk in Milo, like old times," she said. She reached out and touched the back of my hand with quick, dry fingers. "Good."

I heard Ozro moan. "Oh, Lord, I don't need this. He promised me faithful."

Ozro was staring off up the tracks toward the west and what he saw was Bluenose Trogdon strolling in like a man on parade, walking between the rails and hitting every other crosstie in that lanky stride of his. Bluenose was weaving enough to let you know that he wasn't too far from his last drink, and he was hoorahing folks in the crowd as he passed along the tracks. He was carrying something under his arm; as he drew closer, I could see it was a live chicken, although whether hen or rooster I couldn't make out. Just to look at him, I couldn't tell that he had changed for the bad so much as Ozro said. I mean Bluenose Trogdon was the kind of man who could show up at a political rally with a chicken under his arm without necessarily surprising anybody who knew him.

"He doesn't look so dangerous to me, Ozro," I said.

"Give him time. I'll bet you ain't never seen him this drunked up in public before."

"I'll grant you that," I said. Bluenose, although known for the whiskey man he was, had always been pretty discreet about public drinking.

"Well, I don't see how anybody carrying a chicken around can cause too much trouble," Blake said.

Ozro wouldn't be comforted. He just stood there glaring at Bluenose. It didn't help his spirits any when Bluenose got close enough for us to hear what he was saying to the crowd. He was picking out the big Prohibition folks and carrying them high. About fifty yards down the track from us, Bluenose reeled to a halt in front of Bealey Hibbert, Poppa's competitor.

"How you doing, Bealey?" Bluenose yelled. "You let me know when you need another delivery, you hear?"

Poor old Hibbert, a big Methodist, looked like he'd been poleaxed in the privates. Mrs. Hibbert swelled up like a mad goose, all puffed out with sudden suspicion of Bealey, a man who wouldn't take a drink at gunpoint.

"Bluenose, you get off them tracks," Ozro yelled, as if he was really going to do something. "He ain't funny," he added, muttering to himself.

Bluenose didn't seem to pay Ozro any mind, but he did quit pestering the Hibberts and starting coming on down the tracks toward the platform. He was still cradling the chicken under his arm, and as he drew nearer I could tell it was a bantam rooster.

"Look at him!" Ozro fumed. "I ought to arrest him."

"Why don't you?" I asked.

"Well, that's what I ought to do. And don't you go trying to take up for him, either."

Bluenose rambled on toward us. Everyone was watching as he stopped once again and turned to face the people along the north side of the tracks. He executed a low, theatrical bow, waving his old felt hat out in a graceful swoop.

"How you, Brother Pride?" he asked loudly. "Brother Pride Hatton, I'm speaking to you."

Hatton, a Holiness preacher who had a church out on the Fever Springs Road not far beyond Bluenose's house, just stood there, holding his ground at the edge of the railroad bed and ignoring Bluenose.

Bluenose fixed Hatton with a baleful look. "A man'll speak when he's spoke to, Preacher."

"And I'm just the man who'll speak the truth to you, Bluenose Trogdon, drunk as you are," Hatton said suddenly. "I'm going to tell you how I've been. I've been firm in the Lord. I've been washed in the Blood. I've been getting ready to see my Jesus face to face, for we are living in the End Time, Bluenose Trogdon, when all will answer for their days, whether they be cloaked in grace or all smutty with sin, hallelujah."

Hatton's voice picked up that steady rise-and-fall Holy Roller rhythm even as he spoke those few words. "Witness," shouted someone back in the crowd. "Amen," said another voice. Bluenose for his part stood upright and smiled a mean little smile.

"Ain't that a Holy Roller preacher for you?" Bluenose said. He cocked his free hand against his waist and, still cradling the chicken in the other arm, took a couple of fast little steps in a quick, comic dance which ended as he slapped his thigh. "You ask for a hello and what you get is a sermon. Well, Preacher, you answer me this: Does your Jesus love a hypocrite?"

"I ain't never had to worry about that, Brother Trogdon."

"Well, you sure God ought to," Bluenose shouted, "because you're as big a one as ever has been in these parts. You and about half of these folks out here." Bluenose looked around. "I want all of you dry folks to hear this, all you people that's always blowing and going on about whiskey, all of you folks that said the Prohibition was just going to be the best thing since daylight. None of y'all got any business here. Mr. Franklin D. Roosevelt, in case you ain't heard, is for the repeal. He's my candidate. All you dries ain't got the first speck of business here. Go find yourself some Prohibition man to vote for. How come you're down here for a whiskey man's candidate, Preacher, if you ain't no hypocrite?"

"Brother Trogdon, the repeal, if it comes, ain't going to make your kind of whiskey legal, and the repeal, if it comes, ain't going to make Pover County wet. We'll just vote it dry again like we did before the Prohibition. That's because most people in this county are like your good wife, people that try to follow the Lord's will and His way, people that love Jesus and hate the Devil and his old whiskey. Now, you can revile me and you can walk the public roads all over the county just a'shouting your blasphemy, and I'm still going to pray for you because the Lord wants Sister Elmira to have a sanctified husband."

"Oh, amen and hallelujah," Bluenose said. "Elmiry'll be proud to hear that 'cause she surely does love that church of yours and the way you gobble in the tongues like a turkey."

"Tongues is a gift of the Holy Ghost," Hatton said. "I rejoice in the happiness it brings Sister Elmira and all my people."

I could see the preacher wasn't as calm as he had sounded in that last round. His jaw muscles were working under his red, scrubbed skin.

"Yeah, it's a gift, I reckon, and you done give it to my wife," said Bluenose. "She's got the Holy Ghost so bad she's liable to fall out in the kitchen floor any day now, bellowing in the Unknown Tongues like a damn idiot."

Everyone watched in silence. Hatton might be a Holiness preacher, but he was, after all, still a preacher and not to be trifled with in public.

"That's enough," Hatton cried, breaking into his full preaching voice. "The Holy Ghost is not rebuked, but the love of Je-hee-sus prevails against the gates of Hell. It paves the way to Heaven for the vilest old low-down sinner."

Hatton pointed a long arm at Bluenose, stepped out from the crowd, and began moving up on the graveled railroad bed toward Bluenose, preaching as he went.

"Get thee ready, Bluenose Trogdon," Hatton roared, getting right up to Bluenose. "Hear me, Israel."

Hatton picked up a good chorus of amens. The crowd, weary of waiting for the train, was ready for a little excitement, I guess, and Bluenose looked keen to give it to them. So did Pride Hatton, to give him his due. He was not one of your timid preachers.

"The fiery sword is coming! Angels are going to ride in the air like a storm, hallelujah."

Amens rippled through the crowd again and people began to press in toward the two men.

"Holy shit," I heard Ozro whisper to himself, an utterance barely audible and full of awe.

"The dragon days are at hand. We are in the End Time, Bluenose Trogdon."

"Let me tell you something," Bluenose shouted right back, his face only inches from Hatton's. "Anybody believes that hooting, hollering pack of lies you preach ain't got sense enough to go to Heaven. But you let Bluenose Trogdon get ahold of you just right and I'll thrash plenty of sense into your sorry hide."

The breath went out of the crowd and came back in a faint, outraged murmur, a sound like water running loosely over rocks. Hatton raised his face to the sky, his eyes closed, lips working furiously in silent prayer.

"Go get Bluenose," I told Ozro, taunting him. "This is your last chance to stop him."

"I can't do nothing with him, Brant. You know that."

"Some constable."

"Well, I made him promise not to come. What else can I do?"

"Your job," I said, "keeping the peace."

"Why don't *you* go get him if you think it's so easy?" Blake said.

"I don't get paid for it."

I jumped down and stepped out on the railroad tracks. Bluenose was turned away from me, still eyeballing the preacher, so I covered the short distance between us without him seeing me.

"A man could look like a damn fool walking around with a rooster under his arm," I said.

Bluenose spun around. "Hell, I thought I spied you standing up there, Brantley." He shifted the rooster from his right to his left arm and shook hands with me. "This ain't no ordinary rooster you're looking at. This is a genuine fighting cock. Bought him off'n Carther Rooks at a big rippit over at his place last night." Bluenose stroked the little rooster with his hand, as relaxed as if Hatton, who stood maybe two feet behind him, did not exist. "Course, I'll tell you the truth, I ain't got no stomach for making a rooster fight like those fellows over at Carther's. I just took this one cause he was pretty. You want him?"

"No," I said, "what I want is for you to come over here and talk to Blake and me."

"Well, actually, I was planning on speaking some more with

my wife's preacher." Bluenose glanced over his shoulder at Hatton. "I reckon I'm going to whip him."

"Come on, forget him. Blake's just jumping up and down to
talk to you."

"Well, all right. I reckon I can deal with him some other time."

Bluenose came on without another look at Hatton. We left the
preacher standing in the middle of the tracks, flush faced and a
little stupefied, as if he didn't know whether to be mad for getting cut off in mid-sermon or glad for having missed a thrashing. I
could see by this time that this was no fresh drunk Bluenose was
carrying, for he had passed over into that state of embalmed
lucidity in which high good humor and anger are interchange-
able, one mood following the other on the instant. That was
lucky for all of us, I figured, for otherwise I doubt I could have
lured Bluenose away from the preacher.

Ozro, of course, jumped him as soon as we got within earshot.
He was just full of authority, now that everything was under
control.

"I'd like to know what you're doing here," he said.

"Well, I come to see Mr. Franklin D. Roosevelt like everybody
else. I don't figure all these other folks turned out just to see you,
Ozro."

"You broke your promise," Ozro said as we reached the platform. "You promised me faithful you wouldn't show up today."

Bluenose laughed. "Was that what I promised you? I swear, I
knew I promised you something, but I was thinking it was to
bring you an extra jug of whiskey this month."

"Don't be talking that scandal around me," Ozro snapped, jerking his head around to see if anybody had heard Bluenose.

I started climbing up on the platform, and Bluenose grabbed
one of the support posts and made ready to pull himself up, too.
Ozro took hold of Bluenose's arm at the wrist.

"No, you don't," Ozro said. "I won't have you up here on this
platform creating a nuisance."

Bluenose climbed on up anyway.

"Hell, Ozro, any town that elects you don't mind a nuisance. I aim to get up here so I can talk to Brant and Blake whilst I wait for Franklin D. Roosevelt."

Ozro gave up his grip on Bluenose's wrist and backed away from us, defeated. Bluenose, for his part, couldn't have been feeling any better now.

"How you, Miss Blake?" he said. "This fellow here ain't your boyfriend, I hope."

"I don't know what you'd call him," Blake said easily. "I don't think the boy knows himself, but there are some few who hold out hope he'll come to his senses."

"I wouldn't wait on that if I was you. Lasters ain't exactly famous in these parts for being quick learners."

Bluenose, taken with his wit, gave me a shot in the ribs with his elbow.

"Hey, Ozro," he called out, "you hear the one I got on Brant?"

Ozro, who had slunk off to the far end of the loading shed, ignored Bluenose and made a big show of studying the little speech I had written for him. Giving up on Ozro, Bluenose turned back to Blake and me, bringing his rough face down close as if ready to share some secret. It was a dark thundercloud of a face—ugly, but ugly in a way so extraordinary as to give it a kind of natural grandeur. The skin was coarse and colored along the jawbone with a stubble of whiskers so thick and tough that Blue-nose looked in need of a shave the minute he stepped away from the razor. And at this range I could see quite clearly in the skin of his nose the tracery of deep, enlarged veins and dark pits that had earned Bluenose his nickname. His nose was bulbous and whiskery and in certain lights actually looked to have a faint bluish cast to it.

Bluenose jerked his head toward Ozro.

"Touchy, ain't he?"

"Just nervous about the train stopping," I said. "I'd say you've been squeezing the grape a bit."

"No, Brantley, weren't no grapes involved. It was corn, you know that."

"That was a figure of speech," I said. "A little joke."

"Not much of one," Bluenose said. "But you cain't help that. The Lasters just ain't very funny people."

"Amen," said Blake, who was enjoying watching Bluenose work me over.

"You've noticed that, have you?" Bluenose asked her. "I don't know why it is, but they have always been a humorless line of people."

"Unlike the Trogdons, who are natural-born wits," I said.

"You cain't fight the truth and that's a fact," said Bluenose. "Another fact is, I ain't, as it might appear, took drunk for no reason. Fellow I know was making some medicinal spirits and he needed me to taste it, see if it was made right. A man's got a duty, I say, to test out spirits that might be of a help to widows and poor little children and the like of that."

"That's a load off my mind," I said.

"I hoped it would be. This fellow I know would probably be real interested to hear what a new-educated man like you thinks of the value of his potion to the healing arts. Here."

Bluenose pulled a half-pint bottle of clear whiskey from his overall bib, took a quick nip and handed it to me.

"Sort of a graduation present, you might say, Brant. Hey, what the hell you looking for?"

"My old man," I said, scanning the crowd. I capped the flask and slipped the bottle inside my shirt without drinking.

"Son, he wouldn't take a drink if you offered it to him."

"That's another fact. I'll taste this out later."

"Well, I'll be damned," Bluenose said. "Look yonder. That fellow is just a hog for trouble."

I looked out toward the tracks and saw Hatton and about

twenty of his people heading toward us. They marched up to the edge of the platform and hailed Ozro over.

"You ain't going to let that drunk stay up on the platform, are you?" Hatton asked. "He ain't got no right up there when decent folks are standing down here where they cain't see a thing."

"Well, I'm doing the best—"

"Don't make excuses!" Hatton wagged a finger at Ozro. "You're the constable. These folks want you to get Bluenose Trogdon off that platform or give your job to somebody that can."

"Why don't you take that job, Preacher?" Bluenose asked. "You can get as many of these fellows as you need to help you."

"I will not be moved to violence, Brother Trogdon."

"You're fixing to be moved by it, though, unless'n you quit calling me brother. I wouldn't be brother to no Holy Roller coward like you."

"Well, Brother Ozro," the preacher yelled, "we're waiting for you to do something."

"Hatton," Bluenose said, "I ought to whip you myself, but I'm going to give you a match that suits you better. Defend yourself."

With that, Bluenose flung his rooster down on Hatton. The bird hit the preacher full in the face, its wings flapping and its feet scrabbling at the preacher's shirt. For all its flapping and Hatton's flailing about with his arms, the rooster didn't do any real damage in the way of pecking and scratching. But, in the nature of birds when surprised, it did let fly a nice load of the finest barnyard fertilizer all down the preacher's front.

"Look here!" Bluenose shouted. "My rooster shit all over this chickenshit."

That set off the damndest commotion you ever saw. Everybody in Hatton's crowd started yelling at Ozro all at once. Folks out along the tracks, seeing the stir, surged in toward the platform. Then Bluenose yelled that whoever caught the rooster could have it, and every boy within earshot commenced cutting around underfoot. Hatton was dancing up and down, making a show that he was having to be held back to keep from forgetting his calling, but you could tell he was about as eager as a man on his way to get a tooth pulled. Ozro was running back and forth along the edge of the platform, trying to calm down first one and then another of the Holy Rollers. Bluenose was having a good time pointing at the preacher and horselaughing him.

Blake leaned over and whispered in my ear: "Welcome home to the country where the life is pure and sweet."

Suddenly, everyone who had been pressing closer and closer around the platform paused, fell silent. Here and there a hand shot out, pointing toward the west. Heads turned as if on military order. The surge reversed itself and people rushed for their old positions along the tracks as they caught sight of a plume of smoke shooting up above the trees out beyond the point where the track curved into sight. The plume kept coming at us above the treetops and then there was an engine under it as the train broke into view, first the engine, then a coal tender and a half-dozen passenger cars. The engineer hit three blasts on his whistle when he saw the crowd. Deserted by his backers, even Hatton drifted off, offering only a last disgusted look at the lot of us up there on the platform.

Bluenose threw a headlock around Ozro.

"Here comes your man, Ozro. Even if he don't save the country, he's already saved your ass."

Ozro shook free and gave his speech one last reading.

"Brant, you sure I cain't give the long speech?"

I nodded that I was sure, watching the train come on toward us. Ozro had come equipped with a five-page oration of his own composition. I had written him a two-sentence welcome on the back of one of his pages. I didn't want him to flounder around and embarrass the Bankheads if the train did stop.

"Hey, Ozro," Bluenose drawled, "I wonder if Mr. Will's got Tallulah on that train."

At the mention of the congressman's free-spirited daughter—a

sore subject thereabouts—Ozro shot Bluenose a wild look, but he
decided to leave Bluenose be and attack the crowd which had
clotted up between us and the tracks. He made motions with his
arms like a swimmer parting water.

"Hey! Y'all get away. Clear this out in here."

"Dammit, Ozro, leave those folks alone and get your speech
ready," I said.

The big engine was coming at us at a slower pace, and for a
moment, I thought Ozro was going to get his big e-vent. But
when the train got closer, I couldn't hear the brakes chafing, and
the pace, which had looked slow at a distance, now looked steady
and indifferent. Ozro was looking at his two-sentence speech,
then at the train, his head jerking up and down as the engine
passed in front of him, moving for the Georgia line. About halfway down the length of the train, a young man in a suit leaned
out from between the two coaches and yelled something about
them being late.

Out to our right, the people along the tracks were waving and
now, for the first time, cheering as the last car passed them. It
clicked past us, too. Senator John Bankhead was on one side of
the little platform at the rear of the car, and his brother, Congressman Will Bankhead, was on the other. Between them was
the candidate, holding the arm of a tall young man I guessed to
be the son who helped him around. Roosevelt looked maybe a
little tired, but there was that big, confident face and he was
smiling broadly. As they drew away, the senator looked right at
Ozro and gave him a special wave. The people around us were
making a lot of noise now and yelling things about beating
Hoover, and I was amazed that Roosevelt could stir that kind of
response in that dazed, beaten crowd.

Beside me, I could hear Ozro yelling, too.

"Welcome to Milo, Mr. Roosevelt. I'd like to welcome you to
Milo."

His voice was lost, of course, in the cheering, and then they were well past us, rolling steadily for Atlanta, and I felt sorry for Ozro. He had his hands cupped around his mouth, yelling out over the crowd, "I'm Ozro Jenkins, a Democrat." The train bore them away and everyone surged out onto the tracks. They waved and cheered as it moved off, the men on the train waving back for as long as we could see them. They all looked fine and victorious, especially Franklin D. Roosevelt.

"They didn't stop like they said they would," Ozro said.

"They were running late," I said. "You heard that young fellow."

"Mighta stopped anyway if you'd held out that bottle, Brant," Bluenose said. "Fellow crippled up like Roosevelt probably rather have a little snort than hear another gas bag speechify hisself."

"Ain't you done enough today, Bluenose?" Ozro said wearily.

"Yeah, I reckon so. Think I'll go get a snort myself. I'm so near sobered up now it's scaring me. That medicine man's liable to be working down to the river tonight, Brant."

"He's got plans," Blake said.

"Lucky boy," said Bluenose.

The crowd, silent once again, was shuffling past us, moving back up the road toward the Y through the heat and rising dust. Blake spotted my father among them, going away with the crowd, not looking toward us at all.

"Call him over, Brant," she said. "I haven't seen your daddy in so long."

"Let him go. He knows you're here, he knows what he's doing."

"Call him for me, Ozro," she said.

Ozro the obedient just bellowed like a steer, that's all he did. Poppa stopped, looked our little group over, and then started working his way toward us against the flow of the crowd. He didn't have much choice.

"I like that, Uncle B. B.," Blake said, flattering him with the honorary title. "You're bound to have seen me up here and there you went, just walking right on by."

"Well, now, I figured Brant would bring you by the store to see me."

"You're too old to start telling them whoppers, B. B. Laster," Bluenose said. "We both know why you didn't come over."

My father looked at him and, to my surprise, smiled like a candy thief.

"Well, Bluenose," he said cordially, "they do say a man is known by the company he keeps."

"So they say," said Bluenose. "I didn't aim to keep you away from these young folks. You got fine children here, B. B. Right kind of children are a blessing to a man."

He jumped down from the platform, landing beside my father.

"That's what my old pap used to say, B. B. Can you imagine the joy to have a son like me?"

CHAPTER THREE

At 7:30 that evening, people had these positions: Franklin D. Roosevelt was in Georgia; Bluenose Trogdon was in the Sipsey River gorge; B. B. Laster was in his house on the Crane Hill Road; Blake King was in her father's house on the Fever Springs Road; I was above my grandfather who was sleeping in Jesus. I was taking some whiskey and thinking:

—That future historians will not want to overlook the cemeteries of America, least of all that of Milo, Alabama. In it is buried Elroy Laster, my cousin, a Pover County farmer who got a job helping build the bridge over the Sipsey gorge and, being unused to work in high places, fell off. He was one of seven so killed, according to a plaque at the bridge. I never saw him. In it is buried my mother, who died young. I did see her, but not for long. In it is buried my grandfather, a reluctant soldier who was drafted into the Confederate Army at gunpoint by conscription patrols from the slaveholding counties to the south. My grandfather, who turned fifteen in the last year of the war, was not alone in his reluctance. The Peace Society was strong in the hill counties because no one owned any slaves to fight a war over. Winston County, just north of us, seceded from Alabama when Alabama went into the Confederacy. This was not wise. The patrols did a lot of hanging and burning in Winston County. In the other free counties, most people did what my grandfather did, which was to go on to the war and surrender the first chance he got. I always counted his action most admirable, an adjustment to things as they were. Since he survived it, the war was an adventure for my grandfather and I think it made him a man.

—That the chief adventure he had was the dog in the road. When the war ended, my grandfather started walking home from Virginia. In South Carolina, there was a dog in the road. Nearby was a plantation house of the type built by people who had a reason to fight the war. There were people watching from the portico of the house, and my grandfather asked them to give him food and also to speak to their dog on his behalf. They did neither. The dog had its head down and was growling. It was a big dog and meant to kill him, my grandfather judged. The people meant to let it. He was afraid that if he killed their dog, they would kill him. On the other hand, his options were limited. He stunned the dog with the first lick of his staff, popped its head like a watermelon with the second. The people watching from the big house never said a mumbling word.

—That this was a family legend. I never saw my grandfather. He was buried under the long, elevated granite slab upon which I sat as if on a park bench, drinking whiskey. The slab's inscription said:

BRANTLEY LASTER

1849–1890

ASLEEP IN JESUS

—That my grandfather was part of what I called the Historical Mistake and what one of my history professors used to call "the perfidy of the mountain north." For a while, this professor was a very important man in my life. He was from Montgomery, and he claimed he was very close to the family of the girl who had married the writer F. Scott Fitzgerald—an "honorary cousin" he called himself. He said that people like Fitzgerald's wife would guarantee the perpetuation of the "Confederate nobiliary tradition" in American letters. There was a time at the University when I believed such shit, when I could have slit my throat for not being from that rich and gracious, mist-shiny country where Scott Fitzgerald got his wife.

—That my enlightenment began the day the honorary cousin of Fitzgerald's wife lectured about "the hillbilly-nigger alliance" in the Reconstruction. He made us copy down a quotation from a Montgomery *Advertiser* editorial from 1870. He held up the fragile, yellowed old paper, said it had been in his family for years. It moved him very much to read it:

> South Alabama raises her manacled hands in mute appeal to the mountain counties. The chains on the wrists of her sons and the midnight shrieks of her women sound continually in their ears. Is there a white man in North Alabama so lost to all his finer feelings of human nature to slight her appeal?

Had they heard my grandfather when he asked for help?

—That I figured out the lie for myself, which is the only way you can learn about it at the University. You will not be told by the professors from Montgomery and Mobile and Selma, who have decided to spend their lives teaching the lie of their fathers, that they were the sinned-against rather than the sinners, that men like my grandfather were history's villains and its fools. No, they will stay there until they are old men, telling the lie; and they will send their sons to Sewanee or Davidson or Washington and Lee, where the sons can learn to tell the lie in all its high Episcopal splendor, so that conceivably the lie can get better and deeper and more like truth with each generation, until finally even the niggers and sons of hillbillies will believe it, and perhaps the gentlemen-scholars themselves can forget how their people had started a war too big for them and had to make other men fight it for them and lost it anyway and finally were reduced to begging our help to make the free slaves keep on picking cotton for nothing. Of course, they got their way in the end. Even the Reconstruction, for all their wailing about manacles and nigger-rape, was not more than an inconvenience. In the end they had had to suck up to the new Yankee money in Birmingham, but they came out of it running the state the way they ran the University, which was why the last road cut, the last river bridged, the last school built was always in the hills, the land of the nigger-dumb white slaves. The gentlemen-scholars taught none of that, but I learned it anyway and kept it to myself. When you do not believe the prevailing lie, it is best to keep silent, lest you get something like Winston County got, something that will not please you.

—That losing Blake was part of my education in regard to the true meaning of the Historical Mistake and how it reached across the years to dictate the direction of all things trivial and grand, who would win and who would lose. I remembered walking in the darkness down University Boulevard, listening to the whiskey dances going on in the fraternity houses. I remembered dry October nights and the rich boys' laughter drifting down with the music from the verandas where their women moved like clouds. I knew then that if I ever lost Blake it would be to that other South, their world of ease and twilight laughter.

—That the best times I ever had were during my freshman year at Alabama, the year before the letters started coming. The train bringing me from Tuscaloosa would pass on through Atlanta and before long it would be pulling slowly into the little Decatur station, long, curling clouds of steam whipping back past the windows on the winter air. I would look out and see the red-brick buildings of the college set back in the oaks, and Blake would be waiting there on the platform, hugging herself in the frigid afternoon light. Then she would spy me through the coach window and run to meet me, her long coat flying.

The flask was half empty, and I had taken just the right amount of whiskey—enough to help, but not enough to show.

I got up from my grandfather's grave, left the cemetery and

walked on out the Fever Springs Road to Blake's house. It was the only house around Milo that had a lawn of grass rather than swept dirt. Riley King was something of a gardener. In fact, he was an educated and civilized man and for that reason lonely, a man out of place, living testimony to the fact that staying in Milo was a habit you needed to break early and for good. I knelt down to pet the Kings' old dog, one of those long-haired curs we called shepherds on the theory that a dog of that type could be trained to herd sheep in a country that had sheep.

Blake's voice came out of the darkness of the porch.

"Daddy wants you to come in," she said.

I heard the porch swing squeak as she got up and came to the top of the steps to meet me. Her silhouette moved in front of the yellow window; light from the window spilled across the yard beside me. The dog stood in the light.

Riley King just wanted to tell me how proud he was of us. In all the years he had been principal at Pover County High, he said, this was the first time that two people from the same class had finished college. He said Blake was going to teach for him in the coming year and that he wished he had an opening for me.

I thanked him and said I didn't think teaching was in my line anyway. Standing there in Riley King's house with his daughter made me feel guilty about reviving the old poaching joke with Ozro, guilty but a little powerful, also. Riley King was a widower. He had raised Blake from an infant by himself. She meant the world to him, and I had spent a lot of years worrying that he would find out about Blake and me. Blake, with that damnable boldness of hers, had never feared getting caught as much as I had. Yet, once it started between us at so young an age, there was never any question of stopping. Having Blake became as necessary as breathing. All the time we were growing up, I couldn't escape the feeling that I was doing Riley King some deep and cutting harm. But I knew this, too. I could have set him on fire and watched him burn rather than give up his daughter.

"Thanks for being so nice to him," Blake said later, as we strolled down the road toward Milo.

"It was nothing. I'm nice to everyone. It's just the way I am."

"I know," she said softly.

"For god's sake, Blake, I was being sarcastic."

I looked over at her walking beside me. Her face was indistinct in the darkness.

"I know that, too," she said, "but it's still true. You were always the kindest, most gentle person in everything we did."

There, she had done it, touched the first tentative finger to the stinging nettle of our old physical familiarity. For years I had been her gentle lover, more led than leading. Losing her had changed that. I had learned that the secret to getting laid in Tuscaloosa was to be exactly the kind of man the gentlemen-scholars professed to despise—to be brutal, a liar, a man of faint honor, to be exactly what their old fathers, by the proof of history, had been. I say I learned it, but the learning was not altogether in my control. A certain rage was involved and that, too, had to do with Blake.

"Are you still nice?" she said, not without a mild, elusive sarcasm of her own. "Is Brantley Laster still a nice boy to know?"

"Don't be coy," I said.

"Why do you make this so difficult? I just came back to see how you are. Aren't you glad to see me at all?"

"Surprised," I said, "more surprised than anything."

"You're not giving an inch, are you?"

"You broke me of that, two years ago."

We walked on down the deserted road toward Milo, walked without touching, as if the first brush of arm against arm could obligate us back into all the old intimacies. It had been more than two years, in fact. Late in my second year at the University, I began getting letters from Blake that were not like all the other letters she had written.

"You broke me of that when I started getting those wonderful letters saying how you were no longer the most homesick girl at Agnes Scott. I won't lie to you, Blake. I quit loving you in self-defense. That was what I learned at the University, and I learned it better than anything else."

Which was a lie. I had never learned it so well at all. But there was no mistake about what the letters had done to me. They had burned themselves into my memory, until I could think of nothing else. I had thought about the letters until I knew I would be headed for Tuscaloosa's other famous institution if I did not teach myself to stop. The letters. At first, there had been only the casual mention that she had decided to go to some parties as a cure for the pain of being away from me. I should do the same, she wrote; it would be good for both of us; she was making good friends, but it was nothing serious. Then, came the letters about the special good friend, patiently explaining how it might be something serious in a way she didn't quite understand yet, but we should keep in touch. That summer I went home for my last trip until I graduated, but Blake was not there. She was on holiday, Riley King told me, with good friends from college.

"It didn't have to be that way," she said. "You chose the way it would be, that we wouldn't stay in touch."

"You gave me a wonderful hell of a choice," I said. "You were going to belong to somebody else, but I could keep writing you letters if I wanted, and I would get back letters from you saying how wonderful it all was. It didn't seem a very promising way to live."

"It wouldn't have been like that," she said.

"How would it have been?"

We had reached the Y, which was vacant now of the mule wagons, Hoover wagons, the few cars and trucks that had brought the people in from the sticks to see Franklin D. Roosevelt. Blake and I stopped walking and paused for a moment to look out across the broad, hard-packed dirt expanse where the three roads met. Milo, our hometown—two stores, a constable's shack, the post office in the crotch of the Y, the railroad shed down by the T&G crossing—in the wake of Roosevelt's passage had settled back already into its high and hopeless isolation. Off across the Y in front of us I could see against the night sky the tall false front of the Good Neighbor Mercantile. I felt in my pocket for the key to the heavy iron padlock on its front door.

"Oh, Brant," Blake said softly, "I don't know, I just don't know."

It took me a moment to realize that she was answering the question I had asked some time earlier. I had not expected an answer. It was not that sort of question.

"Come on," I said. "Let's go open the store and get a Coke."

We drank them in the back, leaning against the cash register counter, burning only a single kerosene lamp. It threw a circle of amber light, steady and dim like the illumination in an old painting. As I stood beside her in that mellow light, I thought of Blake's body, trim and familiar under her light dress, and regret washed through me like a tide.

"I don't believe what you say about choices," she said, watching the Coke bottle as she twirled it in her fingers, tracing lines in its skin of moisture. "Life isn't like that. We were together for a long time, then we had to be apart, and now we are together again. You live each time as it comes. No one can change the past for you. You must live as if it didn't exist."

"That's the way you lived in Atlanta," I said, "—as if I never existed. It's a talent I don't have, Blake, ignoring the past. Not to know everything that's happened is like being kept from some great secret. You not only don't know the secret, but you don't know if others think you a fool."

Blake listened with her head lowered, her hair swinging forward along each side of her face in curving brown curtains. I knew I could put my hands in her hair, lift her face, kiss her if I wanted to, have her right there if I wanted, and that if I did that, all my resolve would be gone and, if I had learned anything, my survival, too.

"Can't you see you want to be treated like a child, Brant,

wanting someone to make everything perfect for you? You have to take the rough with the smooth."

"Don't condescend to me," I snapped.

"I'm sorry, Brant, but I want you to see how crazy it is. Who cares about us? Who is it that is supposed to know this great secret, to think you a fool?"

"You know the answers," I said.

"I just don't see how it matters."

"Maybe you really don't," I said. "I've thought about it so long and have it so straight that maybe I assume you have it figured out, too. Maybe it never crossed your mind the way I would feel or maybe you didn't want to think about it. Look, I know you, Blake. I know the way you are in love, how you don't hold anything back. So now you've been with someone else and what can you tell me except the truth about the way you were with him? And the truth doesn't leave us anything, because when I know that, I can't go on."

I stopped. Just to talk about the way she might have been in other cities, with other lovers, stirred that old lust for vengeance, those old self-defeating obsessions it had taken me so long to conquer. I had spent a lot of time learning how not to think of things; I didn't want to go back.

"Maybe you don't know everything you think you know," she said.

She looked at me, fixed me with a faint, innocent smile, holding out the promise that although she might have loved legions after me, she had never gone with them where we had gone. It might have worked, too—hell, would have worked; I'd have taken her back right then, fulfilled all Miss Sarahgrace's predictions in a minute—but for one piece of knowledge that scratched around inside my brain like the single grain of sand that makes the oyster build its pearl.

"I know enough," I said. "I know plenty of things that might surprise you."

"Surprise me," she said, holding the same confident, patronizing look. And I wanted to surprise her, but to tell Blake what I knew and how I had come to know it would cost more than it was worth. Even if I could never have her, I wanted her to think of me in a way she could not if she knew everything I had done to find out about her.

"What could I say to surprise you?" I said. "You know everything you did. I only know a little."

Blake put her Coke bottle down on the counter and moved in closer to me, putting herself within my reach. I felt myself buffeted by the power she had when she was turning her whole attention on you, making you feel like the only person in her universe.

"You talk like a detective," she said, "always going on about what you know. Maybe you should pay more attention to what you feel. That's why I came back here, Brant, because here with you I always felt like a whole person. I wanted to feel that way again, that oneness I had when I was with you. When I didn't have you, there was always something missing. Doesn't it mean anything to you that I came back?"

"Yes, it means something," I said. "It means you got ditched. Your wonderful Georgia Tech man dropped you like a bad habit."

"We just don't see each other any more," she said.

"I thought that would never happen," I said. "In your last letter, you said you were feeling so sure you were going to marry him it was unfair not to tell me. You were very considerate. You said I had a right to know."

"I was wrong," she said. "I didn't love him that much."

"And him?"

"I don't know. Maybe he didn't love me all that much, either."

"After all you did for him," I said.

"You bastard," she said softly, backing away from me a little. "Don't you realize I could have had any of them, kept them I mean, anybody over there I wanted. You just don't know what it was like over there."

"I know more than I want to," I said. "I know you got ditched by your fine blond-haired fraternity boy."

And I realized suddenly that I had gone in further than I had intended, said more than I should have said. I had given the actual physical description of a man I was supposed never to have seen. Yet Blake just stood there, looking puzzled, and I thought it surely must be an act. I might have saved us both a lot of grief if I had told all I knew right then. For I thought I knew a great deal, and as it would turn out, I did not know the main things at all. What I knew was no more than one thread of the hangman's rope.

"Is that supposed to be a joke, the thing about the blond-haired boy?"

"Yes," I said, "a joke, a little riddle." Thinking she was still lying, I added: "Don't pretend you don't know what I'm talking about."

"I swear I don't," she said.

"You're really getting quite good at this," I said. "Would you like a drink?"

I took out the half-empty whiskey flask and held it out to her, but she had withdrawn into her own fierce and puzzled beauty, into that damnable strength she had. She folded in upon herself, became a rock, beyond me, beyond curiosity about anything I could say.

"I think I'm ready to go home," she said.

So I closed down the store, left it in darkness, and walked her in silence back out the Fever Springs Road, past the cemetery, past the high school where she would teach, back to her home, where we stood in the black shadows of the porch.

"I don't understand why you treat me like this," Blake said at her door.

"You try," I said. "It's not hard to figure out. You might say I know the truth and the truth has made me free. I have adjusted to things as they are."

"Don't talk that way," she said. "It's just a way of making yourself distant from me. You know that you were as free of me as I was of you."

"Yes, I accept that. We both made our choices."

"I hope your choice will make you happy, Brant. Will you be happy being free of me?"

"Maybe I will."

Then she went inside and I went out in the night thinking I had done what I had to do, ripped it with her for fair and all and ever.

Free of Blake is another lie, of course, a way I never was. Even after I became good at not thinking of her, I always had the dream I had gotten on my last trip to Atlanta. I had caught the train without warning Blake that I was on my way, believing like a fool that I could change her mind if only I could see her one more time. The trip had remained my secret; I never let Blake see me. But after that I always had the dream with its images of blasted landscapes flickering past the train window—first the dead steel mills of Birmingham, then the linthead factories of Georgia where the Scotts piled up the money to build their fine college for ladies, next the dreary sprawl at Atlanta, and finally the college itself, the fine buildings, their bright windows shining down through the trees at dusk. Whenever it came, the dream brought back the foolish feeling of finding myself in the darkness outside Blake's dormitory, my only baggage the packet of fare-well letters from her, and only then realizing what a fool's mission had brought me there unannounced, unwanted, a reminder of an accident which had happened a long time ago in her life. Everything was in the dream, every detail of how I found her free and happy with the blond-haired young man in the fine clothes; seeing Blake again revived the dream in all its power, and the memory of it cut like a new razor falling through flesh as easily as through air, cutting to the bone. The dream was enough of itself, but it was also the symbol of much more, for if there had been me and then another in my place, there was the possibility of an infinity of betrayals I had never dreamt of. I had had the dream long enough to know it had no cure, but I went to find the medicine man anyway.

CHAPTER FOUR

Bluenose was standing knee-deep in fast water pouring through a single narrow break in the dam. His left hand rested lightly, for balance, on a mooring line which disappeared into the jumpy, breaking water behind him. I knew the line led to a fish basket sunk out of sight at the base of the chute. The other end was tied to a sapling up on the high bank where I squatted, looking down at Bluenose. Because of the noise of the water, Bluenose had not heard my approach, and it made me feel like a real woodsman slipping up on him. What if I had been a Revenue agent, what kind of shape would he be in now? I rested my hand on the rope. The current had pulled it tight as a guitar string. I gave it a jerk to surprise Bluenose. His hand fell away from the rope and he swung his head slowly toward me, searching for my outline against the steep, dark mass of brush and trees along the bank. He did not move like a man surprised.

"I hope you ain't back already for some more free whiskey," he said, even before his gaze came to rest on me. "I ain't in this trade for charity, you know."

"Just looking for company," I said. "Doing any good?"

"They's a few coming through. I feel 'em bumping my legs some. Must be big rains upstate, the way this river's rising."

Bluenose had more or less inherited the place where he stood, although he didn't actually own any land down in the gorge. This stretch of gorge territory was simply the Trogdon preemption, theirs by right of use and tradition for three generations now, and nobody had ever bothered to argue any different. Old man Trogdon, Bluenose's father, had built the dam long years before, finding a shoal in the river and piling up rocks from the bottom to divert the flow of the river over against the north bank and through a gap maybe ten or twelve feet wide. When the river was on the rise, you could sink a funnel-shaped net at the foot of the sluiceway, and most every fish that couldn't slip through the cracks in the dam wound up in the net.

Suddenly, Bluenose went down on his knees and the water piled up against him the way fast water bulges up around a boulder and almost covered him.

"Hey, you all right, Bluenose?"

He wouldn't say anything. He was thrashing and groping around on the bottom and once his head went under. Then he sat rigid in the water. "Brant, I got hold of a sure enough Mister Gentleman of a fish down here." He shifted ever so slightly and I could tell he had hold of something strong. "There. Oh, yeah. There. I done got you now, ain't I, uncle. Brant, fetch my burlap bag that's tied out over yonder."

I found the bag and untied the cord which cinched its neck shut. I could feel that there were several fish in it already. I stepped carefully into the chute and fought across the strong current to Bluenose.

"Now hold that bag open. I want to pop him right in that bag before he has time to flounce. He's stout."

Bluenose came up out of the water, both hands dug deep in the gills of a big fish. Spray flew, the moon gleamed on the fish, and I could see it writhe powerful and slow against Bluenose's hold. He got the fish over the bag and threw it in. I shut the top and the big fish went to war in there.

"Damn nice buffalo," Bluenose said. "Bet the son of a bitch will go fifteen pound." A buffalo is a big rough fish something like a carp, but reddish in color. Bluenose watched the sack jump in the water with the rushes of the fish. He laughed. "Too late for that," he said. "You tore your ass the minute you run up on Bluenose Trogdon."

I could feel the current beat the fish against my legs and feel them all kicking in the bag. I thought of how the buffalo had looked, as red in the moonlight as copper or dark blood. I thought of the hold Bluenose had gotten on the fish and I could feel its big, blunt head butting against my legs through the burlap.

"Oh my God, ain't it a wonder, ain't it a heavenly wonder that our jug has come through my fight with that great fish unbroken?" Bluenose said. He was stumbling around in the chute, tripping over the rough rock bottom, letting the current beat him and hauling on a piece of sash cord that was tied to the hammer loop on his overalls. "I have found," Bluenose was saying, "after many years that the longer the cord is, the safer the jug is." He kept hauling on the cord which was stretched out tight downstream. "Yessir, Brant, after long years of observation, I have found that if a man will stand right here in this gap, stand here, by God, and fight this river where she's boiling through, if he'll stand here and let his jug out way down stream"—he was still hauling; he must have had thirty feet of cord out—"why that jug will swing out behind him in the still water and ride on the end of that rope and never break. Man wants a drink, he ain't got to climb the bank and fetch the jug. That's the point."

Stumbling around with that crazy balance a real veteran drunk gets, Bluenose hauled in the dripping gallon jug. He held the jug up between himself and the moon to check the level. "Brant," he said, "see here. We gotta hurry and kill a mess of these fish so we can get to work on this fine whiskey. Serious. This is as good as I've made in a while."

And standing in the water, we drank. The half pint had about worn off and I took a long pull, hoisting the jug atop with one arm since I was still holding the fish bag.

"I want to know one thing," I said. "How in hell did you catch that fish?"

"Ain't nothing to it, Brant. I just grappled him. See, when he comes through the chute, a big fish is just a churning against the current, like this"—he made a weaving motion with his forearm—"and so he's just kind of hanging there and sliding backwards a little at a time. When I feel one swish agin my legs, I make a grab. Lots I miss go in the net, anyhow. It's just something to pass the time while you wait, a sport, you might say."

We drank again, standing braced against the current. Bluenose was looking up the river in the dark tunnel of the overhanging trees. "Hey, boy," he said, "you going to marry that girl?"

"I don't know."

"Well, it don't take anybody real smart to see she's got it on her mind."

"How would you know that?" I said. I laughed, hoping to break the conversation off into some kind of joking.

"You can tell. Well maybe you cain't. I can," he said. "I can tell by their eyes, the way they act. You ought to marry her. Make a good wife."

"You can ruin a mighty good girl friend, making a wife out of her," I said, still trying for the easy joke.

"According to Ozro, y'all been what you might call married for a long time." He turned to look at me with a knowing smile, like he was proud of me for something.

"That son of a bitch," I said. "He needs a kick in the ass to jerk his mouth shut."

"Don't get riled," Bluenose said. "Me and Ozro, we kind of get on, you know. We tell each other things we don't tell other people, on the sly, of course. Man of his high degree can't consort with known moonshiners," Bluenose laughed.

"Well, Ozro ain't quite as up to date as he thinks he is," I said. "I'm not studying getting married."

"It's no nevermind to me either way, but if I was one to give advice, which I ain't, I'd say grab her whilst you got the chance."

"That's the problem," I said. "I think somebody else has already grabbed her, grabbed her good."

Bluenose studied me for a moment, then guessed correctly. "Jealous, are you?"

"Something more than that," I said.

"Ain't no future in grudges like that," he said. "After five, ten years, none of that stuff you think is so important matters a hoot in hell."

"I can't see it like that," I said.

"That's because you're young and hot," he said. "You think everything's happening the first time. Well, there ain't nothing new."

"It's damn sure new enough to me."

"Yeah, that's the hooker, ain't it? Well, you go ahead, Brant, you won't be the first son of a bitch drove hisself loony over something that wouldn't amounted to a hill of beans if he'd let it alone, just let it smooth right on out." He made a sweeping outward motion with his left arm, as if indicating a diminishing line of ripples. "Just let things fade on away, that's the way to do."

"Why are you talking this bullshit to me?" I said, more sharply than I intended. "Goddammit, everything matters, everything counts. You can't just forget what doesn't suit you."

"Goddam if you wouldn't hit it off with Elmira," Bluenose said. "All that stuff you just said is her right down to the ground. I ain't got no call worrying you, though, you're right about that. Ain't no point trying to change your mind when I ain't never been able to change my own wife's."

"I thought you and Elmira got on all right," I said.

"Not the best in the world, to tell the actual truth," he said, "especially since she got hooked up with that Holy Roller bastard. She's always been peculiar about religion, but nothing like since Pride Hatton got ahold of her. Other hand, I ain't been carrying off no prizes in the husband line neither."

Bluenose sloshed over and sat down on a rock at the end of the dam. I found a rock, too, and sat down close to the water so I could dangle the fish bag in the current. Bluenose took a pull on the jug and passed it over to me. The river slipped by at our feet.

"Me and Elmiry ain't none of your worry, though," he said. "Trouble with us old drunks, we get rattlemouthed."

"Aw, you ain't old," I said. "Just ugly."

"Son, it ain't how far you've gone, it's how hard you've traveled that tells the tale. Course, I'll tell you, I wasn't all that hard for the ladies to look at when I was your age. And Elmiry, God-amighty, she was a pretty, choice thing when she was young. I wish them Holiness buzzards coulda seen her back then. She was something all right. She made me court her right, but them first few weeks after we married, she loved me like she invented it. I reckon it was this place right here ruint all that."

Drunk or sober, Bluenose was a big talker, but the thing about Elmira had popped out of him with a momentum of its own. He reclaimed the jug without asking for it.

"Kind of a luxury for a natural-born windjammer like me to have somebody to talk to down here," he said after a long drink. "Less'n you leave right quick, you're liable to hear a true and untold tale from the life of Bluenose Trogdon."

"Hand me the jug," I said.

He leaned down, held it out to me.

"My pap died just before me and Elmiry got married," he said. "I called myself farming and I aimed to leave the whiskey making alone, 'cause that's the way she wanted it. I hadn't even been down to the river since he passed over. One night, summer like this, we're laying in bed, and I'd been working just as hard as I could go on making that first young'un of ours. It had come up a good shower—a real chunk-floater, I mean—while we was laying there. After the rain, I could hear Elmiry breathing easy, satisfied and gone off to sleep. Hey, you didn't take that thing to raise, did you?"

I passed it back to him.

"Like I say, after the rain, I'm laying there and smelling that fresh smell from the rain, and I know that this river is rising and in a little she'll be shooting hard through Pap's old fish trap. Well, I eased off from the house and came on down here. I reckon I got drunk and was a little longer than I planned getting home, longer by a day or two.

"Now this sounds funny and I wouldn't credit it myself if I hadn't seen it, but that one little bit of business turned her against me. I mean it weren't no gradual thing either. It was just like blowing out a candle, that sudden.

"She never said word one about it, but from that time on she never had any use for me, just tolerated me. I told myself, 'Well, now you've hurt her feelings. This thing will pass,' but it never did. I thought maybe having all those children would change her, but it never did." He paused, took a short drink. "Shit, I tell you a man ought to get more of a chance than that."

He sat quietly then, cradling the jug in his lap with both hands, his eyes on the water rushing through the trap. "Son of a bitch," he shouted suddenly, "you know what else she done. I don't know if you ever noticed it, but there's an old Clabber Girl calendar hanging in the corner of our kitchen. I got that calendar for her over in Jasper when we were buying stuff to set up housekeeping. It's hanging right where I nailed it, turned to the month it was on the night I ran this trap for the first time after Pap died. She won't hear of me even touching it. I oughta tear the goddam thing down, but I let her do as she pleases and I do the same. Well, that's the story. Here, let's take one more pull out of this jug and we'll get the fish out of the basket. I bet we got a load."

Bluenose stood up, splashed back out into the water and threw his head back, drinking as if he was watching the moon through the bottom of the jug. The line that held the jug draped down from its neck and from where it was tied into Bluenose's overalls and trailed off in the water. He was weaving and staggered backwards, pushed by the current. Then, with the jug still raised, he just tumbled over into the chute and disappeared under the smooth fast water. I watched for his head to come up in the deep water behind the dam. I waited. Then I realized that he had surely been swept right into the mouth of the big underwater basket. The current would push him into the small tail of the funneled net and he would drown, trapped down there. I struggled across the chute toward the riverbank, letting the current carry the fish bag away as I fought to keep my feet. I made the far bank and scrambled out. Up where it was lashed to a sapling, I grabbed the main rope to the fish basket and started trying to haul it out. The rope hummed in my hand. I could barely move it against the current. I fought the rope desperately, imagining Bluenose down there bubbling his life away among the trapped fish.

"Hey, Brant." His voice was faint, far off, and I was glad to hear it. The sound came from down the river and I strained to see him. "The foulest thing has befallen us. I done rolled around on the bottom and broke the damn jug."

I could see him then, way downstream where the trees parted to let full moonlight on the water. Bluenose was splashing and rolling along and hooting through a place where the river came up shallow over a sand bottom.

"Bluenose, goddammit, I thought you were drowning."

"Praise the Lord," shouted Bluenose. "The jug weren't full."

I slept sprawled on the sand like a dog and during the sleep I had the Dream of Atlanta for perhaps the hundredth time. The dream never varied, always showing me exactly what I had done on that weekend over two years before in Atlanta. Each time I saw myself spying through the parlor window as the blond-haired young man, dressed in his tuxedo, came to call for Blake. I watched as Blake came down the stairs in a long white dress. She carried a small discreet suitcase. She wrote in a ledger under the watchful eye of the housemother. Then the young man took the suitcase and they started for the door. Seeing this, I retreated into the dark recesses of the porch until they passed. Being observant and a college man myself, I had recognized the badge of Sigma Alpha Epsilon on the young man's cummerbund. So after buying something to drink and drinking most of it, I took a streetcar back into Atlanta and went to the Georgia Tech campus. The party in the SAE house had been going on for some time and it was quite dark inside and there was no doorman, so I slipped inside and stood in the shadows at the edge of the dance floor. I watched as the young man cheerfully refused when the other men of Sigma Alpha Epsilon offered to cut in and I noticed how this pleased the young lady. And I knew, watching them at their ease, seeing the confidence they enjoyed, that they were all in their proper places here in Atlanta, the capital city of that other South I was learning to fear and hate. These young men, their ladies, the gentlemen-scholars and laughing rich back at the University, they were all riders on the same circuit and Blake was at one with them.

After the dance, I followed them some more and saw things I did not care to think about. On the train back to the University, I had made up my mind to become good at not remembering what I had seen in Atlanta, and I did. But there was no controlling the dream, and it always left me feeling drained and desolate and ashamed, as I did that morning when I awoke lying in the sand under Bluenose's bluff. I lay there for a while feeling the whiskey headache surge and fade behind my eyes, the familiar pain pulsing as if hooked to my heart.

The night before, after Bluenose finished his swim, we had pulled the net and selected out enough catfish for a fish fry. It couldn't have been much before dawn when I either fell asleep or passed out, depending on how you define it. Now the cook fire was dead, the sun was bright on the river, and Bluenose was nowhere to be found.

The place where I lay was upstream from the fish trap, and it, too, was part of the territory Bluenose had inherited from his father, who had it from his father, a Carolina whiskey man who migrated into Alabama after Andrew Jackson ran all the Creeks and Cherokees out. Bluenose's granddaddy homesteaded the farm that Bluenose still lived on, but he had set up his whiskey operations down on the Sipsey just like he owned all that land in the gorge, too. That had been a hundred years ago, and nobody had ever showed up with a deed offering to run any of the Trogdons out.

Bluenose called the place a bluff, but it was actually a small cave which ran back up under the north wall of the gorge like a muskrat den. The front room of the cave had a sand floor which sloped right down into a deep, slow pool of the river. This sand beach was sheltered by a giant arch of gray rock that hung over it like a big umbrella, and the sand was always clean and dry, a perfect campsite. There was even a little brook of clear water appearing from a tumble of huge boulders at the rear of the room and following its own little valley of sand and smooth stones along one wall of the room until it emptied into the river.

After a while, I heard Bluenose working his way toward the bluff along the faint, bushy trail that ran along the edge of the river. Unless you knew the right place to plunge off into the laurel bushes, the trail would carry you right on over the top of the bluff. You could look down and see the water thirty feet below and never know there was a moonshine cave right under your feet. The bushes rattled some more and Bluenose edged into view along the narrow shelf of dirt between the river and the sheer stone arching up to form the roof of the cave. His blue work shirt was soaked with sweat.

"Glad to see you ain't dead," he said, laughing.

"Lucky not to be," I said. "That damn popskull of yours could kill a mule."

Bluenose snorted. "Trouble with you is you never been exposed to any real whiskey. Hell, if I was to die, there ain't enough real whiskey men left in the state to carry my casket." Bluenose walked across the sand to where I was sitting beside the dead cook fire. He sat down on an old piece of a cane chair he had there. I could tell he didn't feel all that sporty himself.

"Popskull," he said. "I bet you know about popskull all right, the shit they sell you boys down in Tuscaloosa. Prohibition, that's what did it. Since it came in, these bastard amateurs have been getting rich making sugar whiskey in them single-run stream stills. Fifteen years ago you couldn't hardly sell that stuff to the niggers in Birmingham and now they got everybody drinking it. Hell, I guess I could have got rich if I'd wanted to move down to Jasper and set me up one of those big raw-shine operations. I guess I just don't want money bad enough. Besides, there's no fun to it. The kind of whiskey-making I do has a lot of pleasure in it. It's like a calling, you know. Preachers are always talking about getting called. Well, that's what it takes to be a sure enough whiskey man—a goddam calling. Take me. That's why I go at my work so serious, especially the tasting part."

Bluenose laughed at what he had said, showing his big yellow teeth.

"Hey, why're you sweating so?" I said.

"Hell, I always sweat when I've been working. If a man didn't sweat, he'd swell up and bust. I got fifty gallon to go to Jasper today. I've done toted thirty-two jugs up to the road."

"I'll help," I said.

"You damn right you'll help, to pay for that whiskey I gave you last night and for losing that buffalo. Nicest fish I've caught in ten years and you drop the fish sack."

"Trying to save your worthless life," I said.

"I tell you what. You let me worry about saving my life."

Bluenose got up and told me to follow him. We went to the back of the cave and, wading in the little stream, threaded our way back through the man-sized opening in the rock. I squeezed through the hole behind Bluenose and we were in a tunnel that slanted up at about a thirty-degree slope. We went up the tunnel, straddling the little branch as we walked. The tunnel was only about twenty feet long and it opened into the cave's hidden chamber, a high circular room which was a good thirty feet in diameter. Although we were a good ways back in the earth now, there was no trouble seeing because of light filtering down a natural chimney that went up through the rock all the way to the surface of the earth. It was a perfect little grotto for moonshining. Bluenose's copper still sat in the pool of diffused light under the natural chimney, and the free-flowing spring that fed the little branch bubbled from the far wall of the room over behind the still. The wall to the left was lined with big bathtub-sized mash vats made of thick, smooth timbers. The wall to my right was stacked with neat twenty-five-gallon kegs for aging and storing the whiskey. The whole place was as clean as any kitchen, and the air was heavy with that strong, dewy mash smell.

"If I wasn't an infidel by nature," Bluenose said, "the way this here cave is made up would incline me to believe in the Almighty. You got your good spring water and you got that shaft right up to the sky for light and to run your smoke out. My daddy used to tell me how excited the old man got when he found this place. Of course, back then, there wasn't all this trouble with the law, so much. My grandpap just liked this water down here because it made a soft whiskey, but the privacy's the best thing about it, nowadays.

"I've seen the whiskey-makers come and go in this state all the way from Birmingham to the Tennessee line, and I've seen a heap of 'em hauled to Atlanta for one of them federal vacations after they'd told me what a crazy son of a bitch I was to work my ass off hauling whiskey out of this canyon. Of course, what I know that they don't is a whiskey man can get away with anything if he just don't remind folks what he's doing. My pap taught me that. Hell, everybody in the county knows I'm down here, but I don't ever do nothing to call their attention to it. I don't never bother 'em while they're ignoring me."

"That doesn't exactly go along with your appearance at the depot yesterday," I said.

Bluenose looked at me and I guess you could say he smiled. "You're a smart boy, ain't you?" he said. "Let's see how stout you are."

He tossed me a six-foot length of cotton plowline which had eight heavy-wire hooks knotted into it at intervals. Bluenose took one of the ropes, draped it around his neck and started hanging gallon jugs of whiskey on the hooks. He indicated the bunch of jugs on the floor and I started loading my own line.

"We'll take eight apiece on our neck lines, and I'll carry the two extras in my hands," he said. "Walk easy now." Bluenose led me over to the tunnel and we started down. I steadied the swinging load with my hands, flinching each time the jugs bumped a rock. At the bottom of the tunnel, Bluenose crawled through first and I handed the jugs out to him. We stopped long enough to scrub the fish skillet with sand, then started the steep climb on a trail that twisted up through the green shade of big spruces and hardwoods. Bluenose moved smoothly, hardly making a noise, while I labored along sounding like a china cabinet in an earthquake.

We reached the road not far north of where it crossed the gorge on that high, shaky bridge everybody up home was so proud of. We hid the bottles in a stash Bluenose had and started walking up the road toward Milo. Before we got to the Y, we cut cross-country on a trail that brought us out on the Fever Springs Road, just across from Bluenose's house. I guessed it to be a little after noon. Across the road, three boys and a girl baby not more than three played in the shade of a chinaberry tree. Beyond them, the big unpainted house sprawled a little unevenly, roof and floor joists sagging here and there. Under the shade of the long porch, two doors and the windows were open. There was no breeze; the thin curtains hung slack at the dark windows. The house was surrounded by cornfields that came right up to the road. We walked on into the yard and the children under the tree stopped playing and, clustered silently like a pack of wild kittens, watched us.

"Elmiry tells them I'm crazy, tells them not to fool with me," Bluenose said.

As we walked toward the porch, Elmira came out and watched us, too. She was slender and hard of figure, not gone to fat like so many country women after childbearing. You could see that she must have been a very pretty young woman, and I understood Bluenose's sense of loss. She still had a certain prettiness now. After all, she was only about thirty-five, but she added years by the bitter set of her face and by pulling her hair into a tight, uncompromising bun. She gave me a bare nod of greeting. "I reckon you're going to town today," she said to her husband.

"I reckon so. Need anything?"

"No," she said, looking out over our heads to the cornfield. "It's a good thing, too, since there's no surety you'd get past the river with it. I reckon that's where you've been these last four nights."

"Three," Bluenose said and started walking off, heading for the barn out back.

"Most likely we'll be at prayer meeting if you come in this evening."

Bluenose stopped at the corner of the porch and looked back. "Give my regards to the preacher," he said.

"Don't think I ain't heard how you jumped him down at the tracks yesterday. How do you expect us to face decent people when you're staggering around drunk and cussing?"

"Tell them you ain't me and that I'm crazy. Tell them whiskey has drove me crazy and I'm going to hell for it." He turned and disappeared around the side of the house. I followed him, feeling Elmira's gaze on me until I was safely around the house, too. I followed him down a long slope to the barn lot out back. All the while we were putting the mules in the traces, I could see her watching us from the kitchen window in the back of the house. After we got the mules harnessed up, we climbed up and Bluenose headed the team up the twin wheel ruts that led around the side of the house and out to the road.

We passed right under the window where Elmira was standing, close enough for her to spit on us. She didn't say anything and Bluenose never looked at her. I couldn't keep from glancing over, though, moving my eyes across her stiff face and looking past her into the kitchen. We were so close I could have stuck my hand through the window, and I saw her calendar on the wall behind her. The Clabber Girl had a starched dress and a fancy apron with ruffles at her shoulders and bosom. She looked mighty cheerful and pretty, considering her age.

In the still, hot midafternoon, we ran a route through the shaded alleyways of Jasper's best section, delivering whiskey by the gallons or twos to the back doors of mine owners, big landowners, lawyers, judges, doctors and the odd rich merchant or drugstore owner or lumberman. Bluenose had gotten drunk again on an extra quart he had fetched from the barn, and he took his usual turn for the oratorical. As for myself, I became very jumpy about the whiskey once we reached town. For the law to catch me with a load of whiskey would be more than Poppa could bear.

"Ain't no chance of that," Bluenose said, "not when I'm up here in my own territory. Because I have learned and operated on the principle that my daddy used, that what high sheriffs and judges and even little old pissant constables like Ozro love is prosperity. They like things to be calm and orderly, and they like money and good whiskey and things like that. That's why I do a little financial business with this sheriff and the sheriff up at Fever Springs and I make sure that old Ozro don't ever go thirsty. Prosperity, see. Me and these lawmen, and all the people that live in these big houses, we're all interested in each other's prosperity."

We had finished our run by then, turned out from the last alley onto the road toward home. The empties we had reclaimed rattled in the wagon bed, and Bluenose had a roll of paper money in his pocket. Sometimes people inside the houses—most often the colored house help—had handed him the money out the back door. Other times, the money would be waiting for him in some back-porch hiding place, and Bluenose would take the bills and the empty bottle and leave the new jug. A system of trust.

"See, the thing you learn in this business," he told me, "the law ain't shit. It's people, the deals you got with people, that count, not the written law. If the law is on your side, if every page of the written law is with you, and folks are out to get you, you're good as gone. And just the opposite is true. If folks is on his side, the blackest murderer is as safe as a virgin holding hands with the Pope of Rome."

Bluenose fetched the bottle from under the seat and let me have a pull. We were on out in the country now, the road sloping down toward the river bridge. "You're too young to believe what I've been telling you," he said. "But you just watch it and see if I ain't right. Some day when I'm gone you'll look back and say 'Well, the old bastard was right.'"

The road wound downhill toward the gorge and we crossed the bridge, its planks rattling furiously under the wagon wheels. "Dead soldier," Bluenose said, chunking the bottle over. It went sailing down in a long arc, spinning. I thought of Elroy Laster, my cousin, spinning cleanly down toward the river far below. I wondered what erroneous vision had led poor Elroy to believe that he could come out from behind his plow and walk steel beams a hundred and fifty feet above that green and coiling river. Perhaps it was just his countryman's lust for cash money, but I hoped, since it had cost his life, he had at least been driven by the deeper, more deadly urge to see the life that was being lived in Birmingham or Tuscaloosa. Before the bridge, the Sipsey gorge had kept Pover County a very private place. Elroy should have been content with that.

Whiskey Man

I was feeling plenty sober by the time Bluenose let me down in front of the Good Neighbor. I wasn't anxious to see Poppa. Scared of him is what I was.

"I got a run to Birmingham in a few days you might like," Bluenose said. "Goes to a cathouse."

"Yeah, I'll let you know." I walked off toward the store. Behind me, I heard Bluenose cluck to the drooping mules. The wagon groaned as he started out toward the Fever Springs Road. When I got inside, Poppa was standing at the cash register, fixing to ring up a sale. The customer was a member of his church and Poppa was talking to him, his fingers poised on the keys. He saw me and paused for a moment in his talk. Then he hit the keys and I saw the figure 73 jump up in the glass window on top of the old register. The bell rang and Poppa, looking at the ceiling now, said:

"'Look not thou upon the wine when it is red, when it giveth its color in the cup, when it moveth itself aright.

"'At the last it biteth like a serpent and stingeth like an adder.

"'Thine eyes shall behold strange women and thine heart shall utter perverse things.'"

"Amen," said the customer, handing Poppa the seventy-three cents.

"Proverbs, the twenty-third chapter, verses thirty-one through thirty-three," Poppa said. He dribbled the coins out into the right compartments and slammed the cash drawer.

"Your daddy sure knows his Bible," said the customer to me.

CHAPTER FIVE

First thing Monday morning I marched right into the post office and asked Sarahgrace Gilliland why she was telling stories about me all over Milo. Miss Sarahgrace, a big, handsome, red-haired woman of about fifty, ignored the question. She came out from behind her wire cage and hugged me. Then she said, "Have you set the date?"

"I don't know anything about dates," I said.

"Well, you better find out," laughed Miss Sarahgrace, "else you're going to be the dumbest bridegroom ever hit Pover County."

"That's just not going to happen," I told her. "No joking."

"Don't try to fool me or yourself," she said, making that flopping hand motion people use as a signal they've just heard a whopper. "Blake tells me different. She knows you're a little frosted at her, all right, but she figures to warm you up soon enough." Miss Sarahgrace patted my arm and went back around inside her cage.

"She's got no right to be talking to you like that," I said.

"Well, I reckon she does," Sarahgrace said, staring out through the diamond-mesh wire of her cage. "Hadn't been for me, the poor thing would have grown up without another female person to tell things to, her mother dead and all. You ask me, I did a fine enough job."

"She turned out just like you," I said. "Head like a rock."

Sarahgrace smiled. "Like iron," she said, "more like iron. A woman best be like that."

She bent over, disappearing behind the counter for a moment, then she straightened up and shoved Poppa's newspaper and several odd pieces of mail through a hole in the wire.

"You keep telling everybody I'm getting married and you're going to ruin your reputation for accurate gossip," I said by way of farewell.

"I got a piece of gossip that might interest you," Sarahgrace said. "It's one-hundred-per-cent accurate and ain't nobody else in the state of Alabama heard it."

"I'm ready."

"I just got a letter from General Drummond. Your Uncle General's coming back."

I let the mail slide back down on the counter. "Not for good?" I said.

"If I had my way," she said, "but you know General. He said he just thought he'd throw a dance at the school like old times and see what happened." She ran a hand roughly up the side of her face. "I hate him to see how I've aged. That's why I keep telling you to go ahead and get married now while you're young. Look at me. I hope you and Blake will have enough sense to do what you ought to do when you're young. Do something and take a chance it'll work out. Otherwise you'll wind up like me, out of bloom."

"That's not true, what you're saying about yourself," I told her, but of course it was. I could remember back when she had been the best-looking woman in our part of the country and how folks used to whisper about her and General Drummond.

"I used to tell myself that I shouldn't marry General until he was ready to settle down, because I couldn't stand life with a rambler," she said. "Well, I should have married him and learned to live with the rambling. At least, I would have had him between trips. I would have had children of my own. I would have had more than I got waiting for perfection."

"It's just more complicated for us," I said.

"You think so now," she said. "It looked so complicated to me. Now it looks so simple I want to cry. Don't be a fool, Brant."

She said don't be a fool, but it was not harsh or meant to ridicule me. It was an instruction, a basic piece of country caution like don't whittle toward yourself or don't prop your foot on the chopping block or don't slap a rattlesnake. I believed in the wisdom of such sayings. That's why I resisted all the good advice I was getting about Blake.

Sarahgrace looked like she didn't need to talk any more. I gathered up the mail again and left the post office. From its place in the fork of the Y, the post office faced south, so that when I came down the steps I was looking off down the Jasper Road, the Mercantile and Ozro's shack to my left and Mr. Bealey Hibbert's place to my right, the two stores facing across the Jasper Road. It was bright midmorning, but unseasonably cool and windy for August, and the wind pushed an occasional pale, rising billow of dust across the Y. I started across toward the Mercantile, where I was doing some work to make things up with Poppa.

Unlike most pursuers of virtue, my father would show a little mercy when he had one on you. He let my all-night tear pass with the one scriptural observation about the wine when it is red. Besides Poppa was busy in those days trying to augur the future through the pages of the Memphis *Commercial Appeal*. Everybody else up home who subscribed to a paper took the Birmingham *News*, but Poppa said he knew Republican writing when he saw it. U. S. Steel had the *News* in its pocket, he said. For him, America had become an elaborate system of disasters and, like Ozro, he knew who was to blame: the man who had given us Hoover hay and the Hoover wagon and who proposed to save the farms by offering, absolutely free of charge, all the Spanish red peanuts a man wanted to plant. "Anybody in Pover County gets his hands on a peanut," said my father, "he's going to eat it."

But politics wasn't first on his mind that day because of our weather, which was of the kind we didn't usually get until October. My father was a great student of the five-day-old weather reports in the *Commercial Appeal*. He had learned from them that the two places we imported our weather from were the Gulf of Mexico and the Midwest. I picked up a ledger from the counter and went back toward the front of the store. While my father searched for unseasonable disturbances at sea or in the cornfields of America, I was documenting that other disturbance, the economic one, by running inventory on what he had left in the way of stock. Yes, strange things were afoot in America and in the state of Alabama, I thought, exercising that sense of irony which I had learned from the literature of my language. Take the politics of our nation—a fat rich man versus a crippled rich man. Take this stiff south wind whipping tongues of yellow grit across the Y. Take Blake King, walking through that dusty breeze, headed straight for the Good Neighbor Mercantile. Take Blake King most of all, the way the wind lifted her hair from her neck, pushed her blue cotton dress back against her, making a shifting valley of cloth between her legs. Take the way she walked into the wind, spotting me through the window and coming on at me, looking like the heroine in a movie. I gave ground, moving away from the window to join my father back by his counter.

"Here comes Blake," I reported.

"Way this wind is, it's probably in the Gulf," he said, as if I hadn't spoken. "Course, you cain't always tell by the wind direction."

I went to the box and got out two Cokes and opened them. Blake came through the screen doors, stopping just inside to tilt her head and raise a hand to shake her hair straight.

"Well, I hope you know I ain't satisfied with the kind of greeting I got the other day," Poppa called to her, all smiles now.

"That's why I'm here," she said, "just to hug your old neck, Uncle B. B." She came back, did that.

"We're mighty proud of you," Poppa said, as always a little embarrassed by such displays, but pleased.

"You want a Coke?" I held it out to her.

"No, thanks."

"It's already opened," I said. "It'll ruin."

She took the Coke and sipped it without appetite. Poppa said for us to mind the store while he went over to the post office. He was missing a bill he had been expecting and wanted to make sure Sarahgrace hadn't overlooked it, Poppa explained, allowing himself a lie.

"Good old Uncle B. B.," Blake said after he left. "He knew I wanted to talk to you."

"There's nothing to talk about," I said. "We settled everything the other night."

"You don't think I'm going to let it end like that, do you, when I've committed myself to spend a year up here in these damn hills just because I felt I had to see you again?"

"How would I know?" I said.

"I believe we can be happy again," Blake said. "I believe you can learn to see those two years we were apart as a time we had to go through to grow up."

"Infidelity as part of the well-rounded education," I said.

"We weren't married, Brant, for God's sake."

"In a way we were," I said. "Just like you and your blond-haired friend were, in a way."

"Brant, who is this person you keep talking about?"

"That is cleverly put," I said ,"but it is not a denial."

"Brant, I don't know who you're talking about, I swear it."

"That is not even cleverly put," I said. "That is a lie."

"Brant, you're impossible," she said. "What do you want from me?"

"Nothing," I said. "I didn't come to you."

"You'll always have that, won't you?"

"Yes, I tried to tell you last night. Mine eyes have seen the glory. I am adjusted to things as they are. Of all things, there are those which can be changed and those which cannot."

"I hate it when you start talking like some damn book you've read," she said. "Why must you always do that?"

"I don't know. I like it, I guess. Finish your Coke. No use wasting what's already been opened."

"Just shut up. I didn't come to get in this fight about what I did and when and where and with whom. The past is no place to live. I'm not going to give up and let you be crazy about it."

"That's not a kind word to use," I said.

"Don't start, Brant, please. Just do one thing for me, if you ever loved me. Come pick me up Sunday afternoon."

"It's no use."

We could see my father coming up the steps.

"It's not much to ask in the name of so much time together," she said. "Say yes, right now."

"Yes," I said, "but really . . ."

"I can do without the rest." She walked off, passing my father midway through the store.

"Bye-bye, Uncle, B. B.," she said.

"Bye-bye, hon," he said. "Come back in a hurry."

He came on back to the cash register. "A real thoroughbred," he said. "A genuine thoroughbred, that one is."

Standing there beside my father, watching her go down the steps and out in the wind—it was at her back now, pressing cloth against her—I could feel hope, which springs eternal in the human breast, stir like a serpent in my gut.

My father shuffled his *Commercial Appeal* once more, hunting omens unfavorable to Herbert Hoover. He sought signs that all over America and in the state of Alabama balances were shifting. I sat on a Coca Cola crate and thought this:

—That if I sometimes talked like a book, as Blake said, it was only because at the University I had become a serious student of literature. In the literature of man, we find a singular record of the mind turned inward, the blunted expectation, the cyclical dream or waking fantasy, the single idea festering until each man

59

becomes his own Iago. There is instruction to be gotten here. Salvation lies not in combating these things directly, but in avoiding circumstances in which dream and expectation may prosper.

—That crazy is not a word to be used loosely. In Tuscaloosa, the chaste lawns of the asylum for the white insane adjoin the campus of the University. The visitor would be hard put to tell where one ends and the other begins. On Sundays, the inmates of the asylum are allowed to picnic with their families under the oak trees of their lawn. I have seen them perform for their guests the humorless laugh, the tuneless song, even the rolling, grass-snatching frenzy fit which sends wives and children, mothers and fathers scurrying with their fried chicken baskets back to the depot to catch the train to Andalusia or Cullman. That was, in its own way, an education, too, about matters relating to dream and expectation.

—That the elderly gentlewomen of Tuscaloosa have made a regular little industry of letting their spare rooms to gentlemen-students. After Blake put me away, I abandoned the dormitory and took an upstairs room in a fine old house, a suitable base for new operations. The room had its own set of stairs snaking up the outside of the house like a fire escape. The widow-lady who owned the house said she had added the stairs to spare her tenants the worry that they might be imposing. The stairway had other advantages which she did not mention. For instance, a gentleman-student who chose to abuse the privilege of tenantship could bring guests to his room without the landlady being the wiser. Thus, the landlady would be blameless in the eyes of the neighborhood should this abuse of hospitality be discovered. Could she be expected to see through walls? I brought as many ladies up the stairway as I could convince to make the climb. I always waited until after dark. I like to think my landlady and the other widow-ladies of the neighborhood appreciated my caution. After all, these were prosperous old ladies from fine families all. They did not get that way being careless.

—That the girl who made the climb most often was a fair, slender town girl who had breasts small and perfect as lemon halves. Before she met me, she had never done anything with a boy. She had her reasons. Although her father tended a vat at the paper mill, her folks still lived in the old family house, which had the look of a place built for governors and planters and such like. Once her family had boasted such men, long before the genetic accident which had produced her father, a dull day-laborer born out of Alabama's old high lineage. Yet through all the years that the father had returned to his gentleman's parlor in sweat-stained millhand's clothes, the girl's mother kept up appearances, for she knew what she knew and had taught it to her daughter—that among quality people nothing is ever lost, that their name alone could secure for the daughter a marriage which would be the entire family's redemption. Yes, the name alone would be enough if sanctified with that tenaciously preserved virginity which is the last and highest stamp of certifiable quality. The daughter guarded herself just that way, tenaciously, for her mother's sake, for her own. Whenever I went to their house, the mother's hatred enfolded me like a fog. She had heard my name; she knew it didn't count for anything. In the way of such things, this made the daughter like me more. Before long she was saying that she had never intended to go as far as we had gone, but I convinced her she had done nothing wrong. She said she would go that last step only with the man who loved her enough to marry her; I agreed that was the thing to do. One night I just up and said that I was, by God, that very man, and I thought of Blake as I did the Tuscaloosa girl out of the one thing that mattered above all else to her and her quality family. In my dreams that night, I confronted the blond-haired young man about Blake. I said, "Go ahead and marry her, you son of a bitch, then I'll have had your wife." He smiled. He cocked his head. He said, "Marry her? I'm only passing the time."

—That I took my diploma in the football stadium of the University of Alabama from the hand of its president, an old man beaten down by the heat. He had wispy white hair. Water stood in his eyes. He shook my hand with a dutiful, cultivated boredom. He had no idea who I was. That night the Tuscaloosa girl lay in the curve of my arm. I looked down her body, studied her belly's gentle sloping-down to the patch of brown hair, light and warm and new looking.

"Why can't I come to the depot to see you off in the morning?" she said, turning her face up to me.

"It'll be too early," I said. "Besides it will make leaving too hard."

"I'm going to miss you, Brant. I won't be a whole person without you."

"It's only for a few weeks," I said. "Then I'll be back for you."

—That the train left the next morning without me. In fact, I never had a ticket. I kept my rented room in Tuscaloosa for some weeks into the summer. I wrote my father that there was important business to do at the University: I had been selected above all others. I kept to my room. I read books. I listened to the radio, heard how the Bonus Marchers were persuaded to leave our nation's capital. I remembered a saying of Ozro's: "A Republican wouldn't throw a dipper of water on you if you was on fire." God bless Herbert Hoover. I listened to the nomination of Franklin D. Roosevelt, heard "Happy Days Are Here Again." I lay on my bed and studied the wallpaper. Its pattern betrayed no grand design. Having been through commencement, I was waiting for something to commence for me in the United States of America, some transforming event, the dog in the road. I waited. I studied the wallpaper. Time did not break into a new and freer calculation for me there.

I presented myself on Sunday, as promised, and Blake, with her lawyer's guile and that damnable strength and boldness she had, tricked me.

"No problems today," she said as soon as I walked up on her porch. She was sitting on the swing, one leg tucked under her, the other extended as she traced with her toe a regular small oval in the floor; one slender leg, extended like the marker of some recording instrument, mapped the course of the swing's slow, hypnotic travel.

"What does that mean?"

I watched the leg, its calf tapering down to fine-boned ankle, the little rich valley just forward of the Achilles tendon. The map became a graph of my unadmitted desire for her—regular, closed, insatiable, constant and hopeless, incurable as a planet's orbit.

"It means we just don't talk about problems. You told me it was no use, that we have no future. I believe you. I accept that, so there's no need for us to argue about the time we were apart."

"Where does that leave us?" I said, angry now, for I had come only to interrogate her about the life she had led in Atlanta. I wanted details—names, dates, places—the proof absolute of the rightness of the decision I had already made in self-defense. I had enough of the story to believe I had been right, but I knew, too, that without her final, full confession, the memory of her would haunt me forever. I needed her cooperation in our final severance. Now, with hardly an effort, she had cut away my only solid ground for questioning her by saying that she had abandoned all plans for our future.

She stood up and put her arms around my waist. "It leaves us with some time together. We can have fun together, like in the old times. If that's all I'm to have of you, I want as much as I can get."

"It's not that easy."

"Yes," she said. "It's that easy. No past. No future. No plans and no arguments."

I looked down at the clean line of scalp where her hair parted. The hair lay smooth and shiny on each side.

"All I want is time," she said. "Hold me, please."

"Where's your father?" We were hugging in front of the screen door.

"He's gone."

"It won't work."

"Why?" Her face was against my shoulder. "What else is there to do in Milo?"

"Only what we always did," I said.

"That's what I want now."

"It won't mean anything."

"I am a grown woman," Blake said, moving out of my arms, looking up at me with steady eyes, gray as clouds. "My father said we could get the car out. Will you take me somewhere in it? Take me somewhere and treat me the way you treat a grown woman who talks this way."

"Yes," I said. "I know a place for that."

"You did fine," Blake said. "Was it good for you?"

"Yes," I said. "Yes, it was . . ." I had to shut up.

"Was what?"

"Just fine. I had forgotten how good you are, how much better than anyone else."

"That sounds like a confession," she said, sitting up from the quilt we had spread on the sand. Blake smiled and leaned down to kiss my face. I felt her breasts hang lightly against me. "Are you saying there were others?"

"Why do you ask? Are you making fun of me?"

"No. I just want to know."

"I don't suppose it matters now," I said. "Yes, I did all right." I said this proudly, too dumb to see what Blake was leading me to. "I had more practice than some."

"How well I know." A laugh. "What did you tell them?"

"Whatever it took."

"Lies?"

"Only if I had to, and then very harmless ones."

I lay flat on my back, my hands clasped behind my head.

"I didn't know you believed there was such a thing as a harmless lie."

"Well, none of them ever hurt me," I said, thinking back to the girl in Tuscaloosa. Did she still wait to hear from me, believe in my return? "Harmless lies are the ones you tell other people, like the ones you tell me. Don't they seem harmless to you?"

She put her hand flat on my chest and pressed down, leaning closer to me. "I never lie to you, Brant. It is better not to say anything than to lie. I haven't done anything that I want to lie about."

I slipped out from under her hand and sat up so that my eyes were level with hers. I took her shoulder in my hand, felt it curving small and warm under my hand.

"That's the whole trouble," I said, "that you don't consider any of it something to lie about, to hide. You've got that quality, that deep division in you. You can live your life in one place and then pick up and live it just as completely in another place with some other person. I'm not like that. I can't accept that. It's the deepest kind of disloyalty there is to have that division within you like you have, Blake."

Blake looked at me for a long time before she spoke. "I know you feel that way," she said finally. "That's why I made the rule. There's no use in talking about it, is there? It's the right rule."

Blake stood up, naked and familiar above me. "All those girls, Brant, I don't mind that. Maybe I would if I were like you, but I'm not." She started walking toward the river, then stopped and looked back over her shoulder at me with just the smallest whimsical smile. "All those girls," she said. "Old Brant just did the things there were to do. Imagine that."

Then she walked on across the sand toward the water, her body white against the rise of gray stone and greenery on the far bank. I watched her slim back and the curving bloom of her hips which were ample without going all to sprawl and dimple. That was an erotic thing about Blake that I could never get out of my mind: the firmness of her body, how all her surfaces were smooth and hard and sagless. She went into the water and I followed. We dived in the long, slow pool in front of Bluenose's bluff. Then I swam over to the bank and lay in the shallow water with my head resting on the sandy beach. Blake was out in the deep part, treading water.

"Why did we never come here before?" she said.

I told her about the whiskey still hidden back in the cave, not a hundred feet from us.

"An outlaw place," she said. "I like it here. I like old Bluenose, too. Would you bring me down here sometime when he's here?"

"Maybe."

"Didn't you think he was wonderful the other day, the way he told off that silly Holy Roller?"

"His timing could have been better," I said.

"Who cares about that?" Blake said happily.

"Not you, I'm certain," I said, but she did not hear me.

She had taken a quick gulp of air and rolled over into a surface dive. As she plunged for the bottom, her legs swung into the air, held straight and close together, then sliding smoothly down into the green water and out of sight. In a moment, I felt her grab my leg, which was lying, with the slope of the bottom, in deeper water. Her hands came up along my body and she swam right up beside me where I lay. She gasped air and giggled. "You've got company." She stretched out against my side, her head resting on my shoulder and I cradled her shoulders in my arm. We lay there for a long time and occasionally I would look down at her body under the clear water, the slender and perfect weapon she had used to shatter my last defense.

So be it, I told myself. I will take her body and leave the other alone. What difference does it make as long as it is good, the best, and you can have it down along the river and on lonely, nighttime roads, and a few minutes from now, lying on your back on the sand with her sitting down on you, sitting up there looking down at you, looking down at your hands on her body, then leaning down hard on your hands and sitting down and then up and then down again and then her mouth coming open and head going back and maybe making that funny, far-off animal noise that you love to drive out of her? As long as all that happens, none of the rest matters and you don't have to worry about it, I told myself.

"You are thinking," Blake said, still lying against me in the water. "I can feel it through your skin."

"A man can't help what he thinks," I said.

"A man can keep it to himself."

"I haven't said anything."

"I can feel it."

"I was thinking about other people making love to you."

"Why?"

"Because it drives me crazy."

"Then don't think of it."

"It would be so easy for you to deny it."

"It would make me feel like a piece of flesh, like it wasn't my life I was living."

"Just one question," I said, "one thing I have to know."

"No, there wouldn't be just one. You must play by the rules."

"What difference does it make now, really?"

"I want to tell you something again," she said. "I want you to understand it. I came back up here because of you. I could have gone other places that I like a lot better than this hillbilly sinkhole, but those places didn't have you in them. I came back because of the way we used to be. I never got over that. I tried to, and you say you won't forgive me for that, and I understand why you feel that way. I came back on my own, so you don't owe me anything, I want you to know that. I took my chances, but if I can't have the main thing, I want everything else. Everything. I believe you when you say it is ruined for the long run. Now I am just trying to live. If you will crawl up on that quilt, I will show you some more living."

I did that and it was as I had imagined. She sat on top, astride me, so that she could control the pressure within her. After a while, the little noise came out of her like a small animal which had been trapped inside.

Of course, I knew what she was doing. She was smart and tough and knew that she had the terrible advantage of that division within her. I had been divided out of her life and now without warning back into it, and for the first time I began to toy with the idea of ignoring all I had learned about the blunted expectation and the cyclical dream and where they lead. Blake was over me and her hair a tent around my face and with each upward push now I made her mouth come open and the noise come wilder and wilder, ringing off the gray sheltering rock above us, a high, abandoned sound loosing itself in the dense and humming summer heat. The river rushed with its faint respirant murmur through pool and shoal, and Blake had me where she wanted me and where, goddammit all, I wanted to be, the one place in America and the state of Alabama where I truly wanted to be.

CHAPTER SIX

I am utterly unwilling that economy be practiced at the expense of starving people," said my father, quoting Franklin D. Roosevelt. He plopped down the old *Commercial Appeal* which had come in the Tuesday mail.

"Ain't he got a dead aim on old Hoover? I'm telling you, people are going to go for that kind of talk, yessir."

"We gwine to win it, all right," Ozro said. "We gwine to stomp 'em."

Ozro made Poppa read him the whole story again, because it told about a speech Roosevelt had made at the Memphis depot earlier in the same trip that brought him through Milo.

" 'In Memphis,' " Poppa read, " 'Roosevelt repeated his contention that a shortage of circulating money, not overproduction, is at the heart of the economic depression now gripping the nation. The candidate contends that if more money is put into circulation, people will be able to purchase the quantity of goods the nation's industry and farmers are capable of producing, and thus, prosperity will return.'

"He's got that right, just right," Poppa said. "Brant here just finished running inventory. We ain't got no stock. If times was good, I wouldn't even open the doors on what I got in here. But people ain't got the money to buy what little there is."

"Shore he's right," Ozro said. "He's a educated man, got some sense."

"Education's not going to help him in Alabama," I said. "What's important is how you ignorant folks are going to vote," I said.

"Don't sass me, young man," Ozro said. "I got enough to worry about. That peckerwood Pride Hatton's been talking up the notion that the churches ought to run somebody agin me as an independent. I got Bluenose Trogdon to thank for that, I reckon."

"I wouldn't worry about that," Poppa said. "No Holiness man's going to get enough votes to beat you." He glanced over at me. "Course, you could have handled things better, Ozro, down at the tracks, I mean."

"Well, I don't need no opposition. I'd feel better if the train had stopped. Folks might hold it against me for getting 'em out there for nothing."

"I reckon they're pretty mad about missing your speech, all right," I said.

"Boy, you are testing me," Ozro said. "Make yourself useful and fetch me one of them soda pops."

"Give me a nickel."

"What for?"

"For the soda. I been meaning to tell Poppa I think it's about time you started paying your way around here. It just doesn't look right, us giving stuff to a public official."

"Well that just suits me," Ozro said. "Ain't nobody going to accuse Ozro Jenkins of being a freeloader." Ozro worked his hand down into his pocket, finger-walking it past a great roll of fat that stretched his trousers tight as a sausage sack. Finally he brought out a nickel and threw it on the counter. My father picked up the nickel and the joke.

"Never thought of it before, but it could be taken wrong, like we was trying to bribe the law." Ozro hadn't said anything. Poppa looked over at him. "Ozro, just to keep the record clean, you might want to pay for the sodas you've drunk over the years. Let's see, you've been constable sixteen years and I'd reckon you drink about two hundred dollars worth of these a year at the retail price. I'll settle for three thousand even."

"If that's the way you two feel, I'll just carry my business across the road."

"All right, I'll take wholesale, Ozro. Let's make it two thousand."

"Hell with all you Lasters," Ozro said. He started for the door and I saw that he was really hot. I caught him and grabbed him by the arm.

"Ah, come on, Ozro, we're just kidding you."

"Accusing a man of taking advantage of his position," he said, "that ain't so funny."

I led him back up in front of the counter. Ozro made a show of still being mad, but he was all right now.

"Tell him he doesn't have to pay, Poppa."

"You know I don't begrudge you a few sodas, Ozro," my father said, "but I sure ain't going to give back this nickel. First one of yours I ever got." He reached for the key.

"Give him something about politicians," I said.

My father rang the sale and without even pausing to think, he said, " 'For we hear there are some which walk among you disorderly, working not at all, but are busybodies.' "

"Like I said, to hell with all you Laster's," Ozro shouted again. Jerking free of me, he bolted for the door again.

"That's Second Thessalonians, the third chapter, eleventh verse," my father called after him.

Ozro stopped at the door. "Hey, Brant, you come on over to my office. I got something I need to show you." Then he laughed and waved his hand at my father in mock disgust and went on out.

"I'll go see what he wants," I said. "I'll be back in a minute."

Ozro's office sat beside the road about fifty feet south of the Mercantile. It was a small frame building, not over eight feet by twelve. I caught up with Ozro as he was unlocking the door. It was powerfully hot inside. There was a desk and two chairs. Ozro started throwing up windows. There was one on each wall save the front, where the door was.

"I didn't know you ever used this place," I said, looking at the scatter of papers on the desk.

"Oh, more than I used to since you been gone," he said. "I'd use it more often if I could talk the county commission into buying me a coal stove and some coal for it. Cheap farts. All they care about is the courthouse. Gets cold as a welldigger's ass in here in the winter."

"What you got to show me?" I said.

"Hell, I ain't got nothing," he said. "I just wanted to know if you been doing any poaching."

"You horny old goat," I said, "that's kind of personal, don't you think?"

"Don't get touchy, boy. I just like to keep tabs on my friends, so to speak. I could just tell the other day she was mighty anxious to see you alone, that's all. I been wanting a report."

"Poppa wasn't far off in that verse," I said, truly not wanting to talk about it. The old jokes did not apply any more.

"Well, since you've got me down for a busybody I'll go ahead and tell you that this laying out all night with Bluenose Trogdon is no good, neither. You stay clear of him, you hear."

Ozro sat reared back in a groaning old swivel chair in front of his desk. Even sitting still in that heat, he was sweating and breathing hard.

"How'd you find that out?" I said.

"Never you mind how I find things out. The thing is I'm telling you to stand clear of Bluenose. I've been friends with him since we was boys—ask your pa about that—but he's run his string out with folks, just like I told you the day you got home. You saw what he did down at the train depot. He's gone wild and there's no good to come to you from hanging around with him. You hear?" Ozro rocked forward in the squealing chair. He planted both feet on the floor and leaned over, one hand on each fat knee, toward where I was sitting in the other chair. He wasn't kidding, either. "You mind what I say," he finished.

"You mind your own goddam business," I said and went on out.

As luck would have it, as soon as I hit the ground outside the constable's shack, I saw Bluenose walking in on the Fever Springs Road, moving fast in that loose, comfortable gait of his. Ozro, standing in the door behind me, saw him, too. Bluenose came on over.

"What you and the fat man plotting?" he said.

"Ozro's just been warning me about running around with you."

"That a fact? Well, I got one that will shake his tree. I got that cathouse run Thursday. You want to go?"

"Why don't you just leave him be?" Ozro said, glaring down at Bluenose from the doorway.

"Hell, Ozro, I'd take you, too, but I'm afraid if we got you laying down, we'd never get you up again," Bluenose said. "How about it, Brant? I'm leaving Thursday morning."

"Bluenose, you ain't doing right by B. B.," Ozro said. "You ain't got no call getting his boy mixed up with you."

"Boy'll get to be a man, you don't watch him all the time," Bluenose said. "It ain't none of your concern."

"Y'all quit going at one another," I said. "I better not go, Bluenose. I promised Poppa I'd work at the store every day until I can find a job. Besides, Uncle General's playing a dance over at the high school Friday night, and I promised to take Blake."

"General Drummond," Bluenose said softly. "Son of a bitch, there's a rounder for you. We had some fun in the old times. I reckon he's just passing through to break poor old Sarahgrace's heart again."

"Story like that'll die out if you'd just quit telling it," snapped Ozro. "General Drummond ain't been through here in five years, and you still talking that rot about him and Sarahgrace."

"Aw, listen to him," Bluenose said. "Listen to the biggest gossip between Nashville and Miami in Florida. He don't like that story though. Fact is, Brant, the constable here taken hisself a shine to Miss Sarahgrace long years ago. But Sarahgrace, she was by General like Blake is by you. She just couldn't see nobody but him."

"Don't you believe a word of that," Ozro said to me.

"Tell you what," Bluenose said, "I'll put my Birmingham run off till Saturday morning. I can just wait and do my bottling Friday evening and you go right on to your dance and we'll light out Saturday at daybreak."

"Well, I hate for you to do that on account of me," I said. "I ain't really that hot to go, to tell you the truth."

"Shit, boy, where's your vinegar? This is a first-class cathouse, I'm telling you. I'm running a hundred gallon and I aim to take most of my pay in trade."

"Don't pay him no mind, Brant. You're talking sense now," Ozro said.

"Don't think I don't know what's got your back up," Bluenose said, looking up at Ozro. "I heard about pissant Pride Hatton's little sermon agin me last Sunday. That pissant preacher's got you scared crazy for your pissant little old job."

"I ain't studying Pride Hatton," Ozro said. "I just don't want you getting Brant in no trouble."

"Ozro, there's something you need to be careful about," Bluenose said.

"I reckon you're fixing to tell me what it is."

"I am," said Bluenose, "and here it is. Don't go thinking that little badge is going to enable you to go interfering with a man that's got real power."

"That would be you," said Ozro.

"It would."

Ozro laughed. "What kind of power you claiming these days, Bluenose?"

"Spiritual power," Bluenose told him, shaking a long, knotty finger at Ozro as he dropped the words. "The spiritual power of an absolute, stump-snatching, natural man, and that would be me, all right."

"Times change," said Ozro.

CHAPTER SEVEN

My Uncle General was either a one-man traveling carnival show or a bum, depending on who you listened to. Uncle General called himself a vagabond minstrel, last guardian of a vanishing tradition; he was full of it that way. Poppa held the second view, but because General was my mother's baby brother, Poppa had always shown him the courtesy of the house, even after she died. When I was a kid, General had worked our territory pretty regular. Two or three times a year he'd pass through on his way from Sand Mountain toward the southern leg of his circuit down around Parrish and Dora and Cordova. Down in those mining towns below Jasper is where he picked up material for his famous fiddle tune, "Blind Mule in Flat Top Mine." General taught me how to beat straw on the guitar for "Blind Mule" and a lot of other tunes, and it used to be about my biggest thrill to accompany him when he played a dance in Milo or Fever Springs. General had to do some tall talking to get Poppa to let me play rhythm for him in public, but Poppa finally wound up giving General money to buy me a guitar of my own. I'll never forget the day General showed up with it, a handsome six-stringer with a box about three-quarters regular size on it. I asked him where he got it, and he put his hand on my head and said, "Son, I got it from a man who had it to sell." I thought that was about the cleverest saying I would ever hear. Of course, that was years ago, when General used to come drifting in like a magical hillbilly gypsy, back when I was a kid and, come to think of it, Miss Sarahgrace Gilliland had been a toothsome young woman. I hadn't seen General in a long time now, and in a way I dreaded the dance. I had a feeling that General was the sort of man who was at his most appealing when you were a kid. So much of my life in Milo was turning out that way, I didn't see how it could miss with General.

Just before dark, I went over to Blake's house. She came out in a starched gingham dress, the kind of dress a city girl would buy to wear to a party out in the country. The way she looked revived the feeling I had at the railroad tracks that she was only a visitor here in this place which would always be my home no matter where I lived.

"Thank God for a party," she said when we were out of earshot of her father. "I've been about to go crazy up here. I hope you had the good sense to bring some of that whiskey Bluenose is always bragging about."

We came down the walk and turned out into the road toward the schoolhouse. I tried to match the elevated gaiety in her voice. "Not tonight," I said. "No proper schoolmarm can be drinking on the county premises. A cold sober party if ever there was one."

Blake took my left arm with both her hands, holding my arm lightly but close against her as we walked. "One deacon in the Laster family is enough," she said. She reached across my front with her left hand and felt along my belt for a flask hidden under my shirt. "All right, where is it?"

I smiled down at her. The hand passing across my belly moved a rush of desire lightly up from its path. It twisted through me with the kind of rising, doomed feeling you get from the sudden, flashing sight of a deer in the forest.

"The habits you picked up in Atlanta," I said. "Always ready to fire the sunset gun."

I said that for my own benefit, really, a tribute to the vision I had of her drinking whiskey from small polished glasses with handsome people, men with yellow neckties, girls in dresses like clouds, all taking drinks from trays carried by the silent, obedient niggers of Atlanta. I thought of myself as one of the niggers, in the way that you will drive a splinter deeper under the skin by running a finger over and over again across its blunt, exposed stump.

"The sunset gun?" she said, her voice rising happily.

"It's a saying the British have. You're supposed to wait to hear the sunset gun before having the first drink of the day."

Her hands tightened around my arm, making a little band above my rolled cuff. "Maybe I misjudged the quality of education at the University," she teased. "Such a worldly boy they sent me back. Well, I want to fire cannons tonight. I want to raise some dust." She nudged me with her arm. "But where's the ammunition? Come on, the old flask in the hip pocket maybe?" She reached again, behind me this time, to slap my rump, once on each empty back pocket.

I laughed. "Don't worry. I trust my uncle to take care of that. He has a way of sneaking whiskey into these affairs."

We had come back toward Milo far enough to see the church off down the road toward the Y. We could see other people walking up from Milo, couples and a few larger groups coming on toward us in the new darkness. We beat them to the side road which turned off toward the high school and we walked down it out of their sight, passing into the dark little hollow which separated the schoolgrounds from the main road. Blake pulled me to a halt on the wooden bridge which crossed the wet-weather branch in the bottom of the hollow. She turned to face me, running both arms under mine and holding me lightly, her hands in the small of my back.

"Cold sober kisses for a happy time," she said. She turned her face up to me, kissed me. She moved her body lazily against me, as if time and privacy did not matter. "Let's have fun tonight," she whispered, her lips moving against the side of my face.

"Why not?" I said.

Blake leaned back against my arms, which circled her waist, so that she could look at me directly. "You're the only one who can answer that question," she said. "I wish you would, once and for all."

I started to snap back that I had the answer, but I was no longer so sure. When Blake was around, it was not so easy to imagine a life without her. That was a neat trick she had, putting all the burden on me, as if the thing she had done had no bearing. The trick was working well enough, too.

"Come on," I said. "Let's go find Uncle General."

We went up the rise to the open schoolyard and around to the side of the building. We crossed the clay basketball court and went into the auditorium. Uncle General was on the elevated stage at the far end arranging kerosene lamps around his chair so everyone would be able to see him. Miss Sarahgrace was up there with him, making every step General did. There was another person with them, a tall young man I didn't know. He was the only man in the house wearing a necktie and something about the smooth way he looked, his clothes, the soft curly hair worn rather long, struck an immediate resistance in me.

"Who's the new boy?" Blake said.

"I've never seen him before," I said, guiding her toward the stage through a crowd of forty or so people.

"Definitely not a local," said Blake, and I knew that the transformation was already taking place, changing her from the girl with whom I had been alone in all the world only moments before, her division already dividing the world as I would have it.

Uncle General spotted us as we came up the low steps to the stage and rushed to meet us, almost dancing a jig as he came. For the first time in my life, he struck me as a little ridiculous, a skinny, fox-faced little man who played a little too hard at being a dead game sport. He had aged in the way such men do, into a kind of declining false youth. The skin on his face looked tight as a drumhead, as if he had tried to stretch the wrinkles out.

"Godamighty, Brantley, it's good to see you. How's the boy?" He grabbed my hand and swished it side-to-side instead of pumping it up and down. He beat on my back with his free hand.

"Why didn't you come by the house to drop your gear?" I said. "Poppa was looking for you."

"Say he was?" General said. "Well, I didn't want to put your daddy out." He circled my neck with his arm and pulled me in close. "Besides you might say I got me a lodging commitment."

I looked at him, raising my eyebrows. In times past he and Sarahgrace had kept up appearances. He read my expression perfectly.

"I'm getting too old to sneak around, I reckon," he said. "You cain't tell, I might work out something permanent."

He threw his free arm around Blake, kissed her on the cheek and hustled us over to Sarahgrace and the stranger.

"Goddam, this here was the best straw man I ever saw for a kid," he said to them. "Where you been keeping the past four-five years, Brantley?"

"Away from here," I said, trying to sound as thrilled as he did about our reunion. "But I hear you've been scarce yourself."

"That I have," he said. "I been all over. I spent a right smart of time playing dives in Georgia. I was trying to get on the radio show in Atlanta. I just left over there."

"So did Blake."

"That a fact?" said General. He let go of me and gave Blake another big kiss on the cheek. "Prettiest girl over there, I bet. What'd you do in Atlanta, honey?"

"I was going to school," she said.

"A Scottie, I'll bet," said a voice from behind me. I turned around to see the necktie man smiling at Blake. He glanced at me, then turned his attention back to her. "A Scottie," he repeated. "I'd bet anything on it."

Blake brightened, turned her smile on him. "How'd you ever guess?" she said.

"No guesswork," he said. "You simply have the look, although what you're doing up here in this place, I can't imagine."

"Blake King, this wiseacre is MacShan Satterfield," said General. "He's from down there in the Black Belt where everybody's got first names that sound like last names."

"Like Blake's," said MacShan Satterfield. "Maybe she should be from the Black Belt, too." He kept on smiling at her.

"MacShan's been following me around ever since I got back to Alabama," General went on.

"Whatever for?" said Blake, offering her hand to MacShan Satterfield. He took it and leaned his thin, long face toward her.

"It's this insane project I'm doing at the University," he confided in her. He turned to me quickly then and we shook. "Miss Gilliland tells me you went there—Brant, isn't it?"

"I thought y'all might of knowed each other, but MacShan says he didn't recollect you," said Sarahgrace.

"What fraternity were you?" he said.

"I didn't have the time for that," I said evenly.

"Well, it can be a bore, can't it? I know just what you mean," said Satterfield, not meaning it. "I'm sorry we didn't meet. Perhaps I'd have found your uncle sooner. He's been quite the lifesaver on this idiocy Poulain Pickett has saddled me with. Did you know Poulain at the University?"

"I had Civil War and Reconstruction from him," I said. "I had all I wanted of that and of Scott Fitzgerald's wife."

"Ah, you do know Poulain. Did he ever lecture on his mad theory about the new Renaissance in the South? I'm sure you must have heard it"—Satterfield began mimicking Pickett's high, phony voice—"'A new Elizabethan era, a natural outgrowth of the Confederate tradition, the flowering of the last Anglo-Saxon aristocracy.'"

"I've heard it preached," I said. I had to laugh at Satterfield's imitation of the strutting little gentleman-scholar who had, quite unintentionally, educated me about the Historical Mistake. I laughed, but I wasn't fooled. Satterfield might make fun of the honorary cousin of Fitzgerald's wife, but you could bet that deep down inside he believed the very same things. They all did.

"I think you see it's nonsense," he said. "So do I, but Poulain got me drunk at the Deke house one night and made me promise to do a master's thesis in literary history, in which I have but the faintest interest. So here I am, examining the music of native wizards like my friend General for traces of the Elizabethan minstrelsy. Poulain claims he's going to use the thesis in a book which will absolutely revolutionize Southern literary scholarship. Who cares? Anyway, he'll never get it written. He spends all his time drinking with us over at the house. The man is a fool for good corn."

"Who ain't?" said General. "If you'll shut up, MacShan, I'll wet us all down and make some music before we have a riot."

The crowd had leveled off at about seventy-five now, and they were pushing up to the stage. Some of the old hands were teasing General to start playing. I had had all of Satterfield's talk I needed or wanted Blake to have, so I took Blake's arm and walked her back to a crate of opened Cokes sitting against the wall at the rear of the stage.

"See, I told you Uncle General would take care of the refreshments," I said.

"Those Cokes look suspiciously pale," she said as General joined us.

"The color does fall off a little when I doctor them up," General said, "but oh my, it does give 'em more body." General bent over and handed a bottle to each of us.

"Give me one for MacShan," Blake said.

"Let that jackass get his own drinks," I said. "Where in hell did you pick him up anyway, General?"

General minded me. He straightened up with just his own drink. "He does talk a line, Brant, but it don't do to be too harsh on a boy that's footing all the bills. The lad is positively made out of U. S. cash. His family owns something big, I forget just what."

"I know his kind," I said. "Tuscaloosa's full of them. I know those bastards, all right."

"You think you do," said Blake. She bent down and got a bottle and took it over to MacShan. She handed it to him and flounced around in front of him, making conversation. General raised his eyebrows at me and we drifted back over. "Is Rebecca your cousin?" Blake was saying when I walked up. "When we were at Scott, she got me a date with some boy from down in Demopolis who went to Emory. Oh, I wish I could think of his name."

MacShan showed his teeth. "Oh my God, not John Sharp Kelsey, I hope."

"Yes, that's it. I think he's Rebecca's cousin."

"Both our cousins," said MacShan delightedly. "We're all kin in some terribly complicated way. They say everybody that counts in the Black Belt is kin. I hope John Sharp wasn't too insane. The boy has absolutely no reserve."

"It was quite an evening," said Blake. She glanced over at me as she took the first sip from her Coke bottle. Her eyes were wide with a kind of defiant innocence, the pretense being that she didn't know what she was doing to me. At that moment, the evening took on a certain inevitability.

"All right, y'all want to listen a minute, we'll get this shindig started," I heard Uncle General say. He was standing at the very front edge of the stage now, his fiddle tucked under his left arm. As he talked, he slapped his bow in a little rhythm against the starched leg of his overalls. "It's been nigh on five years since I played for you here in Milo, but the price ain't changed."

This brought a little murmur of approval from the crowd. Then a slick-haired man about General's age spoke up from the back of the crowd.

"Hey, General, you musta been down in Flat Top for the past five years. It ain't just everybody that's got a dime these days."

"I was about to say my price ain't changed, but unfortunately the President ain't changed yet neither. But I wouldn't deny no human being music, nor a Republican. So if you got a dime or nickel or whatever, drop it in the bucket up here sometime this evening, but if you ain't, dance right on and pay me when you can."

The crowd began shuffling back toward the sides of the hall. I told Blake we should get down off the stage and finish our drinks. Satterfield said he would just stick with us, if it was all right.

"Wait," General announced, "there's one more thing. Buddy Gilliland's going to beat straw for me, but he ain't here yet. I suspect he's out sparking his girl a little before he has to go to work. Anyhow, my nephew, Brant Laster here, has agreed to beat straw until Buddy gets here, and Brant's pretty good. I know, 'cause I taught him."

The words caught me at the edge of the stage, just fixing to jump down and catch Blake down after me. I turned to General, shaking my head no. I heard Satterfield hit the floor and looked back in time to see him take Blake by the waist and swing her lightly down. He did not look to have that kind of strength in his arms. I went over to General, who was finishing up his spiel.

"Brant's shaking his head 'no' at me, but I don't believe there's any college can ruin a good straw man in just four years," he hollered. "Besides, if Brant don't do it, there won't be any dancing till Buddy gets here. Come on back, Brant."

General handed me the guitar and smiled.

"Goddam you," I said. "I didn't come down here tonight to beat straw for you."

"It won't be for long," he said. "MacShan will keep her entertained for you."

"Yeah, I can see that all right," I said.

General cut his eyes up at me as he lowered himself into his chair. "Son, if you got one that won't stand hitched, ain't no cause to get mad at me or MacShan. If it wasn't him, it'd be somebody else. Mind the beat."

84

General jerked his head toward a chair situated to his left and a little behind him. His beat-up guitar was propped against it. I sat down and took the brush of broom straw which was stuck in the strings high on the guitar's neck. I picked up a beat from the tapping of General's left foot and began striking the strings with a sweeping downward motion of the straw brush, while I chorded with my left hand. Brushing a guitar for rhythm was an innovation General had worked on the pure old-time fiddling style. The traditional and accepted way was for the straw man to beat time on the fiddle strings themselves while the fiddler was playing on the same instrument. Two men playing both rhythm and melody on one fiddle was an art in itself, and I have seen other fiddlers climb all over General for using a guitar. They wouldn't let him come near their contests with one, which didn't bother General over much. He liked playing the dances, and the deep, thumping sound he got out of the guitar was better for dancing. Besides that, General just liked doing things his own way and I think he counted it a bonus that his way happened to piss off the other fiddlers.

After I had brushed along for a while, General threw his fiddle to his chin and jumped right into "Down Along the Canebrake." Several dancers came away from the walls with some whooping and yelling. The men came out first for a run of buck dancing, there being a big element of the peacock strut in these affairs. Carrying their hands clasped behind their backs, they danced alone and in place with high, slamming steps which made the floor thunder. As these solitary dancers wore down, couples began coming out on the floor, arranging themselves in groups of four couples each. The women danced with a light, skipping gait, letting the men drive each group into a slow rotation with loud stepping which was a toned-down version of the buck dance. The groups squared and circled below us, and General did a little calling from time to time as he fiddled. He chanted in his clear nasal voice the catchy quatrains which went with certain tunes, verses like—

> Bow and scrape, bow and scrape
> Head down along the old canebrake
> Ladies turn back and count to two
> If he ain't gone, he'll marry you

—and such as that.

Uncle General drove right on without a break to "House Afire," a really fast one that brought more dancers onto the floor and also started the showboating in earnest. All over the hall, one man and then another would break out of his group and launch into some fancy bit of extra footwork, head thrown back, heels flashing out and back in a blur. The shrill, brief yelps from the men rose from one part of the room and then another, like scattered reports from up and down a firing line. It had been a long time since there had been anything to yell about in Milo.

MacShan and Blake had found a couple of straight-back chairs and they were sitting with the chairs angled toward one another. Satterfield had taken a notebook from his shirt pocket, and every time he wrote in it, Blake would lean in close to watch. Once they were amused by what he had written and she held his arm to steady the notebook before her while they laughed. She was having such a good time and MacShan, that MacShan, he was really something, nothing short of the living embodiment of the truth I had first sensed at the University. To the last man, his people had that air of indifferent superiority which let them ignore all their defeats, which allowed them to maintain their grand, casual contempt for everyone who was not from the Black Belt or one of the sanctified cities of the old plantation days. I think in the beginning owning other human beings had done it to them, and now they passed on from father to son like a blood trait that indolent nostalgia for the old days, passed on, too, the undentable confidence that they were still masters of a world in which people ought to obey them and be willing to suffer for them and render them tribute—the last aristocrats. Of course, there was no way to change them, but I could at least give MacShan a memory.

When General figured he had things worked up just right, he looked up from his fiddle and hollered, "Blind Mule in Flat Top Mine." The whooping broke out again and dancers who had dropped out streamed back to the floor. It was the ideal buck-dancing tune, fast but mournful, just right for the rigid, trance-like style that the best dancers have. Old General really let it sail, too. You could almost see those old work mules bumping along sightlessly down in the dark corridors. Flat Top was notorious all over north Alabama. It was a prison mine down in the coalfields near Jasper. The state leased prisoners to the owners, who provided room and board and guards to kill anybody who tried to loaf or run. Of course, you could figure a man had at least done something to deserve Flat Top. It was the mules that got to General. Once a mule went down in Flat Top to work, it never saw the light of day again. All the mules went blind soon enough, but by that time they had learned to pull the carts by feel and not to move unless led. Well, the U. S. Steel needed that coal down in Birmingham.

Right after we finished and were getting ready to take a break, Blake came running over and stopped right below us.

"MacShan said would you please play 'Blind Mule' again right now, General," she said. "He's almost got the melody line written down."

"Hell, no," I said. "Let him wait like everybody else."

General swiveled his head around and gave me a look. "Ain't you a pistol tonight?" he said. Then he hollered, " 'Blind Mule,' one more time," and I had no choice but to follow him into it.

Blake went back to her musical scholar and he looked up from his notebook long enough to smile at her, sealing his fate. Buddy Gilliland and his girl finally wandered in as we finished up "Blind Mule" and General motioned for Buddy to come on up. General announced he was going to keep right on playing since he had a new straw man. The crowd clapped and laughed when he said he'd done worn out one time-beater already. "Let's see if you can hold up any better dancing," he told me loudly and everyone laughed as I climbed down from the stage.

Blake met me before I reached her and her friend. She took my arm and slipped her hand into mine, leading me toward the dance floor. "Thanks for playing it again," she said. "I swear that crazy man would have had me humming 'Blind Mule' all night, if you hadn't." Her voice and the laugh which came after it were light and high as a fox's yelp.

We joined a group and started dancing with them, but I stayed with them only a couple of rounds before breaking out on "Jump Rabbit Ridge" to dance by myself. I went at it with an angry vigor, driving each foot forward and pushing back from it in that fast stepping which never carries you far. Blake stood watching me for a moment and then, instead of waiting for me to finish up and take her back into the group, she did a thing which was not done. She faced off from me and began moving in a dance which was a delicate counterpoint to my own, her feet moving in a similar, quick step, her hands on her waist, arms propped forward and out like wings. Dancers from the other groups stared at us as their rotations carried them past us, but Blake ignored them, fixing me with her smile. She was daring me to make her quit, but I wouldn't be backed down. I kept up my own dance. It was a rooster dance and I could feel myself swelling like a rooster with it, getting all primed for a real barnyard flogging.

We danced through that tune and then, without speaking a word, went back to where MacShan was sitting. He had been to get us a round of doctored Cokes and had them waiting. He was still turning it on.

"I swear I love that dancing," he said. "I can certainly see why they call it buck dancing, although that's hardly the right term in your case, Blake. It's quite sensual, don't you think, like a mating dance. You two were terrific."

Blake curtsied. I could have choked her. She took her chair

beside him, leaving me standing before them. They were having a good time playing to one another.

"We've just got to get Rebecca to have you down for one of her parties now that you're both home from Scott. You'd love that old place of her daddy's. Of course, the dancing's nothing like this, but we could run over to Gee's Bend and watch the niggers one night. Daddy's got a timber camp down on the Tombigbee, and I swear, they're just absolute Africans down there. Daddy says we've got the blackest niggers and the tallest cypress left anywhere."

"Blake's not coming down to your nigger heaven," I said. They both looked at me in surprise.

"Oh, I'm sorry," MacShan said without rancor. "Of course, the invitation would include the both of you. These parties are really quite huge."

"I got enough of you people at the University."

"Really? I should think you hardly knew us." MacShan stood up, extended an open hand toward me for emphasis. "Honestly, Brant, you've gotten the wrong idea. Seeing you tonight, playing and dancing so well, I've quite given up any illusions of beating your time."

"I haven't given up on whipping your ass," I said, stepping up close to him. Although shorter, I felt compact and dangerous up beside him. He looked down, awareness of what he was into creeping into his face.

"Really, it can't be all that bad," he said, forcing a smile.

"It's bad enough. Come on outside. I'm going to whip your ass."

"I think you ought to know that might not be so easy as you imagine."

"I'm not studying that," I said. "I'm going to burn you up, you son of a bitch."

"That'll do it," he said. "That name you called me will do it just fine."

The music stopped. I looked around to see General leaning

down to talk to Blake, who had slipped away while we argued.

"I'm going to take a break now and get a little air," General announced. "Them that's got dimes don't be shy to bring them up while I'm gone."

Satterfield and I went out the side door and he followed me out toward the basketball court. Looking back, I saw General and Buddy Gilliland come through the lighted door, walking fast. Blake and Miss Sarahgrace stopped in the door. Blake leaned against the jamb and crossed her arms.

"Here comes your uncle," said Satterfield.

"He can't help you," I said.

"I hardly counted on it. I've heard you people stick together." He said "you people" as if he was talking about the niggers down on Gee's Bend. I took it for a brave show.

"What you want to fight Brant for, MacShan?" General said when he reached us.

"It's not my idea," said Satterfield. "Your nephew has been seized by jealousy, I think."

"Well, this here is a nice place to settle it," said General, looking around at the expanse of the hard-packed clay court. "You got plenty of room. Let's don't see no knife work now."

"I had assumed we would fight like white men," said Satterfield.

"Here, Buddy, take my watch," I said. I took my time digging it out of my pocket, holding Satterfield in the edge of my vision. I figured to turn quickly and let him hold a good one before he could get his hands up. The first lick usually tells the fight, and I had learned the hard way not to be timid about taking it. "I need to talk to you when this is over," I told Buddy. Then I spun around and let fly a right, starting low and aiming at his chin.

Satterfield leaned back from it and popped a very nice short left high on my cheekbone. Then he came quickly with a right that took me in the throat. It was much too clever a punch to suit me and I had the bad feeling that he had not thrown it with everything he had. I felt a surge of fear, which up until then had been obliterated with anger, but I fought it down and backed away, giving myself some room.

"I think this is a bad idea you have," he said, moving toward me by sliding his left foot forward and drawing the other up behind it. He knew, of course, that backing me down was better than whipping me. By taking another left, I managed to drive a good shot into his middle, feeling my fist slide in under the ribs, just where I wanted it. He lost some air, but managed to land a right under my chin hard enough to back me up. Then, using his reach, he nailed me dead on the nose with a left before he stepped back to wait on me, as if he wanted me to have every advantage. I felt the blood starting through my nostrils and I backed off far enough so that I could lean over safely and let the blood run for a moment.

"What you got hold of there?" I heard Bluenose say.

I turned around to see him standing beside General and Buddy. By this time, part of the dance crowd, at least fifteen men, had found us and they, too, lined the side of the court. Beyond them, I could see a clump of women around the doorway.

"A son of a bitch that's been in a fist fight before," I said. "What you doing here?"

"Thought I'd come see the party. Glad I did."

Bluenose and the crowd settled me some instead of making it worse, as I would have expected. The fear subsided a little and was replaced by a rush of desperation, which is always your last best chance against a better fighter.

"Are you quitting now?" said Satterfield.

Instead of answering, I went at him with a wild, flailing rush which I hoped would carry me past those long, stinging jabs. It did and once inside I finally got in a good one on his ear. He took it and stepped away, circled quickly to the right and faked at me with the left I had learned to respect. I dodged the fake left and he gave me a right to the mouth so hard I hoped to God he wasn't holding anything back. I went down on my back. I lay there being glad he believed in all those rules about not hitting a man when he's down. I watched the sky and waited for my head to clear. Suddenly I was looking up into Bluenose's face.

"Now that was a nice punch he put on you," he said, leaning over me. His voice dropped to a whisper. "If you get up, you better butt that son of a bitch. That'll be your onliest chance."

I did get up without much stomach for it. Satterfield was standing there shining, still in his necktie. He had his hands up, held loosely, ready to put me down for good now, not bothering with conversation this time. When I closed on him, he made his first mistake, going with the right lead again. I caught it off and moved inside, never throwing a punch. I grabbed his shoulders and lunged up with everything I had. I caught his face just right, feeling after the first impact of flesh the sharper jab of teeth cutting into my scalp. I felt his hands come down on my back, trying to hold on. I crouched and gave him another butt, catching him under the chin this time. He came loose and fell back full length. I ran over and kicked him as hard as I could in the ribs.

With a dazed, dismayed look on his face, Satterfield rolled toward me, trying to catch my feet. When he did that, I got him another one with the point of my shoe right in his belly. He curled up like a sleeper, holding his gut, twisting his face into the hard dirt. I was ready to go ahead and stomp him good, walk him like a road.

"I reckon that's enough," Bluenose said, stepping in front of me and pushing me back. "You've done covered yourself with honor."

"What's that supposed to mean?" I said.

"What's the difference? You the last man standing, ain't you?"

General came up and bent over Satterfield. "MacShan, you get to feeling better, come on in and I'll give you a drink."

Satterfield looked up at us with disgust. His necktie was splayed back over his shoulder. He groaned.

"I hope you didn't break no ribs, Brant," General said.

"I hope that Black Belt son of a bitch hasn't broken my nose," I said. We walked back toward the school building as I dabbed with my handkerchief at the thin trickle of blood still seeping from my left nostril. I felt ashamed about what I had done to Satterfield and expected everyone else to, but Blake met me smiling. Stopping me in the bar of dim light falling through the door, she ran her fingertips over my face, touching all the scraped and puffy places, pressing gently against my bruised lips.

"What a way to treat company," she said.

"I'm lucky that bastard didn't knock my eyes out," I said, holding still for her examination.

"You ain't woofing," said Bluenose. He was leaning against the building in the shadows, watching us. "If I hadn't been there to talk you into not fighting that gentleman like a gentleman, you'd be the one laying out there in the ball yard."

"I take it by you being up here gallivanting around that the trip is off," I said.

"Oh, no, boy. I'll be there sure as sunrise. I just come to watch you dance."

"His dancing's through for the night," said Blake.

We moved into the shadow with Bluenose. Blake leaned against me, ran an arm around my waist.

"That last dance Brant got was a mite rough," Bluenose said, laughing.

Suddenly it struck me that they had all enjoyed the fight a lot more than I had, but I didn't know which of them had enjoyed it most, General or Bluenose or Blake.

We left Bluenose there and started walking down the driveway to the main road, passing down into the hollow to the little bridge where we had kissed. I pulled Blake to a stop there.

"I've got to go back," I said. "I forgot to get my watch from

Buddy." What I had really forgotten was to tell Buddy that he was my alibi for the Birmingham run. I had told Poppa that Buddy and I were going trotlining up on Brushy Creek for a few days, the way we used to in high school.

"Forget it," Blake said happily. "I've got something else to pass the time." She handed me a half-pint bottle of whiskey she said Bluenose had slipped her. She held the bottle up and waved it back and forth in front of me. "Buddy will take care of your watch. We've got other things to do."

"You had a hell of a good time at the fight for someone who tried to stop it," I said. We started walking again. I gave up on the alibi. I would take my chances. It was something I was learning to do, I thought.

"I never tried to stop it," she said.

"I saw you go get General."

"I just didn't want him to miss it," she said. "You know how he loves a little excitement."

"You're disgusting," I said. "How can you talk about excitement after what you made me do to Satterfield?"

We had come to the main road. It stretched left and right before us, moonlit and abandoned. The fiddle music from the schoolhouse drifted in from behind us in a faint whine.

"No one makes anybody do anything," she said. "People do what they want to or have to. Isn't that right, Brant? You've always been the philosopher. Isn't that right?"

Her voice was reckless and a little drunken. It reminded me of my own when I had been baiting Satterfield. I watched as she uncorked the flask and passed it to me. After the whiskey cut with Coke, Bluenose's pure product tasted fiery and clean.

"Well, isn't that right?" Blake demanded.

"Yes, Blake," I said wearily. "It's right enough for you. You did what you wanted to, didn't you? You did what you wanted to all over Atlanta, I reckon."

"Oh, Brant, I wish I could be upright like you." She said it mockingly, in that way she had that always made me feel I was about to lose control of her utterly. It was only another of the many divisions within her, the way she could swing so easily from the appearance of obedience to rebellion, the way she could treat the most serious things as jokes. She moved in front of me, circled my waist with her arms and ground her hips against me. There was no predicting her, no way to avoid being lost in her doubleness. "Are you upright, Brant?" she said in a drunken, ardent voice. "I want you to be upright. I bet I know how to make you upright."

Still grasping my waist, she leaned back from me, her hair swinging out behind her. We still touched at hip and thigh. "My upright boy," she said, her eyes closed. Her face, after the excitement of the drink, the dancing, the hubbub of the fight, looked slack and careless. The thought of her being like this, loose and available, with someone else sent a flash of rage down through me, and I fought down an urge to hold her by the hair and slap her hard, back and forth across the face. But my anger dropped off into another feeling, the one Blake could always rely upon to solve things. Letting go my waist, she ran her right hand up the side of my face and into my hair. She pulled her fingers back, saw the color of them from where Satterfield's teeth had cut into my scalp. The cut place under the blood-matted hair stung a little from her touch.

"He hurt you," she said breathily, "but nothing like what you did to him."

I did grab her hair then, grabbing it close to the scalp with my left hand, doing something I had never tried to do, to hurt her. What an incredible, blood-keen, blood-rutting bitch she was. I pulled her by the hair up hard against me. After the smallest sigh of surprise, she made no sound. She watched me with eyes which betrayed no fear, but widened when I grasped the placket of her dress with my free hand and ripped it down and out. Dress front, slip and all tore away in my hand. I heard her gasp more sharply.

It was not her sudden nakedness which moved me so much as the very familiarity of her body, bare now to the waist in the public road—the smooth, outward-jutting breasts, long nipples, the smooth slim barrel of her body, the twin ridges of muscle down the center of her belly.

Suddenly, I was the one hurting, struck from above by a pain that sagged my knees. Blake had snuck her hand up behind me and sunk her fingernails deep into the cut on my scalp. She dug them in and raked back. I let her go and she scrambled up the roadside and into the trees. I caught her easily a little way into the woods, spun her to face me.

"Goddam you," I started, "I'll make you hum, all right. I'll . . ."

"Don't talk," she said. "Do something."

I felt tall, mean, and full of blood, an upright man, no shit. I backed her against a tree, leaning against her hard. There was blind fumbling and more tearing of cloth to get us joined, still standing. Her breath came in long, ragged jerks and there was no crying out this time, for in this deep, violent conjunction we had gone beyond that. Finally, as we stood still bound together in the close, steamy woods, stood clutched and sweating, listening to the floating fiddle music and the more distant intermittent music of a belling hound and beyond that even the far, brief and dangerous yip-yip of a fox, Blake began to laugh. Her body shook against me and something about the sound, the sheer, unexplainable joy of it, moved me in a way I had not dared hope. I felt what I had never expected to feel again, a love for her pure and undiminished and without agony, as if in whipping Satterfield I had somehow vanquished every phantom of jealousy and exposed a love and desire which ran through my being like a vein of gold. A vision was born there of reclaiming Blake with a possession so pure, so complete, so stunning and brutal that nothing which had gone before could matter. It came to me that I could conquer the Dream of Atlanta by mustering an audacity to match her own. I dropped my head to kiss the curving line from neck to shoulder. Blake pulled herself tighter to me. I imagined having her in all the sacred places of Milo: schoolhouse, our homes, the Mercantile, post office, church, graveyard, our lives becoming one long audacious clasping to take us beyond the debts of history. I imagined her on my grandfather's grave, leaning back on that cold stone bed, her dress torn away in front as it was now, head thrown back, lips parted in the expectation of some sustained, unbearable long climax, legs parted, knees raised, heels planted firm against the stone, ready for the push and thrust, the upward working toward that sweet and final exhaustion.

"What a fighter you are tonight," she mumbled, moving harder against me.

She had felt me come up within her once more. Her breath whistled hot against my ear. From far off, the whine of General's violin drifted through the trees, a tune fast but mournful. I thought it was mighty early for him to be doing "Blind Mule" again, but there it was.

CHAPTER EIGHT

Bluenose had not lied. He was there sure as sunrise and, in fact, well before it, waiting on me. I trudged wearily into Milo on the Fever Springs Road, having left Blake only a few minutes before. We had passed the night in the most fantastic exercise, breaking all our records from the days when we kept up with that sort of thing. I walked across the Y toward Bluenose's wagon, which was pulled up beside the constable's shack. I felt purged and sober, drained of all emotion save a lingering sense of conquest, of having recaptured what was rightfully mine. I smiled to remember how Blake had clung to me as I left her.

Bluenose's mules were standing calmly in their traces, munching on several ears of corn he had thrown in front of them. Bluenose was slumped over in the seat, sleeping soundly. The back of the wagon was heaped with ears of dried corn still in the shucks, and sprawled atop the corn was the form of yet another man. When I got to the wagon, I could see that it was Uncle General, sleeping in a pile with his duffel—the cased fiddle and guitar, his small traveling bag. So much for permanent arrangements.

"Hey, is this here the wagon to the cathouse?" I said loudly.

Bluenose came awake with a little jump and looked at me. " 'Bout damn time you got here," he said.

"Hell, you said daylight and there ain't enough of that to wake you up—or your passenger."

"Kindly don't mention my passenger," Bluenose said. "Miss Sarahgrace ain't never gwine to forgive me if she finds out I helped the little son of a bitch escape the very day after she lays hands on him."

General slept on, propped head and foot on his gear. I threw a canvas sack up under the seat and climbed up beside Bluenose.

"What's that?" Bluenose said.

"My fishing tackle. This is a fishing trip I'm on as far as B. B. Laster is concerned. I told him I was going trotlining with Buddy up on Brushy Creek."

"Well, this is one fishing trip I hope we don't catch nothing on, if you know what I mean." said Bluenose.

"Like the clap," I said.

"Amen," came a voice from the back.

As Bluenose clucked the mules into motion, I turned around to see General's foxlike face grinning back at me. "Looks like y'all could get this trip underway without disturbing a working man's sleep," he said.

"What the hell you doing here?" I said.

"That's what Sarahgrace'll want to know when she wakes up to that empty pillow," said Bluenose.

"Hush up," said General. He made a delicate running motion with his fingers, as if rippling them along a keyboard. "I'm just easing along, you might say, before I wear out my welcome—and before your daddy hears about that little flap at the dance last night. Ain't no doubt who he's going to blame for it. He wasn't never too crazy about me anyhow, B. B. wasn't, especially after your angel mother, God bless her, went on. Not that she was any too pleased about the way I drifted around, but I was her baby brother. She had loyalty, you know what I mean? Ain't nothing like loyalty." General grabbed my shoulder and squeezed it, gave me the little shyster's smile which had been his stock-in-trade all these years. "Say, old MacShan didn't puff your face up near as bad as I figured."

99

"Where is your friend?" I said.

"Aw, I sent him on over to Fever Springs with some folks. Told him I'd meet him over there today sometime. MacShan's going to have hisself a sore mouth to hum his tunes through. I was proud you had sense enough to fight dirty when the shit got thick."

"He can thank me for that," Bluenose said.

"If you're going to meet MacShan in Fever Springs, what're you doing going to Birmingham with us?" I said.

"Aw, I just told him that."

"Some loyalty," I said.

"Rich folks don't need loyalty like the rest of us," General said. "They got something better."

"What has Sarahgrace got?" I said.

"Aw, Brant, you're just trying to make your old uncle feel bad," General said. He slapped a hand on my shoulder and squeezed it again, so I would know how sincere he was. "I counted on staying, I swear I did. I mean I've always thought the world of Sarahgrace, but I'll tell you the Lord's plain truth, I ain't never been much on old women. Now Sarahgrace is a handsome woman, don't get me wrong, but I got to say she's aged something fierce since I was last through here."

"Goddam, man," Bluenose roared. "You looked at yourself lately?"

"It ain't the same thing," General said and he flopped back on the corn to rest some more.

The wagon creaked down the long incline from Milo to the river. The town was well behind us now, and the mules had an easy go of it. They would pay on the climb out of the gorge, once we crossed the steel bridge. Weary from our separate labors of the night before, we rode on in silence, off in the dim gray light, off in the cool morning for Birmingham. It was almost fifty miles and a hard two-day trip by wagon. We spent Saturday night at a campground ten miles south of Jasper, sleeping on blankets spread under the wagon. It was late Sunday afternoon before we reached the outskirts of Birmingham.

Whiskey Man

The last ten miles or so carried us through a region of forlorn mining towns where the big company commissaries were locked and shuttered, and rank upon rank of abandoned coke ovens lined the hillsides like catacombs. Even so close to Birmingham, the land out there still had a rural character, but it was a land ruined for farming by the opening of the mines and ruined for living by their closing. The people we saw along the road looked shrunken and hungry, and when we got closer to Birmingham, we could see, spreading down the ridges to the west of us like the quarters of some peasant army, its vast ramshackle nigger-towns and Hoovervilles. It was the landscape of some fanatical, medieval allegory, and it fit Bluenose's mood well enough, for he had gotten started on Pride Hatton. Hatton had preached for thirty minutes the Sunday before on Bluenose's blasphemy on the day Franklin D. Roosevelt came through. Hatton had called Elmira a saint and said that if Bluenose didn't repent and quit making whiskey, the Lord would strike him down. His text had been "Vengeance is mine saith the Lord," Bluenose said.

"Sounds like he thinks vengeance is Pride Hatton's," I said.

"Aw shit, I don't know," Bluenose said. "Elmira sure thinks he beats Billy Sunday all to hell, I know that for a fact. Let's talk about something else, like this here cathouse. You're fixing to see how a real high-tone bunch of ladies treats a quality moonshiner, yessir."

We had reached the foot of Enon Ridge, the last line of hills separating us from Birmingham's smoky valley. Bluenose guided the mules off the main road and down a little side road which ended in a grove of trees. In the shade of the trees was an overflowing spring which bubbled into a concrete basin. Bluenose climbed down and tethered the mules so they could reach the water.

"Ain't this a pretty place," he said. "I ain't never found out who owns it, but I always stop here. Y'all get out and stretch."

"How long we going to be?" I said.

"Until after dark. I ain't got any arrangement with the law

here, so I don't want to hit town proper in the daylight." Blue-nose found a grassy spot and stretched out. "Might as well get a little sleep, boy. You gonna need all the energy you got to keep up with the old man tonight."

Bluenose thought he looked pretty good when we got to town. He had on, despite the hot weather, a thick black suit of the kind country men keep on hand for funerals. He was wearing a white dress shirt, open at the throat and collarless, and his black hair, which he'd wet down in the spring, was combed and shining. Bluenose had produced the change of clothes from a sack under the wagon seat. I put on a clean shirt I had rolled up in my canvas bag, and General, of course, looked as if he'd just stepped out of a hatbox. He had taken the precaution of having Miss Sarahgrace iron and starch him a fresh pair of overalls before he bedded her down. With his creases like knife blades and his sharp little mustache, General could have passed with most folks as the moonshiner and Bluenose in his rumpled funeral suit as a backwoods deacon.

The whorehouse was out near the steel mills in a big two-story house. We drove the wagon right up into the back yard and Bluenose went up to bang on the back door. The door opened inward and Bluenose said, "Ask Miss Lottie to come out here." Bluenose came back to us and stood beside the wagon.

In a few minutes, a big woman came through the back door and down the steps. When she walked on up to the wagon, I could see she was about fifty, a tall, heavy woman built like an opera singer.

"Good evening, Miss Lottie," Bluenose said, bowing a little.

"Hello, Bluenose," she said. "You bring me a hundred gallons like you're supposed to?"

"Don't you know it?" he said. "Don't I always treat you right, Miss Lottie?"

"Last time you showed up with eighty-five gallons," she said.

"Oh, yeah," Bluenose said. "I forgot about that. Ran into one of my best Jasper customers that was in a real tight for a big party they was planning up there."

"I know," Miss Lottie said, "but that didn't help me any. It's such a damn hardship when you short me."

"That's the only thing I'd short you, Miss Lottie," Bluenose said. He laughed at his joke.

"Don't be funny," Miss Lottie said in a flat voice. "I'll send the boy out."

"Oh, Miss Lottie," Bluenose said, motioning at me. "This here's my friend, Brant Laster. He just finished college down at Tuscaloosa, but I think he could stand some more educating."

"Well, you bring him in when you get everything fixed up, we'll see what kind of laster your Mr. Laster is."

Miss Lottie turned to go in, but Bluenose stopped her again. He indicated General with a jerk of his head.

"And this here is Brant's uncle, General Drummond."

"Goddam, Bluenose, why didn't you bring the whole county?" she snapped.

"I didn't mean to impose," Bluenose said, his humility edged with a faint mockery now. "I know you could always buy your whiskey someplace else. I heared of a fellow out in Pratt City makes a real high grade of sugar whiskey and he needs the business, too."

"Goddam you, Bluenose Trogdon," the woman said. "You know I got more customers come for the decent whiskey than the girls these days. You all come in and do your worst, just please don't short my order no more." She laughed now, the way a person will who realizes he could have lost a dollar arguing over a dime.

"We'll be on directly," Bluenose said, and she went on in.

"You sure it'll be all right?" General said. "I don't want to get in no ruckus down here."

"Sure it's all right," said Bluenose. "Anything I want around here is all right, 'cause Miss Lottie knows I'm doing her a favor. She just takes a little reminding now and then, being a spirited old bitch." Bluenose turned up the quart bottle we'd been sharing and took a shot. "Talk about titties," he said, "You should have seen her fifteen year ago."

After she went in, an old nigger man came out. He wore a white jacket. He and Bluenose greeted one another warmly. "Been a while since we seed you, Mr. Bluenose," the old man said. "You remember me this time?"

"Ain't I here, Booker?" Bluenose said. He reached under the piled corn in one corner of the wagon bed and pulled out a quart jar of whiskey. Booker smiled, his dark face indistinct in the blocks of shadow cast by the tall house and the high board fence down each side of the yard.

"There's a hundred gallon to go inside," Bluenose told him. "One gallon stays in the wagon to get me home on."

"Yes, sir," said Booker. "In case the snake bite."

"Right. Come on Brant, let's go inside. I got to get this boy bred, Booker."

"You sure to God in the right place," Booker said. "That's for certain."

We went inside and sat down in the parlor. Miss Lottie brought us each a drink. Bluenose's was just whiskey poured over ice. General and I had ours with Coke. Bluenose held his glass up and looked at it. "Ain't this something, boys?" he said. "Pover County whiskey over ice."

He was sitting on a purple plush sofa and he looked rough and country there in the room, which was furnished very nicely. In the middle of the room was a round reading table with magazines on it—*Saturday Evening Post* and *Scribner's* and *American Mercury*—just like the reading room in a library. There was a lamp with a glass shade on the table. I sat in a deep chair beside it.

"Ain't things kind of slow, Miss Lottie?" Bluenose asked her.

"Sunday night," she said. "But there'll be some gents in later."

"Don't worry about that."

Bluenose settled back in the sofa. "Whoee, didn't I tell you this place was something, Brantley boy?" he yelled.

A slight frown crossed Miss Lottie's face. Again it struck me how country and out of place he looked in the fine sitting room, which you could see was fitted out for a more polished clientele.

"Now, Bluenose, don't you get too rowdy tonight. I swear the way you get sometimes, it's like you haven't seen a woman in two months."

"That's the damn near truth, Miss Lottie. Tell her, Brant, if that ain't just about the truth, my old lady being the way she is and all."

"I don't know," I said.

"The hell you don't know," he said. "I told you how the whole thing got started." I realized then that Bluenose was pretty drunk from the trip down. He slumped back against the sofa and a deep sadness settled on his face. Miss Lottie gave me a pinched-lipped look and shook her head.

A few minutes later, Bluenose went out to fetch his gallon of whiskey, and Miss Lottie came over to sit down across the reading table from me. We were together in the little circle of light that the lamp made in the dim, finely furnished room. Up close, you could see Miss Lottie had some years on her, but she was a well-kept, handsome woman. She looked intelligent and business-like. She wanted to know if I was working for Bluenose. I explained that I was just out of college and didn't work at all.

She laughed. "Well, you're just off on one of those little tears that the boys take after school," she said.

"I guess you could say that. I don't have any plans."

"Just plan this, Brant," she said. "Plan not to get in the whiskey business, or you'll wind up like Bluenose."

"How's that?" I said.

"If you had known him as long as I have, you'd know what I

mean. These last two years or so, he's gone down fast, gone wild as an Indian. I'm worried about him. I've known Bluenose, been doing business with him, for years. He's just changing, and it's not for the better."

"There's a fellow up home believes the same thing, but I don't know myself."

"It's the whiskey. It gets everybody sooner or later. It gets everybody that will just lay with it long enough, and it'll get Bluenose, too. I hate to see it."

"I don't think it's the whiskey, if there's anything wrong with him," I said, thinking of Elmira, the cold way she acted toward him, and of the Holiness preacher's sermon.

"One thing you'll learn, Brant, you'll learn it's never just the whiskey alone that gets them. It's the years and what happens or doesn't happen that opens up the way; the whiskey is just the last step. You fix things so the whiskey don't get you in twenty years or so."

"I'll try," I said, smiling at her across the table.

"And keep Bluenose out of trouble, if you can. This day and time, a lady can't afford to lose her whiskey man."

"I'll do what I can," I said.

Bluenose came into the room with his jug of whiskey and a glass bucket of ice, which he held up for my inspection. "Look here. Booker done fixed me up for some serious whiskey drinking."

He sat down on the sofa again and started drinking the straight whiskey on ice. Miss Lottie got Booker to set out some more whiskey and Coke and then she left us. Bluenose drank steadily. General, for his part, was nervous as a squirrel, fidgeting on the edge of his chair and sipping without appetite at his drink. A couple of times he got up and peered out the front window. It was hard to figure why a man who had spent his life on the drift would be so ill at ease in a place that ought to be part of his natural territory. The thought occurred to me that my uncle might have something working with the Revenue agents. There was always money to be had for delivering whiskey operators and I had a feeling that my blood uncle was a man whose loyalty couldn't withstand too much money.

But I kept my suspicions to myself and in about half an hour Miss Lottie came back and gave Bluenose three one-hundred-dollar bills. Sprawled on the sofa, his long legs splayed out in front of him, Bluenose flipped through the bills as she watched.

"Right on the money," he said, "just like every time, Lottie." He looked over toward me. "That's the beauty of doing business with quality folks, Brant. You ain't never got to worry about the money. Ain't that right, Miss Lottie?"

"If you say so, Bluenose," she said.

"I do. I do say so," he said. "I'd like to see my girl now. Here, Brant, you keep this money, so's I don't get carried away and give it all to my girl."

"Which one do you want?" Miss Lottie said.

"My girl, like I told you," Bluenose said. "You know who I mean." He looked up at the big woman. His eyes, glazed and red with whiskey, were sinking back into his head.

"You've got no girl here that I know of," she said. Miss Lottie looked composed and polite, but there was a faint iron rigidity in her mannerly voice.

Bluenose stood up. "Don't taunt me, Lottie. Our agreement is I get three hundred dollars and my choice of the girls for a hundred gallons of whiskey. Your nigger's unloaded the whiskey, now I want my choice and my choice is Polly."

Bluenose loomed over Miss Lottie, and I realized that I had never seen him so drunk, not even that night down in the gorge. His hair, long since dried after the combing he'd given it, sprung out wildly from his head and he had a look of hillbilly meanness about him.

Miss Lottie stared up into his face a moment and then came over to the reading table where I sat. She reached down and turned over one of the magazines on the table and studied its back cover for a moment. She was playing for time.

"Bluenose," she said presently, still looking at the magazine, "there's twelve girls upstairs in this house. How come you can't pick one of them that likes you? Polly hates your guts. She's the only one that does and she's the only one you want to go with. Why is that?"

"Never mind why," Bluenose roared. "Goddamit, a deal's a deal. I ain't never gone back on my deal, have I, Lottie?" He glared at her.

When Bluenose started yelling, General jumped straight up. He sidled up to Bluenose and started talking nicely, like a man who is going to work things out. "Now, Bluenose," he said, "you know cain't neither one of us afford to get caught in no troubles. I cain't let you bother Miss Lottie when she's . . ."

Bluenose's arm shot out and he grabbed General's overall bib. He snatched my uncle over so he could talk to him real close; General was up on his tiptoes.

"General," Bluenose said, "when a feist dog barks at me, I kick him. When he bites, I kill him. Now you're just before getting your fiddle-playing ass kicked."

I was anxious to see how General was going to negotiate this situation, but Miss Lottie stepped in. "Both of you just shut up," she said.

"Ain't our deal the way I said it is, Lottie?" Bluenose demanded, dropping my uncle.

"That's the way it is," Lottie said wearily. She left us, went through a bead curtain which hung across a wide, open doorway and called up the stairs in the entrance hall. A girl came down the stairs into the dim foyer and then through the bead curtain. Miss Lottie came in behind her. The girl stopped as soon as she came in. She was turned toward Bluenose so I couldn't see her face.

"Not this goddam peckerwood," she said. "Why didn't you tell me it was this country bastard, Miss Lottie?"

The girl said this looking directly at Bluenose and in a very loud voice.

"See, I told you," Miss Lottie said, not to the girl, but to Bluenose.

Bluenose, still standing in front of the sofa, swung his body back and forth, like a backward child before company. He rubbed his open, big hands hard on his pants legs, as if trying to dry them. "Aw, Polly, honey, don't be like that now," he begged. "You know how much I like you, honey, now . . ."

"Shut up, you goddam hillbilly," she said. "They ain't no way you're getting upstairs with me. I'll quit first, I swear it, Miss Lottie, if you try to make me go with that pig. Look at him. He looks like he just got through plowing. Look at him." I still couldn't see the girl's face, but her voice was shaking. She had on a thin housecoat, and I could tell she was trim and well formed.

Bluenose blinked his eyes rapidly and ran a hand over his drunken face. He looked as out of place in that fancy, big-city whorehouse as he would have in the baptism pool at the Pover Baptist Church. He took a couple of steps toward the girl.

"Don't let him touch me," she yelled, spinning around toward Miss Lottie, and as she turned her face came clearly into view. Seeing Polly's face brought it all together, made it clear why she was the only girl there who interested Bluenose. Seeing that face was like seeing Elmira as she had looked fifteen years before, before the five children and the bitterness and before she began totaling up the sins of her husband, before work and worry and anger had lined and hardened her face. It was the face Bluenose had loved and that had loved him once. The resemblance was unmistakable. Blood sisters couldn't have looked more alike.

"If I've got to take one of them, let me go with him," Polly said, pointing at me.

Bluenose turned toward me, started to speak, didn't. I shook my head and Miss Lottie motioned the girl out of the room. She went through the curtain of beads and I heard her climbing the stairs fast.

"How about one of the other girls?" Miss Lottie said gently.

"How about Grace, Bluenose? You know how much she likes you. I remember when you and Grace used to have a big time together."

Bluenose was making small, strangely delicate motions with his big hands, as if he were fixing to say something. He appeared to be shushing Miss Lottie, but his head was down and he couldn't seem to say anything. Suddenly he bolted from the room, plunging through the bead curtain, across the foyer and out the front door.

"Hey, Bluenose," I yelled, "wait."

Miss Lottie hustled me toward the door. "Go catch him and y'all walk north up this street until you come to the streetcar line. It's two blocks. Take him downtown and get a hotel room. I'll have Booker take care of the team and y'all can pick it up in the morning."

"Yes, ma'am," I said and started for the door.

"Oh, Brant," she said. "Come back anytime and we'll take care of you proper. On the house."

"Yes, ma'am, thank you," I said.

I noticed that Uncle General was hanging back in the living room.

"Come on," I said.

"Listen, Brant, I think I'll just meet y'all in the morning if it's all the same to you."

"It ain't," I said.

"Well, I don't care. I got all my traps in the wagon and I cain't afford to leave them. What if somebody stole my fiddle?"

"You're coming if I have to drag you," I said, more suspicious of him than ever. I wasn't about to let him out of my sight.

Finally General started shuffling toward me, not looking nearly so feisty. "It's a hell of a thing to take advantage of kinfolks this way," he muttered.

Miss Lottie let us out and locked the door behind us. Bluenose hadn't gotten very far. We caught him not a hundred yards up the street from Lottie's front gate. We took him in tow and followed her directions to the car line.

None of us made any conversation as we waited on a corner in a puddle of light from a street lamp. Bluenose sat on the curb, holding his head in his hands. General passed the time like a sulled-up kid, gathering pebbles and tossing them at the metal shade of the street light. Sometime well after ten o'clock, the streetcar came clanging down the wide vacant street, ranging from light into darkness as it passed each corner street lamp and went back into the shadows of the big shade trees which lined the curb. There were no passengers on the streetcar, only the motorman up front and the conductor, who stood by the back door to make change and collect fare tokens. I paid our fares from the loose change in my pockets. Bluenose still hadn't said anything. He staggered on up the aisle to a seat in the middle of the car, stumbling once as it lurched into motion again. General made a point of taking a seat two rows in back of Bluenose. He ignored me as I went past him toward Bluenose's seat. The conductor followed me up and stopped me before I slid in beside Bluenose.

"What you boys doing out here toward Miss Lottie's?" he said. "She don't usually cater to streetcar trade."

The conductor had on a blue uniform with metal buttons, like a cop's.

Bluenose jerked his head around to look at us. "She caters to me," he said.

"You better keep that drunk quiet, boy," the conductor told me. "I ain't having no trouble on my car."

"Who you calling a drunk, blue-belly?" Bluenose said. Bluenose grabbed the seat in front of him and started pulling himself up.

"You," said the conductor.

I tried to push Bluenose back down in his seat, but he shook me off.

"You best just count your goddam nickels and leave me be,"

Bluenose said. His voice had a familiar flat tone, the same one I had used on Satterfield, but we were not before a hometown crowd. The sour smell of whiskey was strong on Bluenose's breath when he spoke. He looked wilder than ever now, real drunken anger showing in his eyes. The conductor came up closer, so that I was pinned tightly between the two men as I struggled once more to get Bluenose into his seat.

"You better mind your boy," said the conductor. "You don't want me to have to seat you."

Bluenose reached over my shoulder and popped the conductor on the chin with a straight, quick right jab. The conductor, caught flatfooted, went down on his ass. I felt the streetcar pick up speed. Looking toward the front, I saw the motorman calmly watching all this in his rear-view mirror as he opened up the throttle.

The conductor scrambled back down the aisle before trying to get to his feet, making sure that Bluenose couldn't jump on him before he got up.

"What a mistake you have made," he told Bluenose in a prim, confident voice. There was a thin trickle of blood at the corner of his mouth, not much though, because the force of Bluenose's fist had been on the bony point of his chin. The conductor came out of his back pocket with a short leather blackjack. "I don't usually have to use this on white folks," he said. "But I guess you're what we'd call white trash, ain't you, friend?"

Bluenose shoved me out of the way and hurried down the aisle toward the conductor. Bluenose was very drunk and the other man was very confident. He was also very fast. When Bluenose swung at him with a roundhouse right, the conductor stepped neatly inside it and laid the blackjack to Bluenose's temple with a short, vicious chop. Bluenose fell like a sack of coal. I could tell that the conductor had used that instrument before. He stood over Bluenose and patted the blackjack in his free hand. It made a fleshy little slap.

"Would you like some, boy?" he said.

"No, sir," I said.

"How about you, shorty?" he said, looking at General.

"Shit, I just run into those fellows down at the whorehouse," said General.

"You move as a group as far as I'm concerned," said the conductor. "You all getting the same ride now." The conductor looked back at me. "What you doing traveling with this trash, boy?"

"We're from the same town," I said.

"Where's that?" he said, still tapping that blackjack in his hand.

"Milo," I said, "in Pover County up north of Jasper."

"Yeah, I know. It figures," the conductor said. He stepped over Bluenose and came past me going toward the front of the car. "Leave him lay," he said as he passed me.

As soon as the conductor left, General crept up and slipped into the seat beside me. He was so scared he was trembling.

"Gimme that money," he whispered.

"What for?"

"Shit, boy, I know this line. It runs straight to the police station and that's where he's telling that motorman to take us right now. Gimme that money so's I can buy us out of this mess."

"I'll keep the money," I said.

"Just gimme a hundred of it, that'll do," he hissed.

"It ain't your money to spend," I said.

General grabbed my arm and squeezed it hard with his strong fingers.

"Godammit, Brant, I gotta have it. I married a woman down here one time. They got papers on me in every court in this town, desertion, bigamy, you name it. If they take us downtown, I never will get out of jail."

"Bigamy?"

"They claim I married a woman up at Boaz one time, too."

I couldn't help smiling. "My mother's bachelor brother."

"You little son of a bitch, I'm going to kick your teeth out if you don't give me that money."

"No, you won't, General," I said.

The conductor looked back toward us. "You two break it up," he said. "Get back to your seat, short stuff."

"You take my seat," General shouted. He jumped up and bolted down the aisle toward the back door. He had worked the lever to open it and leaped from the moving streetcar before the conductor could make a move. I stood up in time to see that General had taken a hell of a fall, rolling and twisting into the street, his arms and legs flying at crazy angles. The damn street car must have been running at least thirty miles an hour when he jumped. He finally skidded up against the curb beneath a street light. As we drew swiftly away, I saw him get up and, holding his body, scuttle off into the darkness. The streetcar never slowed down. The conductor came back to me.

"That'll take the crease out of his goddam overalls for him," he said, laughing. "Was that little dude traveling with you, son?"

"I never even knew him until today," I said, settling down for the ride. I looked back at Bluenose. He was sleeping in great peace. A lump as big as an egg had pushed up under the hair above his ear, but he wasn't bleeding. The streetcar was going down a broad avenue lined with houses and an occasional store. We came on through a district of shops and warehouses, past an open block where the other streetcars were parked for the night. When we got downtown, the car tracks made a sharp turn and I felt the car begin to slow down. It stopped in front of a two-story brick building. I saw CITY HALL cut in concrete over dark double doors. Off to the side of the main entrance a door stood open, revealing a lighted stairway. Lights shone from the windows across the second floor and POLICE DEPT. was written in gold leaf on every other window. The conductor went up the stairway and came back with three cops. They were all talking excitedly and laughing. They all stood over Bluenose. I stood up to meet them.

"Who's he?" A cop with sergeant's stripes on the sleeve of his blue shirt nodded toward me.

"He's with toughie there, but he didn't give me no trouble. No need to book him," the conductor said.

"Son," the cop said, "if you knew Herschel like I do, you'd know how lucky your friend is not to have a hole through him."

Herschel, the conductor, looked proud. "Aw, I done quit carrying a pistol. I handle 'em all with my little head-knocker now." He patted his hip pocket.

"What's the matter, Herschel?" one of the other cops said. "Your preacher get to you?"

They all got a good laugh out of that. The two cops with no rank picked up Bluenose and we all followed the sergeant. Herschel and the driver made their good-byes and went off in the street car. Inside at the booking desk, I gave the sergeant Bluenose's name and tried to talk him into letting me take him on to a hotel. I promised to get him out of town first thing the next morning.

"No way, son," the sergeant said. "The city's cracking down on street fighting and shooting. We got a new judge says he's going to tame this town down. Your friend will get to meet him at nine o'clock tomorrow morning. Now get on out of here." I did just that, walking a few blocks over to the center of town, where I passed the night in a cheap hotel near the Lyric Theater. They were playing *The Public Enemy,* but it was too late to go.

Judge Comer Ragsdale had a bald head. There was a black plaque with his name on it in front of the bench. He gave a speech about how the mayor had asked him to take time off from his law practice and fill in as city judge to try to cut down on some of the lawlessness in the city, particularly gun-carrying and brawling.

There were about thirty people in the courtroom, mostly friends and relatives of the defendants, I gathered. There were white people and colored, and the colored sat behind a little low fence in the back. The bailiff brought in the defendants one at a time through the door beside the judge's bench. The first ten defendants were nigger men charged with drunkenness and disorderly conduct or disturbing the peace or assault and battery and resisting arrest. They all got the maximum sentence the law allowed except for one old man up on a public drunk charge. The judge said he had known the old man since he, the judge, was a boy and he let the old man go on a suspended sentence. The judge made a little joke about the old fellow drinking too much and having too many young-uns and the old man laughed at it.

Bluenose was next. Judge Comer Ragsdale read the police report out loud. It said that the conductor had had to repulse Bluenose's drunken attack in order to protect his life and limb and transit company property. The judge asked Bluenose where he was from and Bluenose told him.

"And what do you do in Pover County, Mr. Trogdon?" the judge asked.

"I'm a farmer, Your Honor."

"If you're a farmer and not just another drifter, what were you doing drunk down here in Birmingham?"

"Visiting friends, Judge. I ain't no drifter. I ain't never been in trouble before. It's just a rare thing for me to even have a drink."

Bluenose looked terrible. His eyes were like two pissholes in the snow and the side of his head had turned dark blue. The judge smiled, as if he'd been told a joke.

"Well, Mr. Trogdon, in view of this good record you're claiming, I might be able to temper justice with a little mercy. From the looks of your head, you could use a little mercy. I'm going to sentence you on just the public drunk, if you'll plead guilty on both the drunk and the assault and battery charges. Do you understand?"

"Yes, sir."

"Guilty or not guilty?"

"Guilty."

"Thirty days or a hundred dollars?" said the judge.

"I'll do the time," said Bluenose.

"Take him away," the judge told the bailiff. "One more thing, Mr. Trogdon. The next time you have one of those rare drinks, do it in Pover County. Don't let the sun set on you in Birmingham when you get out of jail."

Bluenose turned and nodded good-bye to me. I raised my hand and opened my palm so he could see the folded bills, but he shook his head and formed the word "Elmira" with his lips. He followed the bailiff on through the door and it shut behind them. It was too late to start for home that day, so I took my hotel room for another night. That evening I went to the Lyric Theater to see the vaudeville show and *The Public Enemy*. In the movie, this gangster smashed a grapefruit in his girlfriend's face, but he got killed in the end. As a student of literature, I knew it was an old story: how the mighty are made humble. The next morning I went out to the whorehouse to get the wagon. The mules had been tied so they could reach into the bed and feed on the corn that had been used to cover the whiskey. They had water, too, in a big bucket shoved up under the tail of the wagon where they couldn't kick it over. Booker had been around mules before, I decided. I led the mules around to the front of the wagon and started hitching them into the traces.

"Hey, boy," I heard a voice say. The voice came from above me. Looking up, I saw the whore Polly peering over the sill of a second-floor window. Her hair was tousled and I could tell she was lying down.

"Hey," she said, "where's that country bastard you run with?"

"In jail, as if you'd give a shit," I said, continuing to work on the harnesses.

"Boy, you sure do talk dirty," she said in a lazy voice. "You ain't quite as wild looking as that squirrel."

I didn't look back up.

"Hey, boy, cain't you hear me? I said you ain't so bad."

I looked back up at her. In the daylight the resemblance to Elmira was unmistakable.

"Come on up here, I got something I want to show you, boy," she said, rolling over and out of sight. I was interested enough in her invitation, but I thought of how Bluenose felt about her and why he felt that way. I went back to the hitching.

"Ain't you coming?" she said in a minute, sticking her head over the sill again. "I know you'd like to see what I got to show you."

"I don't want to see it," I said, straightening out the reins and looping them around the arm rest on the driver's seat. "I'm not interested," I said. I grabbed the halter of the near mule and started swinging the team around toward the alley driveway that crossed the far end of the back yard to the alley.

"Look here," she said. I did. She had raised up over the windowsill so that she was visible from the waist up. She didn't have any clothes on. She was propped on the windowsill with straightened arms and it was a sight to get your attention.

"Say, those are nice ones all right," I said, squinting up toward her against the morning light. I wanted to go up, but the resemblance to Elmira made me feel funny about it.

"You just tie up them mules and come on," she said. I climbed into the driver's seat. "It ain't going to cost you nothing, if that's what's worrying you."

"That ain't worrying me," I said. "I wouldn't pay you anyhow."

"Good," she said. "What's the matter, boy, ain't you ever had none?" She laughed very lazily at that. I sat there with the reins in my hands, just ready to cluck up the team. They shifted in the traces, ready to go.

"No, ma'am," I said, "that's not my problem. I've had more than I need, I think."

"Well, I ain't going to beg you to take what other folks is pleased to pay for," she said and dropped out of sight again.

I opened the door slowly and looked in to make sure it was her room. She was lying naked on the bed, her long slender legs open. Her breasts were white and round as cantaloupes. The brown skin around the nipples covered the whole ends of them.

"How'd you know which door was mine?" she said.

"I guessed by the position of your window," I said. I could see that she was younger than I was, not more than twenty. I shut the door behind me. She made no move to cover herself.

"I'd say you're some considerable better looking than your running mate," she said.

"Shut up about him," I said, and started taking off my clothes.

"Why is he so crazy about me?" she said.

"It's nothing personal with you," I said. "It's what you might call an accident." I sat down on the edge of her bed as I undressed.

"How's that?" she said.

"Never mind," I said.

"You feel bad about doing this, since he's your friend and all," she said.

"You might say that," I said.

"A hard dick has no conscience," she said. "Ain't that so?"

I didn't want to talk any more. I lay down beside her.

She raised up on an elbow and looked me in the face. "Listen," she said, "you do me some good. That's the reason I called you up here. Most of these fools that trade here hit three strokes and blow their load. I want you to do me some good."

I did that. I hammered on that thing to a fare-thee-well and did her a lot of good. It didn't do me as much good because of Bluenose and her resemblance to Elmira, even though she was a whore. When I went off, it felt like a plug deep inside me had been pulled and everything was draining out through my guts and it burned as it went.

Afterward I felt bad, as I had known I would. I lay on my back, studying the ceiling, tracing cracks which ran out from the light pedestal in its center, ran crazily like rivers in a dry season.

The whore lay beside me, snuggled down like any good girl friend or wife.

"You want to do it again," she said by and by.

"Not really," I said.

"We'll see about that."

She began kissing along my face, down the line of my jaw, my neck, down across my collarbone. I lay back, closing my eyes now, feeling her lips and spreading fingers moving in a light network of touches down my chest and belly. I looked to where she knelt over me, her hair flopped forward in a soft, brushing fan across my body.

She looked up, saw me watching her.

"You don't get much call for this in Birmingham," she said. "Scares all these big men. You ever had one?"

"No," I said. "Why should I lie. Where'd you learn?"

"Same place you are," she said. "In a whorehouse. Not this one. I've been better places."

She fell to her work again, progressing with small kisses toward the place she wanted. My breath went out of me in a long expiration. I had the sensation of being stretched back against the curve of the earth, muscle stretch and tendon pop, a loosening of nerve and joint, as my whole body arched up to the single place she touched me. I thought of the lot of them, Blake, Elmira, Polly, and of how devastated Bluenose would be to see his whore like this. I thought of them fleetingly and without guilt, for she was right, of course, Polly was. A hard dick has no conscience.

On the trip home I had the advantage of a light wagon. Still it was well into Wednesday night when I reached Milo, since I didn't get away from Polly until Tuesday noon. I took the wagon to Bluenose's house and turned the mules loose in the barn lot. There was a light showing in the kitchen, but I didn't bother to try to hail Elmira. I just went on home and went to bed, slipping in quietly to keep from waking Poppa. He didn't wake me for work the next morning and I slept until almost noon. After lunch, I went over to the Trogdon's place to give Elmira the three hundred dollars. When I got there she was sitting on the porch with Pride Hatton, who seemed to be enjoying a little home visitation work in the absence of the master of the house.

I nodded to him and asked Elmira if I could see her privately. The preacher stayed on the porch and he bounced the youngest child on his knee while Elmira and I talked. I could hear him singing a nonsense song to the baby and cooing at her.

"Bluenose said to give you this," I said, handing her the three bills.

"And where is he? Laying out down at the river?"

"He's in jail in Birmingham. He got thirty days for hitting a streetcar conductor."

"A common brawl," she said. "I guess he was drunk as usual."

"I wouldn't know," I lied. "There wasn't any spectacle to it anyway, if that's what's worrying you. He and the conductor had words and exchanged licks and the conductor called the police to him, that's all. It could have happened to anybody."

"That's where you're wrong, Mr. Brant Laster," she said, suddenly spiteful. "It could have happened to anybody out selling whiskey and drinking. How am I going to explain his being in jail to the children—and the preacher?"

"Don't explain it," I said. "It's none of his business anyhow." I nodded toward Hatton. "He don't live here, does he?"

"I can see Bluenose has been filling you with all kind of talk against me and Brother Hatton and the church."

"I brought you the money. That's all I came for," I said.

"Whiskey money," she said. Her eyes looked hard and unforgiving, and you could see the years of anger and stored-up spite telling on her in the lines of her face. Still it was not hard to see that once she had been pretty enough, like Polly, but slimmer of hip and less full bosomed.

"Whiskey money or not, it'll spend all right." There was a pause. "And you see if Brother Hatton throws any of it out of the collection plate."

"You get off this place, Laster," she said, low and fierce. "And mind you, Bluenose and his like don't fool me. None of you fool me. I'm marking all this down. Now you get off the place."

"Yes, ma'am," I said, bowing toward her. "I'm good as gone." Behind her, Hatton was still playing with the baby girl on the porch. The baby seemed happy and comfortable with him. "Good-bye to you, Brother Hatton," I said to him with mock friendliness. "I'll let you get on with your visitation."

"Good day, Brother Laster," he called back in the same tone.

I headed across the dusty yard toward the road.

"Oh, Brother Laster," the preacher called. I looked back. Elmira was already standing by him on the porch. "We're having a revival down at the church every evening this week. Why don't you come see us? I believe we could help you."

"You best just help yourself, Preacher," I said, letting my gaze move from him to Elmira as I spoke.

"Oh, I am, Brother Laster. I am doing just that," he said in an easy voice. "I been helping myself every day."

"And your help is in the Lord, I reckon," I said.

"Amen."

CHAPTER NINE

Word spread pretty fast that Bluenose was in jail, thanks to Pride Hatton's revival sermon Thursday night—a real stem-winder, from what folks said. Then on Friday, Ozro charged into the Good Neighbor Mercantile waving a copy of the Birmingham *News*. He marched right up to the counter where my father had the Memphis paper spread out.

"Well, I guess he's happy now," Ozro said, hollering like he wanted to argue about something. "You seen this?"

"No, but I'd guess you're talking about Bluenose," said my father.

"My God, is it in the Memphis paper, too?"

"No, Memphis doesn't have to import drunks to fill up its paper," Poppa said, laughing. "I just guessed from the way you waved that paper that Bluenose must have made the drunk list in the *News*. Most all big-city papers have drunk lists."

"Maybe it's funny to you, but Pride Hatton's already got folks mighty worked up about Bluenose. Now this comes in the morning mail."

I took the paper from Ozro.

"It's on page thirteen," Ozro said.

The story, under a small headline at the bottom of the page, said: "Judge Comer Ragsdale convicted a total of 23 persons on misdemeanor charges in Monday's session of Recorder's Court.

"Those convicted and their sentences were as follows: John Ed

Jeffcoat of 137 Second Ave., drunk and disorderly, 30 days; Sidney Porter of Bessemer, assault, 30 days; Eleazer Trogdon of Milo, Ala., drunk and disorderly, 30 days; . . ."

"Mark me, this newspaper thing will really rip it," Ozro said. "Folks'll be saying Bluenose has give the town a bad name. And saying that if I had been doing my job like the Birmingham police . . ."

"Looks to me like most people won't even notice this little story unless somebody points it out to 'em."

Ozro turned toward me. "I guess that's supposed to mean I'm spreading gossip. Well, it's my job to find out how people feel about things."

"And to show them this paper in case they're not too sure how they feel."

Somehow old Ozro didn't seem comical any more. He had his feet to the fire now and he was looking out for himself.

"Don't come down on me for doing my job, Brant. I been after Bluenose to do right for a long time. I told him something like this was coming if he didn't lay low. And I'll tell you this: You're lucky you ain't in that newspaper."

"What's that supposed to mean, Ozro?" I demanded, cutting him a mean glance.

"He knows, Brant," Ozro said triumphantly. "Your poppa knows."

Poppa reached in a drawer under the counter and then skidded my pocket watch across the counter toward me.

"Buddy Gilliland brought this in the night after you left for your fishing trip," he said.

I realized that he had known all week, had let me pick up my old routine at the store without saying a word.,

"Why didn't you tell me you knew, Poppa?"

"A lie ain't the easiest thing for a man to throw up to his son," he said. "Besides you're whatever kind of man you're going to be. I figured maybe"—he stopped, blinked his eyes rapidly behind his glasses—"I hoped you had your own good reasons for lying to me."

"I did," I said. "You were it, Poppa. You're my reason."

"Listen, Brant, I'm sorry I brought it up," Ozro said.

"Oh, shut up, fat man," I told him. "You did what you came to do."

I left the store. It was early afternoon, and I just started walking south on the Jasper Road, following it down toward the river. I had spent a long time dreading the day Poppa found out that the little boy who never told lies had grown into a different kind of man, but now that the truth was revealed, I was relieved. As for Ozro, he had come down to hard knucks and decided that the thing to do was look out for himself. Only a fool would be surprised. We are what we are. I went straightaway down to Bluenose's bluff and dug around in the sand until I struck whiskey. Then I kicked up a pile of sand and covered it with an old denim jumper of Bluenose's to make a pillow. I lay down in the sand. I drank whiskey and thought:

—That all of us in Milo were in a time of reductions. These were the winnowing days, a time for making final choices. It was a time, too, in which all pretense fell away. Sarahgrace had opened her bed to General Drummond and counted it no secret worth keeping. When Pride Hatton looked down from his pulpit, his tongue spoke the Holy Ghost, but his eye was on Elmira. Bluenose Trogdon loved a whore because she reminded him of someone he used to know, and then there was Blake King and there was me and there was whatever we had.

—That I first had Blake King when we were fourteen, had her almost by accident, in fumbling innocence and blood and pain so fine that she clung to me the whole afternoon weeping, and the tears would not stop, but passed beyond loss and became a kind of celebration. The memory of that day in a branch-bottom thicket—Blake naked in the shifting forest light, her slim, girlish body shining on a carpet of crushed fern—that memory could hunt me down in the midst of any happiness and turn it to blank despair. For years after that day, our love had run smooth and clear and green, like the Sipsey's green water finding its way among rock and boulder in the dry summertime. Our mistake had been going into the world, the changing place.

—That there were two Blake Kings: the one who had loved me from that day and had come back to be with me forever, and the other who had no resistance to the life of temptation and possibility. I didn't believe I could handle the second without going crazy, but I wanted the first Blake, my old Blake, whatever there was left of her, so badly I was sure God going to try. That knowledge wrapped its chilly arms around me. My heart lay in my chest cold and still, a lump of ice. Could whiskey ever melt it? Whiskey 'til I die. A good hillbilly song. I play it when I can.

I woke up with a headache that would stun a mule. I mean it was a goddam ground-shaker. I lay where I had fallen asleep, the whiskey jug propped against my side. It was dusk, cool under the bluff. I crept to the river and bathed my face and lay there for a while, very still. The headache settled down to a steady, dull streak of pain right behind my eyes. I have always been a student of the quality of pain in headaches, especially whiskey headaches. This one definitely had character and staying power. I figured the night couldn't be any more wrecked—I felt shaky and rattled by the general suspicion that there was a bad tribulation brewing somewhere—so I decided to take Pride Hatton up on his invitation.

Hatton was preaching from the front steps of his church. His outdoor revival was well in progress by the time I was able to make it out of the gorge, back into Milo and on out the Fever Springs Road to his church. The church benches had been moved into the yard, where the limbs of two big oaks arched over to make a kind of tabernacle. The place was lit by kerosene lamps hung from the oaks. I guess there were a hundred people in all, not all of them Holiness by any means. Plenty of spectators came to the Holy Roller meetings, standing back in the shadows to watch them talk in tongues or dance when the Holy Ghost got them. The Holy Rollers didn't mind. A man that came to gawk might get the Holy Ghost, too, they figured.

Hatton looked good. He had his black hair brilliantined flat and shiny against his skull, and his white shirt starched so stiff you expected it to crackle. He had that lean, shifty handsomeness that you saw sometimes in preachers of those little country churches. Poppa had a saying for slick preachers. He said they "got the call behind the plow," meaning they took to preaching to avoid hard work. That was Hatton all over. But he could preach, and the Holiness people, poor folks, liked his flash.

Hatton held up a Bible. "Who says this book ain't clear?" he demanded. "Who says any man that has eyes to read or ears to hear cain't understand it?" He held the book before him, squeezing it between his two hands. "There ain't no trickery or deceit about it. It's just what you see. A man that claims confusion from the Bible is trying to dodge the Lord. He's lying to hisself. Friends, it's as clear as can be.

"And what this book is mainly about is one thing and that's plain and simple, too. It's God's rules about how to avoid sin." He waved the Bible in the air again, allowed his voice to rise. "If you got a question about anything you want to do, just look in the book. Live like it says, and you ain't got a worry. But if you live any other way, you are living in violation of God's word. You are living in deadly sin. You are living in-ah mortal sin. Yes, sir. And God hates *sin*." He slammed the Bible down on the last word. Amens rose from the congregation. "You better know God hates sin-ah. And hallelujah, I hate it, too."

Hatton rocked back from the lectern, clasped his hands at his chest. His voice got soft again. "Now, I've heard us Pentecostal people criticized for not having our women fancy up and wear paint and frilly clothes. They say we're foolish and old fashioned and silly. They say the Holiness folk carry things too far, that the Lord didn't mean for folks to be always somber and serious. Friends, that's what people say, but that don't count. Tongues speaking words devised of man—that don't matter no more than a rabbit-sneeze in a tornado. What God says, what God says, *what God says-ah,* that's what counts."

Hatton grabbed up his Bible again. It seemed to fall open to the place he wanted. He struck his finger down on the page. "Hear this," he shouted, "God says in First Timothy, the second chapter, the ninth verse: 'In like manner also, that women adorn themselves in modest apparel, with shamefacedness and sobriety, not with braided hair, or gold, or pearls, or costly array.'"

He looked out at the congregation. He was preaching with a rhythmic, barking delivery. "That's what God says. Don't worry about anything else. Don't worry about the talk that says woman oughta be equal of man, and the husband shouldn't be the master of the wife. That's what *people* say. They're writing about it in the newspapers every day. Oh yes, it's big talk up in New York and places like that. But friends, God says in the first book of Timothy, 'Let the woman learn in silence with all *Subjection.*' Now did you hear that last word? 'Subjection' is what the word of God says and it goes on: 'But I suffer not a woman to teach, nor to usurp authority over the man, but to be in *silence.*'"

When Hatton paused to let the amens die down, I slipped inside the circle of onlookers and sat down on the back bench. I was tired of standing. Hatton flicked his eyes up at me as I took my seat.

"Now," he said softly, "ain't that clear? They may think they're smart up there in New York, but they ain't smarter than God—no, sir. That whole city ain't smart as one of you that's got sense to heed what God says." He looked out over the audience again and there was silence.

"Yes, God's word is clear, but God don't always show us right off what His will and His way is." Hatton propped his hands on his hips, struck a pose. "He don't have to. He's God."

There was laughter, a chorus of assent, and Hatton picked up on it.

"The smart Christian just takes his tribulation, keeps on loving the Lord. For them that love the Lord can say, 'My day's gonna come.'"

Shouts: "That's right." "Preach hard."

Hatton's arm shot out, pointing down toward the front row.

"Here's a woman that's been living the word of God every day and in every way."

"Amen," came the response.

"But the way is hard for her. Folks might say—I say-ah *man* might tell you—she wasn't minding the Bible."

Hatton, keeping his long arm extended, started walking down from the steps. He kept moving toward the congregation, slow and stiff-legged, until he stopped in front of the first row of benches. His hand was extended over the bowed head of a woman sitting there. Her face was hidden from the congregation.

"Here's a woman suffers like no good wife and mother oughta. But she is strong in the Lord and she don't complain. 'Cause she knows it ain't God's fault."

"No."

"Don't you come a telling me that-ah. No"—a hand clap—"No"—another hand clap—"*NO*. Don't come telling me it's God's fault."

God, I loved him. Pride Hatton beat any show I ever saw.

"God done all he could," he said. "He give rules for the woman, and Sister Elmira here followed 'em."

Amens all round to that.

"He give rules for the man . . ."

Silence all round.

". . . and Bluenose Trogdon broke 'em ever one."

"Amen." "Well, tell it all."

"Broke 'em fast as he could come to 'em."

"All right."

"He loved to break man's laws, but he'd rather break one of God's holy laws."

"Hallelujah."

"That's hard, I know. But I believe it."

"Yes-unnnh." "Lord."

"If Bluenose Trogdon was here I'd say it to his face. It's hard, but it's fair."

He spun away from the congregation and went up the stairs like a dancer, scooped up his Bible and came dashing back up the center aisle. He stopped about the middle of the crowd, so people in the front rows had to turn around in their seats to watch him.

"But Bluenose Trogdon ain't just disobeyed God's laws of husbandry. No, worse than that. He's worked like the Devil-ah—he's worked *with* the Devil to pull other people down. I don't have to tell you what this man does for a living."

There was a long negative groan from the congregation.

"Now what does God have to say about those that barter in spirits? God's word is clear. Let them that have ears hear it and eyes behold it. Hear this from the Book of Habakkuk, the second chapter and the fifteenth verse, where God speaks in this wise: 'Woe unto him that giveth his neighbor drink, that puttest thy bottle to him, and makest him drunken also.'" Hatton slammed the Bible shut. "You hear that?" he shouted. "Did you hear the word that the Lord used there? It was *Woe*. Yes, sir. 'Woe unto him that giveth his neighbor drink . . .'"

"Amen," came the answer. There was a breathless and rhythmic pulse behind the word.

"And what does woe mean in God's book? I'll tell you what it means. When the Lord says 'Woe' it's a promise, my friends." Hatton dropped his voice suddenly and leaned over as if to whisper some secret. "It's a promise that if a man persists in sin, to his woe, to his eternal woe-ah, he's gonna go to fiery, burning, everlasting *Hell*."

There was a shout from the front and Elmira rose up and then flopped down on her knees, as if praying. The crowd came out of their seats again; the women set up a dull wailing.

"I said HELL," Pride Hatton shouted.

"Uhhhhh," they answered him with a deep animal groan.

He picked up the rhythm of their groan.

"That's right, Hell," he chanted.

"Amen."

"We ain't playin' now."

"Oh, no."

"Burning Hell-ah."

"Oh, Lord, uhnnnnn."

Hatton clipped off his words in pairs, as if calling cadence. "That's right—that man-ah—that sins—will burn-ah—" (That drunken old Holiness pandemonium was loose in them now, as if herds of small animals were scurrying under the benches, jostling the people and making moaning noises.) "—for ever—in HELL-ah." As he preached, Hatton worked his way back to the front until he was standing over Elmira. Three other women were kneeling there, clustered so close they looked to be piled on top of Elmira.

"Look at this poor woman," Hatton said, softly now. "Sister Elmira here praying for a man that lies in jail in Birmingham. That's where whiskey leads, my friends-ah, to dark and lonely jailhouses in strange cities where a man lies down in his loneliness and his shame."

"Amen," the congregation replied.

"And shame is what he's brought on Milo, dragging its name down . . ."

"Amen."

"Down . . ."

"All right."

"Down, with the liar's name . . ."

"Preach."

"The drunkard's name . . ."

"Lord."

"And-ah the fornicator, and-ah the brawler, and-ah the man of reprobate mind. Now that's how low he's got the name of your town-ah."

He shut up abruptly. The hubbub dwindled off into a low rhythmic grunting. The sweat rolled off Hatton's forehead. He looked down at the lectern, as if he had suddenly forgotten this congregation that he was playing like a fiddle. Softly he started again.

"And friends, ain't times hard? Ain't folks right here in Milo going to bed hungry?"

"That's right," someone said.

"But hard times don't bother the whiskey man." He looked up, spoke sharply. "Do you think they do?"

The grunt came up like a heartbeat.

"No. Whiskey money keeps coming in, hard times or good. The drunkard-ah will let the little infant baby go hungry to buy that whiskey, and Bluenose Trogdon and his like draw profit in good times or bad."

"That's right," they said. "Amen."

"Snatching that money from babies and mothers and the old folk-ah—the whiskey man's gonna get his."

Hatton stopped talking. He dropped his hands down to his side, as if surrendering to the sinful world. He stood looking out over the audience. They got quiet.

"What do you do?" he said. "What do you do when a man is shaming his family and town, spreading sin and suffering? What can one man, one feeble, ignorant country preacher do?"

There was a moan from the congregation. They wanted to assure him that he was none of those things. "I thought about it and I prayed about it. I asked the Lord, what to do about it. I asked the Lord to come into my heart. I said, 'Lord, I ain't nothing but a man.'"

Elmira seemed to have swooned, and a fat woman in a print dress was rocking her gently in her arms. Hatton stood over them, a protector.

"I said, 'Lord, I got anger in me from that day at the railroad tracks. I'm wishing I had smited him, Lord, just like old Samson smote the Philistines.' I said, 'Lord, I'm giving this anger to you.' And the Lord took it, hallelujah."

"Praise the Lord."

"So I can tell the world I'm doin' my part to help Bluenose Trogdon, 'cause Jesus helped me."

"Amen."

"He helped me find the seventeenth verse in the eighteenth chapter of Matthew. The Master's speaking there-ah. Says we gotta warn the sinner-man and have our friends warn him. 'And if he shall neglect to hear them, tell it unto the church; but if he neglect to hear the church, let him be unto thee as an heathen man and a publican.'"

There was a good chorus of amens to that.

"So we gonna try to save Brother Trogdon, to bring him into the House of the Lord where he may be bathed in the blood that washes all sin away."

"Hallelujah. Praise His name."

"Now, God's word says a man who will not heed His church is a heathen man."

"That's right."

"And what must be done with the heathen man in the community of Christians? I'll tell you and I'll tell you right now and I'll tell you straight."

Hatton had them locked down now, waiting in suspense for the big answer and he gave it to them in a little sing-song chant, rising on the last words.

"He must be cast out."

"Amen."

"He must be cast out-ah."

A chorus of amens and shouts.

"He must be *CAST OUT*-ah."

They roared back at him and Hatton began pelting them with short sentences and the congregation bent to his rhythm.

"Ain't we got a sheriff in this county?"

"Yes, indeed. Ain't we?"

"Ain't we got a constable in this beat-ah?"

"Ain't we?"

"Well, I say it's time they did what we elected them for. Enforce the law against making-ah whiskey and selling-ah whiskey and drinking-ah whiskey."

"Amen."

"So I'm telling you we're gonna have the law enforced or we're gonna get us some new enforcers."

"Amen."

Hatton was still standing up near the front of the congregation. He reached up and loosened his collar and started rolling up his sleeves. In Holiness churches, this is a signal that the soul saving and talking-in-tongues and the stomping and dancing is about to get underway. That place was fixing to break out in serious Jesus fits.

"But brothers and sisters we're gonna try love first."

He started walking down the aisle toward the rear of the group. The folks up front turned to watch him as he went.

"And I think love will work," he said.

"Praise His love," someone said.

"That's right," Hatton responded. "Praise His love. Praise its power. Before we do anything, we're going to extend to Bluenose Trogdon the open hand of our fellowship and love." He held out his right hand, palm upward and open, all the while walking slowly down the aisle, moving through the soft yellow light.

"We're going to offer him the open hand of invitation to join our fellowship, to join the saved that will see Jesus face to face on that glad tomorrow."

"Amen, brother." "Happy day."

Hatton, his hand still out in that graceful, practiced gesture of giving, had stopped in the aisle near where I sat. His back was to most of the congregation.

"We're going to offer this open hand of our church to Bluenose Trogdon just as I now offer it to Brant Laster, who was with him when he ran afoul of the law."

Hatton had stepped over in front of me and his hand, strangely white and tender looking, was before me. Everyone there was looking at me to see what I would do.

"Prepare a way for your brother Bluenose by taking my hand and coming down to the altar, Brant," he said. "Don't keep on walking that old whiskey road. Turn back before it's too late. Make your daddy proud. Come on home to Jesus."

"Oh, save him, Lord," a woman squalled. I kept my eyes on his hand, trying to think what to do.

"Take his hand, son," a farmer in overalls said.

"Take my hand and come on down, Brant. Jesus is waiting." I reached up and took his hand and clasped it firmly. The congregation gasped in relief.

"Praise His name." "Hallelujah." "Tell the story."

I stood up and threw an arm around Hatton's shoulders and hugged him, pulling his head over toward mine. It was meant to look like my surrender. I could hear a woman crying in a high, shrill, joyful voice.

"The Holy Ghost is moving here," Hatton said. "Welcome to the Lord's love, Brother Brant."

I pulled his head on over until I could whisper in his ear. "Fuck you, you goddam crooked son of a whore," I told him.

I let him go and slipped quickly into the crowd standing behind the benches. There in the back, folks were standing four or five deep, but they parted to let me through.

"Blasphemer. Oh, sinner of reprobate mind," I heard Hatton bellow behind me.

When I got through the spectators, I turned back to see the

preacher staring out into the dark alleyway where the crowd had parted for me. I could see his eyes shine under the lantern light. He ran a hand across his slick hair and pointed into the darkness where I had fled.

"Read the book, brother," he shouted. "Read where it says he that believeth and is baptized shall be saved, but he that believeth not shall be damned."

"Amen," shouted the crowd.

"I said damned," he yelled. "Damned to Hell for eternity."

They came back at him with a roar. I set out down the road for Milo and home. Behind me in the darkness, I heard him preaching and the people chanting and grunting back at him. I knew he'd not let them slow down again, but would push them right on into the talking-in-tongues and that old drunken, frantic, howling craziness that would come when the Holy Ghost seized them.

I had just crossed the churchyard and gotten on the road when I heard someone running at me from behind. I turned and braced, expecting that one of the men was coming after me for a fight. A squat heavy figure came shuffling toward me.

"Go on back to your congregation," I said when he reached me. "You have done tore your ass with me for good."

"Don't say that, Brant," Ozro whined.

"What do you expect me to say after that little deal you pulled with Poppa?"

"Brant, he already knew."

"Yeah, but he was letting it slide until you popped off and didn't leave him any choice," I said. "Go on back and arm up with Hatton so he won't let anybody run against you. You probably rigged that little trick he pulled tonight."

"Brant, you cain't blame me for all your troubles," Ozro said, still panting for breath. "You had no call showing up there tonight. Holiness folks take a heap of leaving alone."

I was pretty well sobered up, even though my head still hurt and I was shaky from my run-in with Hatton, and I knew Ozro was right. Besides I was too tired to stay mad at him, even for stirring up Poppa. "Cut out that tongue of yours and you wouldn't weigh ninety pounds," I said.

"Come on now, let me walk into Milo with you," Ozro said.

"All right, round man," I said and started walking. Ozro shuffled along beside me.

"Hey, what did you say to him?" he said.

"Who?"

"The preacher."

I told him.

"Shit," Ozro said, "that sounds like that crazy Bluenose."

"Speaking of Bluenose," I laughed, "what do you think of the preacher's plan to save him?"

"He'd just as well try to convert John Dillinger, I reckon."

"Well you better hope he can. 'Cause, according to the preacher, if Bluenose don't see the light, they're going to be calling on you to put him out of the whiskey business."

"I ain't wasting my time trying to keep a Trogdon from making whiskey. I'd sooner try to teach a hog to fly."

We had reached the bend of the road which would take us out of sight of the church. I turned around and looked back toward the yellow bulge of light under the big oak trees.

"Well, you tell me this. What the hell are you going to do if Hatton and the Holy Rollers get the Baptists and the Methodists all stirred up, and they all get in behind you to stop the whiskey trade?"

"Why, I'll tell 'em what I been telling folks all these years, the gospel truth. I never seen Bluenose Trogdon actual make any whiskey and I don't know where he does it if'n he does. But if I ever run up on such a place, I'll sure take him in."

"You'll do what you have to do when the time comes," I said. "You better get back up there in case Hatton calls on you to testify."

"I'd a little ruther have a drink of whiskey, if you was to know where to find one."

"I believe I can fix you up, but you know what sinner made it."

"I don't know any such of a thing," Ozro said, and that was the beginning of the campaign to save Bluenose Trogdon.

CHAPTER TEN

Time passed. Franklin D. Roosevelt was at large in America, spreading hope like an infection. There was no immunity, not even for me exiled in the remote high Alabama autumn. As summer died down in the still, dry days of late September, I surrendered fully to expectation; I lived in the careful ignorance of history. Blake and I had a place we went every night, an abandoned farmhouse where I had laid in a store of Bluenose's whiskey and some firewood, and in those nights, as I lay rolled in her arms, forgetting seemed an easy trick. I imagined myself the very kind of forgetful, forgiving man she sought, one of those admirable men for whom the past is past. There was even a surcease of dreaming in those first days of fall. But I too was seasonal. My autumnal peace was a frail thing. All that was needed to fracture it was the tiniest trip-hammer tap, and Sarahgrace, God bless her heart, gave me that.

"I tell you, I been such a fool it makes me sick to think about it," she said one day when I made my regular morning call at the post office.

"What's that supposed to mean?" I said, studying her expression. Her eyes, her whole face had a heavy, dead look.

"You tell me," she said. She flipped a postcard across the counter toward me. It had a picture of the Henry Grady Hotel in Atlanta on it. I turned it over and read: "Sarahgrace—I was just thinking of you. Tell Brant I'm over that fall I took down in B'ham and have no hard feelings. As ever—General Drummond."

"Well," I said.

"You did it, didn't you?" she said. "You and Bluenose hauled him out of here after I ain't seen him for five years."

"He rode with us to Birmingham," I said. "We didn't haul him anywhere. He's his own grown man."

She moved back and forth in the narrow pound of her cage for a moment, then turned from me and started sorting letters on the side counter.

"You could have had the decency to tell me," she said, not looking up at me. "But I guess you enjoyed your little secret, just you and Bluenose knowing what a fool I am."

"I didn't think it would make you happy to know," I said. "You weren't made to look a fool. Everybody knows about General."

That wasn't the right thing to say. Sarahgrace tucked her head to her shoulder and cupped her quivering chin in her hand. The tears rolled down the lined face that once had been beautiful enough to make her a regular stop on my uncle's circuit.

"Oh, God," she said, "why don't you just say it? Everybody knows about General but me, his old wore-out whore." She wept harder, her shoulders shaking.

"He'll be back," I said.

"Yes, he'll be back when he's so old and burnt out with whiskey that it don't matter and he needs a fire to sit by and some old fool woman to take care of him. He'll be back."

"Reckon I could have my mail now?" I said.

"Yes," she said, snuffling. "I'm going to give you your mail." She came back to the front counter and shoved across one of Poppa's familiar bundles, a *Commercial Appeal* and a pack of bills. "I'm going to show you some more mail, too," she said.

Sarahgrace held out a crisp white envelope addressed in a hand I recognized immediately. It was addressed to MacShan Satterfield in Camden, Alabama.

"Give me that," I said.

"You know I cain't do that, Brant," she said. "Other folks' mail—we got our rules. Why don't you ask her about it? This is the second one she's written. She's got two from him, too."

I didn't say anything. I reached out blindly and scooped up my father's mail.

"I didn't aim to tell you until I got that postcard from General," she said. "Then I decided you ought to know how it feels to be made a fool. I wanted to see how you liked being the last one to know the big secret. I thought I owed you at least that much."

I rushed out of the post office, as if I had somewhere to go. A breeze from the west had drifted the packed clay with curled brown leaves from the oak grove over behind Hibbert's store. I started walking slowly toward the Mercantile, and the dry leaves broke underfoot with dull, crushing reports like the gunshots from some distant hunt.

Blake came down the steps with her smile shining, sliding an arm around me as we fell in step toward the road. We went to our secret house. I built a fire. We had a drink, mixing the whiskey with Coca-Cola. Then I had another one.

"Promise me you'll get me in early tonight," Blake said. "I almost fell asleep in class today."

"I can promise you that, all right. I could get you in right now."

"What's wrong with you tonight?"

"How's old MacShan Satterfield these days?" I said.

"Who cares?" she said lightly.

"I know about the letters."

"Oh," she said. "Well, you can bet he's not wanting to see you again."

"Don't be funny."

"I didn't want you to know about the letters unless it became necessary."

"What would make it necessary?"

"If I decided to go to Demopolis for the houseparty he invited me to. There's a big hunt and a dance on Thanksgiving week-end."

"Are you going?" I said.

"I wrote him that I didn't know."

"It took you two letters to tell him you didn't know?" I said.

"No, I wrote him at first saying I wouldn't come because of you. Then he wrote back asking me to think it over some more and I wrote him that I would. It seemed only fair."

"Fair," I said. "Oh, you bitch."

"I don't have any commitments that would keep me from going. Maybe it would be fun for me. Maybe it would be good for you."

"Good for me. God, yes, that's really what I've been needing, just when things are starting to get better for us."

"Are they, Brant? I didn't have any signal from you."

"What about this?" I said, waving my hand around the room.

"This is just what we decided on last summer. I wanted it. I don't have any complaints. But I was afraid to hope it was any-thing beyond what it is, your still wanting to have me in this way."

"Goddam you, you knew I was beginning to think I could make myself get over things, over this goddam jealousy that is like a snake inside of me. You had to know that and now you go and pull this stunt."

"I can't read your mind, Brant."

I lay back, closed my eyes. I felt the heat of the fire beating against the left side of my body, then Blake's hands moving over my body, as if to knead the worry out of my skin and muscle. She opened my shirt, running her hands over my chest. I listened to her voice, which was telling me what I ought to do.

"Why don't you quit struggling so, Brant? I want you to know that no matter where I go, no matter who I am with, even if I marry somebody else, you can always have me, you could be having me if you were there. All you have to do is come for it."

I felt her shift position, her hair brushing against my bare skin, her head resting against my chest. "It's a power I have over you, Brant," she said softly, "and that you have over me. That we have over each other."

I felt her lips against my skin then, tracing slow lazy kisses across my body. I lay drifting, thinking of her doubleness.

"I will show you you can't leave me," she said. Her fingers were at my belt, moving quickly, and her head dropping across my belly, moving in quick, excited kisses, going down and down. I sat bolt upright, pushing her away.

"Where did you learn that whore's trick?" I shouted.

Blake, taken by surprise, pushed her hair back out of her face. She seemed to study my face for a long time. "I'm here with you now, doing what I want to do," she said.

"Don't lie to me," I hissed. "That's some goddam whore's trick you learned in Atlanta."

"You won't believe the truth when you hear it," she said. "Someday I may tell you more truth than you want to hear."

"About the whore's trick you did on your friend in Atlanta."

Blake put her hands together and then pressed them between her knees. Sitting thus, she rocked back and forth a little, as if she had a pain in her stomach. "Do you know what MacShan Satterfield said in his letter? He said he thought you must be crazy, insane with jealousy. He said he'd never seen anyone behave the way you did over any woman. He said he didn't think it was normal."

"Maybe he's right," I said.

"He wouldn't be if you would just live your own life."

Blake took my hand, held it between her hands. "Brant, don't you see it doesn't matter what I've done or haven't done. *I* don't matter. I'm just the thing you use. You don't really want me. You just want this thing you have with yourself. How can I make you see that? I accept your not wanting me, but why do you want to ruin yourself?"

I felt a rush of heat behind my eyes. "But I do want you," I said.

"Then why do you do this over and over and over?"

"I don't know. The humiliation of it, maybe. I can't explain it. Goddammit, I thought I had it whipped, I really did, Blake."

"Brant, I can't make things the way they were when we were kids. I wish I could do that for you. I'd give anything if I could. I took the risks for you, Brant, all those years, but now I've done all I can do."

The heat behind my eyes became tears and I fell over in Blake's lap and wept, my anger displaced by a black and cavernous despair. And she held my head in her hands, held it carefully.

Thus, in the last days of September, Blake's final, small, whore-trick betrayal led me into my season of dreams. The Dream of Atlanta, which I had believed vanquished, came as regularly as sleep itself and with it came other dreams, fantastic and more fearsome. I saw once again the blond-haired young man of the Dream of Atlanta, saw him just as I had imagined him that night in Tuscaloosa, laughing at my credulous, lunatic vulnerability as Blake spun under his indifferent touch. I dreamed the cool, dim rooms of the whorehouse. MacShan Satterfield was standing there, his hands in a woman's hair, turning her head to face me. They trooped through my dreams, MacShan and the blond-haired young man and a teeming army like them, gentlemen-officers all of that plantation empire which acknowledges no defeat, all working their wills on my conquered territory; and everything I dreamed struck me with the force of revealed truth: Each man his own Iago.

In those dream-racked days, I felt the first stirrings of a cold and looping violence. And because it seemed a reckless violence which did not care for consequences—something within me, but not a part of me—I became scrupulous about safety. After seeing Blake home at night, I would wait outside until she had made her passage through the darkened house and the glow of her lamp shone from her bedroom window—my reassurance that I had delivered her safely.

As I entered this season of dreams, I became an actor more skilled than Ozro might ever hope to be. My face became a mask, my eyes as flat and unfathomable as poker chips. I, too, had learned the arts of doubleness, and each person thought of me exactly what I wished. My father thought me reformed as we spent long, idle days together among horse collars and licorice whips, his poor merchandise, talking of the impending, forced retirement of the President of the United States. With Blake I was cleverest of all, and luckiest. After my performance in our secret house, it was no easy trick to convince her that the letters did not matter, after all, that all things worked once more toward our happy future, that the names I had called her were only whiskey-talk. But no lawyer ever argued a better case, and in the end, Blake thought me captured once more in her contentment. Yet even as I held her, I smelled in her sweet hair the year's dusty decay, the very scent of my own autumnal obsession. I lived in perfect deception.

In fact, only one person thought me a liar and she alone was wrong. That was Elmira Trogdon, who, trailing her five silent children, marched into the Good Neighbor Mercantile one fine October day. She was not there to shop.

"Why'd you lie to me?" Elmira demanded, first thing. "I hate a liar."

"Don't we all?" I said idly, not getting up from my nail keg. My mind was on other things.

"Smart talk won't help you no more," she said. "Read this. I had Brother Pride Hatton write the sheriff down there for me."

She handed me a soiled envelope from which I withdrew and unfolded a letter. The letter was typewritten. It said:

"Dear Brother Hatton:

"You can tell Mrs. Trogdon that we do not now have and never have had a prisoner by the name of Eleazer C. Trogdon. She must have got the wrong information about her husband's arrest. Please do not fail to write if I can be of further help. We could use more preachers in our county who have your view on the liquor problem."

It was signed "Sincerely" and I thought, the sincerity of sheriffs being what it is, that this man had probably drunk Eleazer Trogdon's whiskey in Miss Lottie's whorehouse down in Birmingham. I laughed.

"Don't get cute, boy," Elmira said, unamused. "Why'd you lie to me? Brother Pride Hatton says you just made up that jail story to give Bluenose time to hit the road. Now I never will find him after all this time. There's a judgment against lying."

She leaned down, aiming the words at me, her face red and squinched up. She was near to crying. I was still sitting on my nail keg. I passed the letter over my shoulder to my father, who was standing at his cash register, silent witness to all this. I stood up, regarded the scared children huddled behind her, the lot of them imagining no telling what about their father's partner in sin. I took in Elmira again, detecting once again that ghost of beauty in face and body, a failed beauty which not even her floursack dress and yanked-back, Holy Roller hairdo and her grim Holy Roller outrage could mask completely. I understood anew how the sight of the whore Polly had excited a rage of memory in old Bluenose, and I decided to be nice to this woman.

"I didn't lie, Elmira," I said. "Pride Hatton just wrote the wrong jail. This letter is from the sheriff and he's talking about the Jefferson County jail. Bluenose is in the Birmingham city jail."

"I never heard of no place having two jails," she said.

"Brant's right," my father said.

"I believe it if you say so, B. B.," she said. "Well, I ain't bothering Brother Pride to write another letter."

She said this as if I had suggested it.

"I'll write the Birmingham jail for you," I said. I was, after all, as curious as anyone about Bluenose. The time of his sentence had long since passed, but I wasn't buying the notion that he had hit the road for good. Many were doing it, but Bluenose had things to stay for: his trade, his place on the river, if not his home.

"No, it's in the hands of the Lord," she said. "He knows Bluenose's time is short. If he wants Bluenose to repent before the time runs out, we'll know it. I don't want no help from you. I know what you said to Brother Pride. You better get right yourself. You're just like Bluenose. The truth ain't in you."

Poppa came around his counter then, moving between me and Elmira. He handed her the letter and then gave each of the children a piece of hard candy. They took it timidly, betraying no enthusiasm.

"Say thankee," Elmira told them. The three oldest did. They still had the anonymous, wild look of a pack of barn kittens.

"I tell you what, Elmira," my father said, "let me write down there for you. Brant didn't mean no harm, but I can understand how you feel about him."

"I 'preciate it, B. B. I'm most ashamed to face you, the way my husband's ruint your boy."

"Well, that's going to work out all right," my father said. "Now, let me write for you if you're worried. I sure enough don't mind."

"No," she said, after thinking a moment. "It's in the Lord's hands, I reckon. The Lord knows Bluenose's time's near about up. We'll find him when the Lord is ready."

"Well, the Lord's saved plenty of worse sinners than Bluenose Trogdon," my father said, still trying to gentle her. "You'll have plenty of time to work on Bluenose."

"No, there ain't much time," she said, her voice slipping without warning into that fast crazy cadence that lets you know when a Holy Roller's about to start witnessing. "The days are few, the ways are two. Bluenose is between Salvation and the Sword and don't know it. I got me a sanctified vision on that."

She blurted that out, then spun around and started herding the children toward the front of the store. They let themselves be driven before her, silent, obedient, their cheeks caved in on hard candy. Something she had said had shot in cleanly through the fog of my own troubles.

"Hey, wait Elmira, I want to ask you something," I called after her.

"Let her go," Poppa warned, but I brushed past him and caught her on the front porch.

"Leave me be," she shouted, turning on me with a dazed, rapt look. "I know the filth you talk." She drew out the word "know" into a second, rising syllable, like a word in a hymn—"I knoooow-ah the filth you talk."

"No, listen," I said, "I'm not going to say anything bad. What do you mean, you had a vision?"

"No heathen going to understand," she said in that same metrical voice. "Brother Pride Hatton explained it all."

"A vision like a dream," I said.

"I thought it was a dream for just years and years," she said, "but Brother Pride Hatton explained it all."

"But you do have dreams? Tell me that."

"The same dream I've had for all the years. I dream the Blood of the Lamb," she said. "Always. The blood is vengeance, flowing in a river. It carries angels. Each angel has a sword. It's an anointment, like the Tongues."

"Pride Hatton told you that?" I said.

"I ain't bound to tell you nothing," she said. She glared at me. The children drew into a shifting covey around her feet. For the first time I looked straight into her eyes, which were flat and depthless, mere puddles of hallucination. I saw her for what she was, a woman done in by a lifetime of blunted expectation. She had paid a price for being the only person in Pover County who expected Bluenose to be something other than what he was and always would be.

"I ain't telling you nothing else," she repeated, the singsong leaving her voice, as if she was emerging from a trance.

"You don't have to," I said. "You've told me all I need to know."

She turned and took the children down the steps. I watched her go on out the Fever Springs Road, moving steadily away from me, but I knew this: She was headed in my true direction, sure enough.

So I stood on the porch, yet traveled with her as she went out into the pale October light. I walked stride for stride with her toward the declining sun, dust rising in motes of gold around our feet. We moved together in the flow of our histories, vessels carrying the same essential madness. And I thought how only a lucky thing could save me.

That is the way I watched her go—Sister Elmira, my sister, too—and from that day forward, all things were of a piece.

CHAPTER ELEVEN

At the Mercantile, when cold weather came, we circled the straight-back chairs around the heat stove. It was the beginning of the long winter sitdown. Come one of the first days cold enough to keep a fire all day, Ozro found us there.

"Guess who died," he demanded.

"Bluenose," I said, just that quick, suddenly and absolutely sure of it.

"No, no. Somebody important," Ozro said, spraddling his legs and lowering himself, hands braced on his knees, into a free chair. "A real important man has died."

"Franklin D. Roosevelt," I guessed.

"Nope. You Republicans ain't going to be that lucky." Ozro leaned back, ready for me to try again.

"Don't play with us," said my father. He had a high regard for death as a theological event.

"It's old man Herman Giles," responded Ozro. "They found him slumped over his desk at the courthouse yesterday. They think his heart just stopped."

"That'll do it every time," I said, knowing better.

"That ain't funny," Ozro said. He had shifted his gears right quick to suit Poppa. "Why you want to say things like that all the time? This is a fine old man we're talking about."

"I didn't mean any disrespect," I said. "That's just a funny way to put it, saying his heart stopped. I mean, that's why everybody dies, when you get right down to it."

"I ain't got no idea what you're talking about," Ozro said.

"I do," said Poppa, "but there's no humor to it. What you don't know, Brant, is there's a mystery to death. I had to learn that young, right down there in that house where you're living, when your granddaddy died. Maybe a man dies first in some other way and then his heart stops."

"It was a fever took your granddaddy," Ozro said to me.

"No. No. That wasn't it," said Poppa impatiently. His voice sounded remote, somehow flattened out. "My mother used to say that—say a fever come on him right at the end. My momma didn't know. She had to say something. She never knew why my daddy died, no more'n I did. He come in from plowing one day and he knew he was a dead man. He left the mules standing in harness down in the barn lot and he came in and told my mother, 'Martha, I've worked my last day.' Then he went straight on to bed without taking supper. Thirty days later he was dead. He never had any fever that I recollect."

"Well, I never heard none of that," Ozro said.

"You were just a baby then," Poppa told him. "I remember Momma got your pap to go down to Jasper to fetch old Doc Gladney and some young doctor to come up here. My mother gave Mr. Jenkins cash money to pay them in advance. The young doctor said they must operate right then and there in our house, and Doc Gladney said if they cut him open he'd die for sure. Poppa was calm and in his right mind the whole time, and he said for them to get off his place and they did. He said there wasn't anything either one of them could do."

"How do you figure he knew his time was up?" Ozro said.

"Ah, I don't know. When she got old, Momma used to say that Poppa had told her he just wanted to go live with Jesus, but I never believed that. Her mind got pretty bad later on and be- sides"—Poppa paused as if examining this final item before giving it out—"my father was not a believing man."

We all fell silent. I looked over at my father and he seemed vulnerable and far away and it moved me to think of him as a little boy going down in the darkness to tend the mules on the night his father took to the deathbed. I thought of my grandfather meeting death with the same desolate resolve with which he had faced the dog in the road, and how he had slept all these years not in Jesus, but in the irony of final defeat. My grandmother had seen to that, cancelling his heresy with the three graven words which were all he had to carry him into history. I could see her on her widow's mission to the Walker Monument Company down in Jasper, see her standing in the shade of the workshed. Behind and beyond her great slabs and obelisks of granite baked in the fierce Alabama sun, waiting to be named. Dressed in her widow's black, she would be glad for the shade. She would wait patiently in it while the stone-cutter slowly printed her order into his notebook, a stub of pencil tiny in his meaty, granite-dusted hand. As he wrote, she would speak in final, calculated defiance of her infidel husband's willful death, his suicide: ". . . make the inscription, 'Asleep in Jesus.' "

Poppa shifted in his chair, as if shaking himself loose from the memory. "Judge Coxwell will likely take this hard," he said. "Mr. Herman's been his clerk for twenty-five years or better, ever since the judge got elected."

"Now that he's gone, who you reckon will get the clerk's job?" Ozro said.

"Oh, probably some fellow the judge owes a favor. That clerk's job is kind of a political thing." He spoke as if it seemed a stale, dull consideration in comparison to the mystery of death.

"I know that, B. B." Ozro said. "I reckon you don't have to tell me that, me of all people."

Mr. Herman's heart stopped on him the Thursday before Roosevelt was elected, which would have been November third. It was a shame his old heart couldn't have kept going until November eighth. Being a loyal Democrat, Mr. Herman Giles would have enjoyed that election. Roosevelt won because the nation was hungry. Judge Coxwell and Ozro and the other Democrats all got re-elected because Democrats always won in our county. Ozro finally wound up without opposition because he showed up every time a church door opened until the deadline was past for anyone to file against him in the general election. If Mr. Herman had lived, he would have gotten to hear Hoover's last speech before the election. Hoover said that if his opponent was elected, grass would grow in the streets of a thousand towns. The next day down at the store somebody asked Poppa about that speech. "Well, we might have grass in the streets if Mr. Roosevelt wins," he said, "but at least we won't be cutting it to eat."

From my station beside the stove in the Good Neighbor Mercantile in Milo, Alabama, I had time to study all that transpired in those first days of November: how Franklin D. Roosevelt was victorious; how salvation was hanging fire in the long vacation of Bluenose Trogdon; how the first Brantley Laster had left home and family to become an unwitting sleeper in Jesus; how in the matter of Blake King I was a double man. I searched these events for signs of what was to come, and in the end I could count myself no genius for ignoring the clearest sign of all, which lay in the unreliable heart of Herman Giles.

"I don't believe it will be any trouble for you to catch right ahold, considering your education," Judge Coxwell told me. We were sitting in his office in the Pover County courthouse in Fever Springs, where he had just hired a new circuit court clerk. "I can't tell you how pleased I was to get your father's letter. I said to myself, 'Now here's a chance to do a good friend a favor and get some first-class help at the same stroke.'"

"I sure hope I can give that kind of help to you, Judge," I said, sounding grateful, which was not the way I felt.

Judge Coxwell dipped his head toward me as he worked at lighting his pipe. He was a first-class pipe fiddler, all right. Packets of tobacco, a couple of pocket knives, matches and extra pipes were scattered all over his desk. He was forever breaking off conversation to tend to the mechanics of smoking. I watched the match flare up a couple of times between his noisy sucks at the pipe. Then the judge paused.

"I'm not worried about that," he said. "Lasters breed true."

He went back to work on the pipe, sitting hunkered down around it in the fine place he had carved out for himself in the world. Everything looked just right, I had to admit that: the cluttered desk, the packed bookcases behind him, the tall windows with their big panes of variable glass in which sparkled minute, oblong bubbles of antebellum air, and not least, of course, the judge himelf. The judge lifted his face toward me in a cloud of smoke.

"B. B. Laster's been my friend a long time. Friends count a lot in the law. Frankly, I think there is nothing so important in this profession as making friends and holding them." He smiled suddenly across the desk at me. "Of course, judges must be impartial, but we must also be re-elected every four years."

"Yes, sir," I said. I smiled back; it seemed like the thing to do.

"You've thought about the law, then?"

"Well, yes, sir." That was not a lie.

Judge Coxwell gave me that smile again. It was a smile that made you want to be his friend, maybe even be like him. His skin was fine grained and smooth, almost translucent, and above his small face was a thick puff of white hair, so that he had a look both distinguished and elfin. He motioned at me with his pipe-stem.

"Good," he said. "I've every intention of making you think more about it. Young fellow like you isn't cut out to be a clerk all his life, like old Herman, God rest him. You can work here through the spring session with me and have yourself quite a jump on the other fellows starting out in law school. You be thinking about going back down to Tuscaloosa next fall. All it takes is a letter from me to get you in."

"Well, I'll sure think about it," I said.

Judge Coxwell had quit looking at me. His eyes were roaming the bookcases behind me. He spoke again as if I hadn't said anything.

"The thing I want to make you see is, there's opportunity in the law for a young man that's got brains and ambition. The legal profession is one of the quickest ways to get ahead. You run across opportunities. You could go off to school next fall and be back in fine shape when prosperity returns."

His eyes drifted back down, locked on my face. He darted an index finger into the bowl of the pipe to check the ember. "The good times will return, you know." He gave the smile again.

"Spoken like a true Democrat," I said.

The judge laughed. "You're B. B.'s son all right. You see the politics behind everything, even an old man's rambling." He stood up and held out his hand. I shook it and started for the door. He called my name and I turned around, my hand on the knob.

"I hope I'm not telling you anything you don't already know, but being your father's son can never hurt you in these parts," Judge Coxwell said. "He's a fine man, and my dependable friend. B. B. Laster hardly ever asks a favor, but when he does, I take care of it"—the judge raised one of his small clean hands and snapped his fingers—"just like that."

"Thank you, sir," I said. "I think he's a fine man, too."

"You owe it to him to always make him proud," he said. "In fact, now that you're my clerk, you owe it to me, too, to set a good example in the community, watch who you run with and so forth. Do you know what I mean?"

"Yes, sir," I said. "I'm sure I do."

I left his office, came out of the musty book-and-ripe-tobacco smell into the light on the steps of the courthouse, stood there in the clear sun and wind. I recall what Bluenose had told me: "Remember one thing. The law ain't shit. When people decide to get you, they get you." The judge had told me: "Nothing is more important in the law than friends, making them and holding them." The judge ought to know. He was a man with influence in Tuscaloosa and, so they said, in Montgomery, as much influence as any man from the hills was allowed to have in those places. A wise man, he had adjusted to things as they were. You would never catch the judge, I figured, nursing any bitterness about the Historical Mistake or entertaining any illusions about avenging it. He had made his accommodation—and prospered by it. Now, if I would take it, he was offering me my chance. From the high steps of the courthouse I could see most all the main street of Fever Springs: the feed and hardware stores with the lawyers' offices upstairs; the dry-goods store, owned by the county's only Jew; the post office and the garage-livery stable, owned by a mule trader turned Ford dealer, and on the lawn of the court-house the fancy shed over the artesian spring where the first settlers had either cured a fever or caught one. I forget which it was. I stood there, watching the sun on the fields, and wondered if both of them, the judge and Bluenose, were saying the same thing.

It was dark by the time I hitched back to Milo and the store was closed. I walked the half mile on out the Crane Hill Road to our house. My old man was eating supper at the kitchen table when I got there. He jumped up and began fixing a plate as soon as I walked in, acting real cheerful.

"Well, did you get the job?" he said.

"You got the job, Poppa," I said. "I reckon I just went over there to make it official."

It was about as close as I had ever come to speaking to him in anger. He gave me my plate and took his seat again.

"I hated to trick you," he said, "but I figured you wouldn't have any part of it if I told you I had written the judge."

"I just felt like a fool when he started talking about your letter," I said. "Judge Coxwell said you didn't ask many favors, but when you did, he always took care of it. It wouldn't have made any difference if I had been a monkey sitting there."

"That's right," Poppa said with some heat. "I'm glad you figured that out. What you got is a political job. If I hadn't spoke for it, Judge Coxwell would have passed it on to someone else he owed. But I wanted it and he gave it to me because he knows that if B. B. Laster spent the next four years telling his customers that maybe old Judge Coxwell ain't such a fine fellow after all, then he's going to lose the Milo box, and he may not be the circuit judge any more. Don't think there ain't plenty of other people knocking on his door about this job, hard as times are. But the judge owed me something big for all the years I've kept him right on top in this Milo beat, and it's proper for you to have it. Now that's the way of it. Perfection is in Heaven, not down here, and you better adjust to that."

"Yes, sir," I said. "I believe you're right. I do need to do just that thing. I'm sorry I brought it up."

"No, this is the time," he said. "If you don't want the job, don't take it. I just thought from watching you, you needed something to do. You've seemed awful low lately."

"I do want it, Poppa," I said. "I need something to do real bad."

"Good, let's quit arguing about it," he said.

We ate in silence then, sitting opposite one another at the round table in our big bare kitchen. My father worked on his food with the rapt concentration of a man accustomed to eating alone. My father had never before spoken so harshly to me, and I realized that in my childlike acceptance of my father as a man of steady, motiveless goodness, I had clung to some false notions. I had, for instance, always thought being a Democrat was sort of a hobby of his, like quoting scripture at the cash register. I had never thought of him as a man capable of dispensing favors and demanding them in return. I had never known that his virtue, which was real enough, was balanced by a certain cunning, that my father possessed a mind which, even as it pondered the flight of Herman Gile's soul to the bosom of Jesus, could be composing a letter to take advantage of the accident of Mr. Herman's death.

"When did the judge say he wanted you to start?" Poppa said, pushing back from his empty plate.

"Not until the first Monday in December. The judge wants to take a few days off. He said there's still plenty of time to teach me what I need to know before the session starts."

"Good," Poppa said. "You can get in a little bird hunting. Weather's about right and I've got a shelf full of shells cain't nobody afford to buy. You might as well shoot them up."

"I'd like that," I said. "Let me ask you one other thing about the job. Did you tell the judge about me and Bluenose?"

"Sure I did. He had a right to know about you, Brant," my father said.

"I don't see that'll be a problem," I said.

"Sure it will." He cut his eyes up from his plate. "You're going to work for the law, son. You cain't hunt with the hounds and run with the hares."

In a dream I had that night, Ozro and old man Hibbert and my father went with me to meet the T&G train from Atlanta. When the train drew up at the loading dock, a workman opened a boxcar and skidded a casket out to us. We carried the casket up the road to the Y and on across to the Baptist church, where everyone was waiting for us. We put the casket in front of the altar and I took a seat across the aisle from Riley King. He didn't look to be doing good at all. Right in the middle of the first hymn, he jumped up and started hollering. "I'm gonna kill you for what you done to my baby."

Then he reached into his funeral coat and pulled out one of those goddam long old horse-cavalry pistols. He popped off a wild shot at me, and people started screaming and praying and scrambling around. The men of the church ganged up around

Riley King, and I could see the pistol waving around above their heads as he tried to get another crack at me.

I ran, shoving aside old ladies and anybody else who got in my way. As I fled, I could hear them shouting at Riley, asking why he had done it, but I didn't need to hear his answer. I knew Blake was dead and I was to blame, and neither in the dream nor upon waking did I feel any remorse. I understood the tide of history, its cold waters.

I took my father's advice and went hunting the next day under a thin November sun. The first hard frosts had burned the hickories gold, and the cornstalks rattled in the breezes which swept along the high lonesome ridges. At evening the sky turned the smooth dull gray of a dove's wing and breathing the air was like inhaling the smoke of some distant sweet fire. It was the best time of year in the hills, I always thought, and that first day the dogs worked beautifully and I shot very well, and I learned this: Nothing is any fun if you believe you are going crazy during it.

CHAPTER TWELVE

Well, that was the longest thirty-day sentence in history," I said.

"It did run on," Bluenose said. "Just got loose yesterday." He reached out and shook hands without getting up from his chair beside Ozro's desk. I had stopped by the shack to leave Ozro a mess of quail. When I opened the door, there sat Bluenose, looking not nearly so sober as he must have been when he walked out of the B'ham jail. "How you been keeping, boy?" he said.

"I'm all right," I said. "I just need somebody to go bird hunting with me."

"I might be a candidate for that," said Bluenose. "Looks like you're doing pretty good by yourself."

I swung my canvas game bag up on Ozro's desk and counted out a dozen birds for each of them.

"I've been busting them pretty good," I said, "killing them almost as fast as Ozro can eat them. But I sure didn't count on finding you here this evening when I dropped his ration off."

"Well, you caught me at my first stop," Bluenose said. "I had to let his honor here know that the menace to society was at large again in his beat."

"Least you stayed gone till after the election," Ozro said. "I got that to be thankful for, anyway."

"No fooling, why the hell have you been gone so long?" I said.

"Aw, I wound up pulling ninety days in the damn jail."

"How'd you manage that?" I said.

"Big fat guard they had down there took to jawing and going on at me, calling me an 'ignorant hillbilly' and such as that. He thought he was much of a man, seeing as how nobody could get to him to learn any different. One day, he passed by kind of close to my cage, low-rating me as he went, and I just reached out and snatched him against the bars and I says to him, 'All right, gas bag, your time is at hand. I'm fixing to make your day for you.' Then I popped him one right on the end of his snout. Hell, it wasn't that hard of a lick, but the end of his old nose split as wide open as a peanut hull and the blood just flew. It was a funny-looking thing.

"Well, of course the son of a bitch swore out a warrant for me and that same judge gave me sixty more days. Hell, he wanted to give me six months, but I begged him out of it, told him my children would starve. He ain't so goddam tough as they say, that judge ain't."

"Still I bet along about then you were wishing you had let me go ahead and pay your fine that first day," I said. "I never have understood why you didn't let me pay them off. It cost you plenty more than a hundred dollars' worth of business, just serving the thirty days."

"Son, them big fines like that is a trap," Bluenose said, "just a piece of bait the law likes to throw out there. Fellow like me pops up and pays them a hundred-dollar fine, and that's when they really get to work. They figure you have naturally done something illegal to get that kind of money, so they start calling the law in other places checking on you or maybe they just make up something of their own to claim you done, but they'll get you once you attract their attention like that. My pa always taught me this: If you get caught, take the time. You got to do your money paying afore you ever get to court."

"Yeah, maybe you're right," I said. "Still, I bet those last two months were pleasant."

"It wasn't too bad. The guard come down the first day of my

new sentence with this piece of rubber hose he proposed to whip me with. They usually only do that to niggers. Anyhow, I talked him out of using it on me, and he was right nice from there on out."

"I'll bet he was," I said.

"He was. That's a fact," Bluenose said. "I reasoned with him. I told him, 'Listen here, you fat bag of cowshit, you've done got me sixty extra days. Now if you lay a hand on me, I'm gonna kill you when I get out, and if I don't get out alive, I've got a brother that's going to be sitting on your front porch some fine evening when you get home and he's going to cut your guts right out on the ground, you hear.' And he heard me in his heart."

"What'd he say?"

"Not word one. He just marched right back with his hose and never said another word to me the whole time. Good for him, I say. He'd damn sure been a dead man if he'd a laid that hose on me."

"Aw, Bluenose, you don't mean that. You're not the killing kind." I figured in those days I knew who was and who wasn't.

"No, Brant," he said, "folks have kept messing with me till I'm damn near mean enough to do it. I'm just too old and wore out to take much more shit."

For a moment there was a vacant look in his eyes, like the look a dog's eyes get before a fight. Then he laughed and pounded his hand on Ozro's desk.

"I swear," Bluenose said, "it's just struck me how much that fat gas bag of a guard resembled his honor, the constable of Milo. I'll bet you gained twenty pound since I left, Ozro."

"I weigh just what I have since I was twenty year old—two hundred and seventy-five pound even," said Ozro, suddenly petulant, cheating on the figure. "And I ain't no gas bag neither, nor a jailbird, and I don't like being joked at by the likes of you no more, and I'd just as soon you got on. It don't do me no good to have you hanging around the office, you hear."

"What in hell are you talking about?" Bluenose said. "There's been a heap more carrying on to do with whiskey and pussy in this shack than there has been to do with the law. Don't flare up at me after all these years, Ozro."

"Things change, Bluenose, like I told you a long time ago. It ain't nothing personal."

Bluenose stood up, glaring at Ozro. I could see that deep vacancy in his eyes again, as if something pleasant and familiar had moved out, leaving nothing in its place. "The only thing that changes, Ozro, is people that go chickenshit and turn on their friends. I noticed before I left that you was getting mighty picky. I'll bet you ain't too picky to take the free whiskey I've been supplying you with ever since you got elected, are you?"

"Hold on, Bluenose," I said. "Ozro didn't mean anything. He's just trying to tell you how things are around here now. He's right, things have changed some."

"What, other than this chickenshit that turns on his friends? I guess now you're going to tell me that the high sheriff that I've been paying off for twenty years has got religion and is going to shut down all the whiskey-makers in the county."

"Not by his own choice," I said, and went on to tell him about Brother Pride Hatton's sermon. "Since that night I went to his revival, he's been staying right at it and the other preachers have picked it up. I wouldn't be surprised if the preachers go to work on the sheriff and Ozro and the other constables around the county."

"Looks like they already have," Ozro said. "The sheriff called a meeting over at the courthouse for next week. It's about whiskey, sure as the world."

"Well, I'll tell that crooked son of a bitch and I'll tell you just like I told that fat guard. You stay clear of me or they'll be holding one of them special, slow church services and saying 'Don't he look natural' over your dead asses."

"Hold on, Bluenose," I said. "There's no cause to get mad at Ozro."

"I ain't mad," he said. "Despite his shifty ways, I think as much of this fat turd as if he was my brother. But that's the way of it, Ozro. Don't mess with me."

Bluenose went out the door and down the steps to the dirt road. He looked back up at us standing in the door of the shack and said, "Now, Ozro, if any of your Christian constituents get upset about me being in your office, you just tell them I was up there to get a temperance lecture from you. Okay?" Bluenose gave a bow, and after a slight, initial stagger, set out with great dignity toward his home.

"I ain't never seen him act like that," Ozro said.

"He'll be all right," I said, "as soon as he gets over being in jail. Just don't aggravate him, that's all."

"Well, the sheriff ain't kidding. The preachers are after him to bust up some stills in this beat. Old Hatton's got a lot of influence now, even if he is a Holy Roller."

"I didn't think it had gone that far yet."

"Take my word it has. Bluenose may just have to quit making whiskey and go to farming and starving like everybody else."

"That's at the bottom of all this," I said. "People hate any man making a living these days. Plain jealousy. Bluenose will never stop making whiskey. You'll have to kill him to stop him making it."

Ozro let his bulk down into his old, sprung swivel chair. It rolled back under his weight.

"Too damn much talking about killing going on around here to suit me. Bluenose will just have to stop like anybody else. It's the law."

"It's been the law for all the years he's been giving whiskey to you and the sheriff," I said.

"Well, there's something you and Bluenose neither one has got the sense to understand," Ozro said. "The law is like anything else. It changes. The people are the law and what they want determines the law. It ain't just what gets written down on paper that's the law. It's what the people decide to have enforced that's the law."

"Seems to me I've heard that general theory of the law before," I said, "but it wasn't in exactly those words."

Ozro followed me to the door. "Hell, Brant, it ain't nothing personal with me, you know that. If it was up to my say-so, Bluenose could set up his still right there in the middle of the street."

CHAPTER THIRTEEN

On the last day of November, a Thursday I believe, I caught an early ride down to Jasper where I found a clean Ford sedan for sale at what seemed a cheap price to me. I bought it with the cash my father had given me. Even with the store down the way it was, Poppa had cash money laid back in some special hiding places he had. He felt about banks just like he felt about Republicans and the Birmingham *News*, and he was forever warning folks not to trust their money to them. You can believe it didn't hurt his influence any around Milo when banks all over Alabama started folding like morning glories on a hot day.

I was back in Milo right after lunchtime. Poppa closed the store and I took him for a little ride. Then, just before three o'clock, I drove over to the high school and waited for Blake to come out. When the final bell rang, I saw her coming down the wide front steps with the kids and I could hear them calling good-bye to her, calling her "Miss King." Sitting in the car, watching her make her way among them, I thought of all the afternoons we had come down those steps together. She saw me sitting in the car and, waving a final good-bye to the students, came over carrying a load of books in the crook of her arm like a schoolgirl.

"They must pay court clerks a lot," she said.

She stuck her head in the window and gave me that good open smile, her face close to mine. "Oh, there's so much nice room in there." Just then, at that moment, I loved her so much I wanted to cry, and more than anything, I wished things were different, that I didn't have the dreams I had and know the things I knew.

"Get in and I'll give you a ride."

She ran around the front of the car and climbed in beside me. "Oh boy, a ride with a local dignitary."

"Not every day a girl gets a chance like this." I turned the car around in the open schoolyard and we started down the long drive that dipped through the ravine and led out to the Fever Springs Road. The students who were walking along stepped back to watch us pass; some waved. Blake reached across the seat and touched my hand.

"Mustn't let my pupils see any public displays of affection," she said. "I've convinced them I'm a frigid old maid."

"Old maid maybe. Frigid, no." I looked at her when I said that and smiled to make sure she took it right. She did. I wanted to keep it light and friendly, to mask with good humor my own deep frigidity. I wanted to give Blake no hint of the changes within me. I had avoided her by spending my days back along the far ridges with my bird dogs and gun, setting out before first light each morning and using my early rising as an excuse not to see Blake in the evenings. I spent my nights with the dreams.

"What are you waiting for?" Blake asked, startling me.

The car was stopped where the driveway from the school met the Fever Springs Road. I was holding the wheel tightly with both hands, and, my foot pressed hard on the brake, I had drifted away into my own thoughts. "I was just trying to decide which way to go," I said. "Where do you want to go?"

"I want to go somewhere we can talk," she said, and we turned out on the road toward Milo.

"Something serious?" I said.

"Yes," she answered.

"You're not pregnant, are you?"

"No," she said. "Nothing that simple."

"We're too lucky for anything so simple," I said.

I had felt a surge of hope at the thought. I needed some

transforming event, a dog in the road. But I would not be that lucky, so I would do the only thing left to me, which was to hold on against my final passage into the new country of my dreams and hope the last long hope that something would happen in time to save us.

"Are we going to talk, Brant?" she said. "Why are you so quiet?"

"You're the one who said we shouldn't talk," I said.

"I know," she said. "That was when there was nothing to talk about. I think there is something to say now."

"Let it wait. Let's just ride for a while."

"All right," she said. "Have you got any whiskey?"

"I'm out."

"I haven't known that to happen lately."

"What's that supposed to mean?" I said.

"Just that you're not going to be able to drink all the whiskey in the world, no matter how hard you try," Blake said.

"Well, you are looking at a dry man today," I said. "That's me, a dry, dry man. I don't know of a drop of whiskey between here and the Sipsey River."

"Let's go there, then."

"Down to Trogdon's Bluff? That's a hell of a walk, and it's too cold to do what we did last time."

"I'll go—for a drink," she said. "We can't do anything if Bluenose is there anyway." She gave me that warm, open smile again —that invitation of hers to forget all the bad times and get on with the main business, that smile of hers that let me know I was going to get laid. I wanted it, too, needed to sink into her and be lost there, for even as she was the source of my despair, she was sometimes its relief, her and the whiskey.

"After we get the whiskey we'll find a place," I said.

"We do have to talk, Brant," She rested her hand lightly on my arm. "Don't forget."

How could I forget, I wondered, but I did not speak the words.

Bluenose was drunk when we got there. He had just finished bottling fifty gallons and he had gotten into it pretty good. He was lying up under the bluff in the sand with a jug beside him. In a little pit in the sand, he had a fire going against the afternoon chill that had settled into the shadowed gorge. "How y'all doing?" he said. "Don't mind me if I don't get up."

We walked over to him. "You drunk everything you've made since you got back?" I said.

"Oh, hell no," he said. "I'm just testing a load I've got ready to go to Jasper—if I ain't lost all my faithful customers whilst I paid my debt to society."

"You best let me and Blake test it, just in case your tastes are rusty."

"Sure," he said. "Go fetch Blake a keg to sit on."

"No need," I said. "She can sit on the sand with us."

"I swear, Blake, a girl as pretty as you ought to get her a boyfriend with some manners," Bluenose said. He lay propped on one elbow.

"Well, I've got that very thing under consideration," she said, letting herself down on to the sand and tugging her skirt in around her knees. "This fire feels good."

It was getting dark now and much cooler down there along the river. The water was rushing down fast and cold-looking and we sat in the warmth and light of the fire.

"Blake, I'm afraid I ain't got nothing to cut this whiskey with, unless you'd like a touch of water in it," Bluenose said.

"Straight's okay," she said.

Bluenose insisted on demonstrating how to drink straight whiskey. Inhale, drink, exhale. "Blows all the fumes out. Take's the bite off the whiskey. Not that my whiskey bites enough so's you'd notice."

"Here, let me try," Blake said. She hoisted the jug in the Bluenose style. I watched her throat move when, head tilted back, she took two quick gulps of the warm whiskey. She released her breath with a little whistle. Her eyes were bright and watery when she handed me the jug.

"Like drinking fire," she said happily. "Did I do good?"

"Really fine," I said, and for a moment I liked her again without reservation, and wanted her.

We passed the jug until we were all pretty drunk, and it was the best time I had had in a long time. Blake had a lot of fun drinking the whiskey like Bluenose had taught her. A couple of hours after dark, I helped Bluenose carry the load of whiskey up to the road and we put the jugs in my old Ford. The three of us rode back to Bluenose's house, where he and I unloaded the whiskey in his barn. Bluenose had been planning to make a delivery run down to Jasper the next day, which was Friday. I talked him out of it, so we could go hunting. It would be our last chance for a while, since I was starting work Monday, and Poppa was already planning on closing the store so he and I could hunt together Saturday. Sunday was out altogether because Poppa had strong feelings against Sunday hunting, especially with his bird dogs. After we unloaded the whiskey, I drove us back up the wagon lane to Bluenose's front yard. Elmira was standing in the open doorway now, watching us.

"Welcoming committee," Bluenose said, jerking his head toward the silent figure in the doorway. He got out of the car, closed the door, and leaned down to talk to us through the open window.

"You get the dogs and come on over here after daylight," he said. "I'll have Elmiry fix us some breakfast."

"That ain't necessary," I said. "It might make problems."

"It's my goddam house," Bluenose said. "I'll feed me and whoever else I want to in it, and she'll cook it. Don't worry about it." He put both hands on the window frame, ready to push himself upright. "Well, I got to get me some sleep. You young folks done about made me drink enough to get drunk. Blake, I enjoyed having you visit. You get Brant to bring you back anytime, you hear."

"Thank you, Bluenose," she said. "It was good whiskey, but I don't believe a schoolteacher ought to hang around with you two on a regular basis."

"Why not?" Bluenose said. "You've already been a party to the crime of hauling whiskey."

"Promise you won't tell the sheriff," she said, laughing.

"I ain't making no such promise," Bluenose countered. "Me and the sheriff is mighty tight, you know."

He pushed off from the car with a sigh and started for the house. We watched him walk across the bare yard in the moonlight toward his wife, who was still waiting in the doorway.

"Hello, hello," Bluenose called to her. "I know you musta missed me." The woman disappeared from the doorway without a word or gesture, and Bluenose went in and shut the door behind him.

I wheeled the car around in the front yard and eased it out onto the road. "You still wanting to talk?" I said.

"Not just yet," she said, sliding across the seat toward me. "I've got something I want to give you first to sober you up." Blake wrapped her arms around me, pressed herself against me. "I changed my mind about talking. I want to do this now. Right now."

"Well, let me get the goddam car stopped," I said.

"Oh hell, just pull off the road anywhere," she said.

"Patience. I'm trying to think of a place."

She let go of me and took a drink from the jug Bluenose had left us. I could hear her breathing heavily, as if I was already kissing her. She put her hands on me again. "I am getting drunk and I am ready to be laid, dammit."

We laughed together. Blake started climbing all over me while I was trying to drive. She put her mouth up tight against my ear and said, "Pull this thing off the road, country boy."

We were still on the road leading into Milo, not far from where it passed Blake's house. I knew where a dim old logging road went off into the woods and I pulled down it until the car couldn't be seen from the road. Blake climbed over into the back seat and by the time I got there she was ready. Her skirt was up around her waist and when I touched her with my hand, she said, "No, not that. Put it in me. Now."

She lay back across the seat with her legs open, one foot on the floor board, the other leg thrown up against the back of the seat. She waited with her eyes closed while I took off my pants and moved over her.

"All the way," she said. "Now," pressing lightly on the small of my back with her hands. I went to the bottom, felt her shiver. I poured it to her. Her legs came up to circle my waist.

"Oh, give it to me. Oh, oh, that's deep."

"Is it hurting?"

"No. I want it hard. I want it to split me open."

Her voice trailed off into a steady low moan and I laid it in there right. Blake arched up to ride it out and grabbed me hard and the noise that would slip out like a secret little animal came out of her throat in a gasp. The noise came out and I could feel her tears on my shoulder where she had buried her face.

"I wish it would make a baby," she said, and I wished it, too, for a moment.

We sat in the car for a long time and the whiskey smell in the closed car was tart and pleasant.

"We still haven't talked, Brant," she said, after a while.

"I know," I said. "This has been a fine day. Let's let the talking wait."

"Not long," she said.

"Soon. This week sometime, for sure."

"You see how good it can be if you just live your life," she said. "You must see how good it could be forever."

I drove Blake home and waited outside in the darkness until I saw her bedroom light come on. I drove very slowly back into Milo, across the wide, vacant space in front of the stores and on out the road to our house. I drove with the window down. The cold night air felt good on my face and I realized how very drunk I was, drunk and spent like soil which has grown the same crop season after season. "You see how good it could be forever," she had said. That could mean only that she had not been able, after all, to abandon hope for our future. What a wonderful actor I must be, I thought, to have someone want me forever when I am burning down to ash and air inside. Finally now and soon, I would have to say yes or no to our future; to say yes and live all my life with the phantoms of Atlanta and with that dream of violence which would be waiting always to pull me across; or to say no and live forever as I had in all those Tuscaloosa nights without Blake, when missing her had become a palpable thing, a taste in my mouth, coppery and electric, as if a penny had been placed far back on my tongue, like a wafer.

That was the night I woke up crying. In the black air above me, as in a dream, I saw a vision of myself hunting in a cold, dark and lonesome country, armed with a compact rifle, a weapon I neither owned nor recognized. I thought of Elmira and her dream, which was an anointment and a prophecy. Her river was vengeance, she had said. Now I was being swept along by the fixed idea and the cyclical dream just as surely as Bluenose had been borne away into darkness on the Sipsey's moonbright current.

I got out of bed before daylight and struggled into my hunting clothes. After the weeping, I felt detached and peaceful, as if I had drifted out beyond fear and mercy now. Perhaps my river, too, was vengeance, the oldest of hillbilly solutions.

CHAPTER FOURTEEN

Down at Bluenose's fish trap on the Sipsey River, the water in the big pool above the trap was deep and slow-moving. Then as the river funneled down into the sluiceway, the water picked up speed, pouring through that narrow channel as if driven by some terrific motor hidden on the bottom of the river. Whenever I try to think of the events of those next days, my mind always calls up an image of that run of river, its waters gathering ever faster for the plunge down the narrow chute of the sluiceway. And beyond that chute, the river, like our lives, flowed on but was not the same; its currents sought new channels; the old patterns would not hold.

Things began picking up speed that very morning. When I stepped out on the porch, first light was beginning to show at the tree line back in the east. My old man was standing on the porch in his long nightshirt. Our two bird dogs circled the yard, their tails thrashing with that excess of energy bird dogs get when they sense they're going hunting.

"Couldn't sleep," he said. "Thought I'd let the dogs out so's they could do their business 'fore you tried to haul 'em. You oughta have a good day."

"You wanta go?" I said.

"I figure you've already got a second gun."

I didn't say anything. I propped my shotgun against a post and dug in my hunting coat for the cold biscuits I had brought the dogs.

"Well, ain'tcha?" Poppa demanded.

"I'm supposed to pick Bluenose up," I said. "Three guns are not too many."

"For me, it is. I thought I told you about running with Blue-nose."

"I'm a grown man, Poppa."

"So you are, and you got a grown man's job."

"Not yet. Not till Monday. Let's don't argue about it."

"I reckon I've give that up," Poppa said. "Just wish you'd re-member it ain't just yourself you're shaming."

I tossed biscuits to the bird dogs. They danced and squirmed at our feet, snatching the biscuits out of the air with gulps that shook their bodies.

"That Dan dog there—his granddaddy was the best bird dog I ever took in the woods," Poppa said finally.

"This one ain't bad," I said, glad for the lighter talk.

"He'll never be the dog old Toby was. A man don't get but one of them in a lifetime. Just one if he's lucky enough."

We watched the dogs some more. There was Dan and his mother, an old pointer bitch named Dot. She was a good steady dog, too. Seeing my old man in his nightshirt, a plain white gown of heavy cloth that reached almost to the floor, made me realize that age was robbing him of some size. His shoulders had a slight but permanent sag and his chest had started to sink, the first signs of that old fishhook stoop that gets worse and worse until you are old and bent and powerless and so bowed over you must look up to look straight ahead, and finally you are a dead man. Well, that had started happening to my father and suddenly he seemed old and vulnerable to me and I wanted to do anything but hurt him in my life.

"You still seeing Blake, son?" he said.

"Pretty regular," I said. "You know that. Nothing's changed."

"Well, you and Blake been going together for a mighty long time," he said.

"I guess I better get started," I said, fetching my gun from where I had propped it. Automatically, and although I had done the same thing twice already that morning, I broke the weapon and stared down its two empty tubes to make sure it was not loaded. Then I started down the steps.

"I swear, she was about the prettiest little old girl I ever saw," he said. "I was always mighty proud of you two. They say she's doing a good job over to the school. She's been into the store a couple of times to visit me. I think a lot of her, Brant."

"I know that, Poppa." I hesitated for a moment, trying to think of a way to head him off. "I best be going."

"I ain't never said anything to you about her, Brant, but I gotta tell you, girls like Blake are hard to find. She's a real thorough-bred in my book."

The light was none too good. His face was obscured by the shadow of the low porch roof. I've always wished I could have seen his face better the only time we spoke directly of Blake.

"I know that's fact, Poppa," I said. "You're right." I called for the dogs.

"I just wanted you to know, son, I mean, I don't know if you've thought of it, but, even though times are hard . . . I mean, if you wanted to get married, I'd help you any way I could. I've still got a little money saved back."

"I appreciate that, Poppa, but I don't think—it just ain't the time," I said.

"Well, I wanted you to know that if that was what you wanted to do, wouldn't nothing make me any happier. And I was think-ing, Brant, you recollect your Ecclesiastes: 'For all things there is a season.' You and Blake been going together a long time. I ain't saying it's always so, but there are some things that, if you don't do them when they're due to be done, are never quite right. Maybe getting married is one of them."

"Yeah, Poppa," I said, "I guess the trick is figuring out the right time from what maybe just looks like the right time and keeping both of them separate from things that don't have a right time at all. I gotta get started." I whistled the dogs up again. When I was halfway across the yard on my way to the car, I turned and looked back at the old man.

"You know," I said, "in that damn gown, you look like a prophet."

"I'm no prophet, son," he said. "Far from it. Scripture tells us we are not living in the age of prophets."

My poppa knew his Bible. I hoped he was right.

As I drove through the Y on my way to pick up Bluenose, I saw light in the window of Ozro's shack. I stopped for a visit and found Ozro sitting at his desk, all bowed up and cussing the county commissioners.

"You can bet if one of that courthouse gang used this shack, they'd have a stove and a pile of coal like a young mountain," he said.

"It's not that cold," I said. "You're just not used to getting up when the working folks do. What the hell you doing down here this time of day?"

"My duty."

"Well, it's never too late to start."

"I ain't in no mood for your shit this morning," Ozro said. "What're *you* doing, coming in off a drunk?"

"Going bird hunting with Bluenose," I said. "Now what's your excuse."

"I ain't at liberty to say. It's official business."

"I guess you've forgotten you're talking to a county employee."

"So I am, God help us. I reckon you'll find out anyway. I'm waiting for Freddy Dunlap from Crane Hill to pick me up. Sheriff wants all the constables in Fever Springs this morning."

"Must be that whiskey meeting you told me and Bluenose about," I said.

"I never said nothing about no whiskey meeting," Ozro said, "and I ain't going to have you telling it all over the courthouse that I run to Bluenose Trogdon with everything I know. I'll call you a liar as quick as the next man."

"They have really put the fear in you about this thing, haven't they?" I said, for Ozro wasn't kidding. "Listen, that sheriff's not about to give you any trouble about Bluenose. He's been getting a payoff from Bluenose just as long as you have, only he gets more than a jug of whiskey every now and then."

"I'd be careful what I said about duly e-lected officials and payoffs if I was you. People get sued for slumber or whatever they call it."

"Not if it's true, which it is," I said.

"True or not true, let me make you a little advice." Ozro leaned back in his chair. "A man that's got a little education, as you are rumored to have, ought to know that politics is important to a sheriff, especially a sheriff that didn't stand in this election but has got to run again just two years from now. And there ain't no sheriff, least of all this one, that likes to piss the preachers off."

"So the preachers have finally talked the sheriff into going after Bluenose," I said. "That's what you're saying, ain't it?"

"I ain't saying nothing of the kind," Ozro said. "All I know is that a passel of preachers went calling on the sheriff last week, as you would have heard, no doubt, if you had been in church Sunday with the other decent folks. If I was a court clerk that was going hunting today with a moonshiner, I'd make sure it was my farewell visit with him, so to speak, and I'd make damn sure I didn't hang around certain vicinities of the Sipsey River."

"And, if you had any sense, you'd convince the sheriff to lay off Bluenose. He's had about all he's going to take, I'm thinking."

"That's where you're wrong, son. Listen to these years talking. Bluenose is just a man. He ain't near as big as he looks to you right now. He's just a man; he'll take what he gets, just like the rest of us."

We heard tires grinding on the gravel. A car stopped outside the shack, but its motor kept running.

"That's my ride," Ozro said, heaving himself out of his chair.

"Mark this, Brant. I want you to remember me saying it. I told Bluenose last time I seen him what was coming. I warned him and I'm warning you. It ain't nothing personal, but this thing is started now, and the sheriff's got no choice. He's got to cover his ass and you best do the same."

"Just like you're doing, right, Ozro?"

"I don't aim for him to feed me to them preachers, if that's what you mean." Ozro blew out the lamp and walked past me to the door. "Close the door when you leave," he said.

By the time I got outside, Dunlap's car was already backing away from the steps. It stopped and I heard the gears clank and then it moved off down the Fever Springs Road. I watched it go away through the clear blue failing night and I knew that things were not the same with Ozro any more. He was not happy about it, but that did not change anything. Things were not the same with any of us in Milo any more. The car went on out of sight, leaving me alone in my situation, in my cold and dangerous season. I got in my car and faced the task of getting myself out the Fever Springs Road past the house where Blake slept in her illusion of safety and forgiveness, and on to the Trogdons' happy home.

Bluenose was standing on the front porch when I drove up. He had on a clean pair of overalls and looked sober.

"Come on in," he said, "Elmiry's going to fix us breakfast."

"Might as well. No point starting until the sun hits the hillsides," I said. I let the dogs out of the car and they started prospecting around the yard.

"That is right, but I'm always chomping at the bit to start earlier. That's one of them things I never learn, I reckon," Bluenose stopped with his hand on the knob of the front door. "Listen, don't expect no great lot of friendly talk from Elmiry. Seems like that preacher's the only soul she has a kind word for these days."

We went in to the kitchen where Elmira was working at the stove. The three oldest children had just finished eating and she sent them out of the kitchen. "My two babies are still in bed," Bluenose said. He rubbed one of the boys on the head as he passed by, but the child went out without looking up or speaking. Bluenose shook his head and smiled at me.

"Sit down. It'll be ready in a minute," Elmira said without looking around.

We sat. She cooked and started serving, me first; then she went over to her husband's side of the table. I was looking down at my food, but I caught some movement and looked up. Elmira was standing bolt upright beside Bluenose's chair, her small, thin face was red and outraged looking. I saw Bluenose withdrawing his arm from her. He was smiling, a little wildly, I thought. "Guess it's too late for that by a long shot," he mumbled.

Elmira said nothing. She stared over and past us, as if we weren't there. Then, after a few seconds, she served her own plate and sat down.

"Bow your heads," she said sharply. She gave thanks for the food, then said, "And Lord we pray, too, for them living in ignorance and sin. Here in the End Time, let 'em heed your Word in the Book of Ephesians—'And be not drunk with wine, wherein is excess; but be filled with the Spirit.' Amen."

"Amen," I said, and we started to eat. "The way you quoted that scripture, Sister Elmira, reminded me of my father."

"Your father is a good man," she said. "I'm sorry some in my family have part in bringing him sorrow. You heard me tell him that."

Bluenose dropped his fork on his plate with a clatter. "Well, I'll tell you who it reminded me of—the almighty Mr. Pride Hatton, the man who is in direct contact with the Father, the Son, and the Holy Ghost."

"There ain't no greater sin than blasphemy," Elmira said. "I won't listen to it in my own house." She started eating furiously.

"Not even murder is a greater sin than this blasphemy, you figure?" Bluenose asked her.

"There is no greater sin than mocking the Lord," she said.

"Well, good." Bluenose said happily. "Then I won't lose no more credit with the Lord for breaking that son of a bitch's neck then."

"I wouldn't put it past you to shame us even more by raising your hand against a preacher."

"I'm gonna do more than raise my hand if ever I catch him at what I think he's up to. I'm gonna blow him away is what I got in my mind. Son of a bitch slipping 'round my house, preaching agin me till my own babies scared of me." He was shouting at her now. "He better know who he's dealing with. This is Bluenose by-God Trogdon."

Lacking its normal whiskey flush, Bluenose's face looked pallid and bloodless, and for the first time in all the years I'd known him, he didn't seem powerful. There was something desperate and helpless about him, as if he knew he was up against a force he could neither overcome nor surrender to. I've often thought Bluenose must have sensed that morning that everything was winding down for him. Elmira had dropped her hands to her lap and I saw that she was crying.

"Brother Hatton's only trying to save you," she said. "You're going to Hell otherwise, Bluenose."

"It ain't you and him that's gwine decide that," Bluenose said. "And besides, whiskey ain't the only sin they got listed in that book." His voice dropped; he spoke into his plate. "Y'all better look to your own."

I wanted out of that room. I stood up and stepped back against the wall. I realized then that it was the Clabber Girl calendar, hanging to my right, that Elmira had been staring at after Bluenose touched her.

"Listen," I said, "I'll go on out and get the dogs rounded up. Seems like the little girl here on Elmira's calendar is the only one around here that's got a smile today."

When I said that, Elmira came out of her chair like she was spring loaded.

"Just you stay away from my calendar," she shouted. "Don't touch it."

"I wasn't aiming to," I said.

"Well, go on, get out," she yelled. The tears were rolling down her red twisted face, which looked as if it would break into pieces if she cried any harder. She shoved past me and clamped both hands against the calendar, holding it to the wall. "Leave it alone. It's mine. It's my business."

Bluenose, who was still sitting at the table, motioned with his head for me to go outside and I did. I took his signal to mean he wouldn't be going hunting, so I started loading up the dogs. But before I could get away, he came walking across the yard carrying his shotgun.

"Didn't figure you'd be up to going after all that," I said.

"Might as well; there's nothing to be done here. Let's drive up toward Fever Springs a couple of miles and put the dogs out in some of those old, fallow fields."

"All right," I said and we got in the car and started down the road toward the county seat. The fields Bluenose had in mind were old corn and cotton plots that hadn't been tilled since the times turned bad. They had grown up in chickweed and partridge peas and other types of natural quail feed.

"I hope you brought plenty of shells," Bluenose said when I parked the car in the yard of an abandoned farm house. "I'd love to kill a mess of birds. Calm my nerves after all that hoorah this morning at the house."

The dogs prospected around the yard and up onto the porch of the old house, the male wetting down everything in sight. Then they started at an easy run, one behind the other, down the trail that went from the back of the house down to the old barn. The fence gap was down and they went on into the pasture, which was grown up in sage grass and the dead stalks of summer cedar. We followed on down the path.

"Wouldn't be surprised if we got a point right out behind the barn here," Bluenose said. He was stuffing the shells I had brought him into the pockets of his overalls. "You going to be in a tight with nothing to trade for whiskey when we shoot up all of Mr. B. B.'s stock of shells."

"No, sir, I'll be self-supporting by then and a cash customer," I said. "I start to work Monday."

"For the judge, huh?" Bluenose said.

"Yeah," I said.

"Well, put in a good word for me with all the legal authorities and don't forget what I told you about the law. What they got written in them books don't mean a shitting thing but what they decide it means and that's subject to change right often."

"We'll see," I told him.

"Oh, don't take it on my word. You just look around a spell and see if I ain't right."

We stopped at the gap and loaded our guns. Both of us had double barrels, but Bluenose's was the old style with rabbit-ear hammers. My gun was a fine L. C. Smith with concealed hammers. Poppa had given me the gun when I first started hunting on my own.

"By the way, Brant, don't be too upset about that business this morning. That preacher's meddling has about drove her crazy."

"I didn't think anything of it," I said. "She sure threw a fit about that damn calendar though, didn't she?"

"Well, you got to figure anybody that will keep the same calendar for nigh on twenty years is a mite peculiar about it."

"Maybe she knows something," I said. "Maybe when you hit a year that suits you, you ought to hold on to it."

"Near as I can tell she's writing stuff all over the back of it, but I don't know what," Bluenose said. "She made me promise never to look at it. I figure the least I can do is keep my word about that, even if I am going to Hell. Look yonder, didn't I tell you we'd get a point in this barn lot?"

Sure enough, I could make out the dogs locked on point, their white coats showing patchily through the weeds. When we got up to them, it was Dot that had the birds and the young dog was backing. We walked in and it was a big covey and both of us doubled. Then Bluenose reloaded and a lay bird got up and he killed it, while I was standing there with an empty gun telling the dogs to fetch. That tickled Bluenose.

"When you're old and pretty as I am, boy, you'll learn to reload right quicklike. Lots of times you're apt to find a covey with a fool in it. They're an amazing lot like people."

Bluenose got his wish. We stayed in birds all day, and we both shot as well as two men are likely to. After a while we didn't talk much, just stayed with the hunting steadily and let the dogs work. It was one of those days when they couldn't make a mistake either. It was one to remember.

Late in the day, with only about thirty minutes of shooting light left, we got a point on the edge of a big honeysuckle tangle. The birds got up and made straight for the thick stuff. I doubled and I heard Bluenose shoot only one time. But it seemed like the birds never would stop falling.

"Goddam, I got five with one shot," Bluenose said.

"The hell you did," I said.

"All right, by God, I'll show you. You let the dogs fetch your birds. Keep 'em away from over here."

The dogs brought out my two birds in short order. Then Bluenose called them over and made them hunt dead.

They brought two birds out and he kept crooning, "Dead, dead, dead bird here," and pointing at the honeysuckle. The dogs went back in and came out with two more birds.

"That's four," Bluenose said. "There's one more."

"That's the damndest thing I've ever seen," I said.

"See that little opening there?" Bluenose said. He pointed to a break in the vines about the size of a basketball hoop. "I was shooting at one bird going through there and the others all went for the same hole and flew into the pattern."

The dogs went back into the tangle, but they couldn't find the fifth bird.

"Maybe you just got four," I said.

"Bullshit," Bluenose said and he plunged into the thicket, too. When it was almost dark, I tried to get him to come on and hunt the singles with me.

"Hell no," he said. "I know I saw five birds fall."

So I took one of the dogs and went into the open pine woods beyond the honeysuckle and killed three singles before it got too dark to shoot. When I came back, Bluenose was still thrashing around in the honeysuckle and crooning. "Dead bird, hunt dead in here."

"Come on," I said. "Four birds on one shot is more than most people ever will believe."

"But I got five," Bluenose said, coming out of the vines. "I bet I could have found the son of a bitch if you hadn't took the other dog off."

I started laughing. Bluenose wanted that last bird so badly he was actually getting pouty like a child.

"Ain't funny, goddammit," he said, picking up his gun.

"What the hell, it's just one bird. Why does one more matter when you've got more than you can tote? It's not that important."

"The hell you say it ain't important. Why, if I was to die next week you could always tell people, 'You can say what you want about Bluenose Trogdon, but I'll say one thing for him—it ain't everybody that can kill five quail with one shot.'"

CHAPTER FIFTEEN

I gotta have a word with you, Judge," Sheriff Elbert Willis said.

"Then come on in," Judge Coxwell said.

"Alone," the sheriff said.

I shoved back from my desk and started to get up so they could have some privacy. It was my first day at work. I figured it was expected of me.

"Stay where you are, Brant," said the judge.

"Maybe the boy's right to step on out, Judge," said Elbert Willis.

"This boy, as you call him, is the clerk of this court, Elbert. None of its business need be secret from him."

Elbert Willis leaned against the door jamb. "I ain't so sure about that," he said thoughtfully, as if stalling to give Judge Coxwell plenty of time to change his mind.

"Listen, Judge," I said, "if Sheriff Willis wants me to . . ."

"What the sheriff wants doesn't matter in my chambers," said the judge. "You work for me; there can be no question about your trustworthiness. Don't you agree?"

"Yes, sir."

"And you, Elbert, don't you agree now that you've thought about it?"

"Whatever you say, Judge," Willis said dryly, cutting his eyes over at me. "I reckon you know your man here."

"Then go ahead. I'm listening."

"Well, the straight of it is, we've got a mess on our hands.

Bluenose went and cold-cocked the preacher Hatton yesterday. I got a big crowd of Holy Rollers down in my office right now, wanting me to put Bluenose away."

The judge frowned like a teacher getting a report on some fractious pupil. "Tell me what happened."

"Way I get it from them, in church yesterday, Hatton allowed that he had the Holy Ghost so strong that he could save anybody, including Bluenose Trogdon. So the preacher leads a big crowd down to Bluenose's house and they commenced praying for him right there in his yard. By and by, Bluenose comes out on the porch, smiling and acting real meek and friendly. He says, 'Preacher, I'm ready. Come lead me on down.' Naturally, Hatton goes running over to the steps to meet him and just as he gets there, Bluenose lets drive a terrible lick, full in his face. These folks say Hatton went down like a shot hog. He didn't come to till late last night. They think yet his jaw may be broke."

"That front-yard evangelism can be a dangerous line of work," the judge laughed. "I cain't say that I blame Bluenose much."

"These folks don't see it that way," Willis said.

"Oh, I know, I know. We've got to do something all right. Where do you stand on the whiskey thing?"

Willis glanced at me again, but he spoke up. "I got all the constables and deputies ready to go."

"When?" said the judge.

"This Thursday night, I think it is."

"And where?"

"Aw, we're just going looking for some whiskey stills."

"Willis, you trying to make me mad with you?" the judge said.

"No, sir. I just hate to take chances. We're going into the gorge after Bluenose."

"And you talk about chances. Bluenose has got more friends in that posse than you do. If you wait until Thursday night, he'll have heard about the raid from every deputy and constable you've got. Probably from you, too."

"That ain't fair, Judge. You know . . ."

"Yes, I know. That's why I want you to get your people together and go after Bluenose this evening. Now you go tell your
Holy Rollers that everything will be taken care of. I want you to
get an assault and battery warrant and go by Bluenose's house
and arrest him on that if you can. I don't want you going down to
the river if there's any chance of catching him at the house. You
go down to the river, Elbert, and we'll have to make a whiskey
case. And I don't want to try a whiskey case. It would just upset
the whole county. You just bring him in on a simple assault and
battery warrant."

"Well, there may be a problem about the warrant, Judge. Earl
was talking to the Holiness folks and I think he kind of promised
them something a little stronger. I think he was talking to them in
terms of an attempted murder."

"That's Earl all right, trying to make an attempted murder case
on a fist fight," the judge said. "Tell Earl I said to give you an
assault and battery warrant and that's all. Tell him if he thinks
this is attempted murder, he better read some law."

"Well, I think old Earl was just thinking to get Bluenose out of
the way for a while."

"Tell Earl to let me do the thinking."

"I'll tell him," the sheriff said and he went on out.

The judge lit his pipe and blew a layer of blue smoke out over
his desk. He rubbed his forehead with his left hand while he
puffed on the pipe. "That Earl," he said. "Always wanting to put
somebody in prison."

"There's something I don't understand, Judge. I thought the
solicitor had the last word on warrants."

"You know more law than you've let on, Brant," the judge said,
sounding pleased. "There's something you had to be told sooner
or later, so I suppose I might as well tell you now. Earl Gordon is
a good man, but unfortunately—and I mean this in the gentlest
possible way—he is a fool. I found that out right after he got
elected circuit solicitor, and when I did, I began helping Earl out

on the tough decisions, began making them for him, actually. He's just as happy without the responsibility."

"I see."

"It may sound harsh to speak of Earl that way, but he always gets in a bind when he tries to handle things. What we need is some bright young lawyer to run against Earl. That'll happen one of these years and then I'll have to find Earl some kind of little old job around the courthouse. I do feel a certain obligation to him after all these years. But that needn't worry you, Brant. You just look to your own future."

I agreed not to worry about Earl Gordon and went to work studying the big ledgers in which it would be my job as clerk to record all the court's proceedings. The judge said I had to learn how it was done before the spring court session began. Some time later, I heard a light knock at the door and looked up to see Earl Gordon stick his head into the office.

"Earl, Earl, come on in," said the judge heartily. "It looks like we're going to have to do something about Bluenose Trogdon. Did Elbert see you about a warrant?"

"Yes, sir, I give him an assault and battery," Gordon said. "I thought that was the best to start with."

"Good, good," said the judge.

"I told Elbert to just bring him in on that little old warrant and then we'd see about what kind of case we could build."

"Fine, Earl," said the judge, turning back to his reading. Gordon stood there for a moment, waiting to be dismissed. When the judge didn't look up again, he wandered on out, a large, dull man in a shapeless gray suit. I wondered how Earl Gordon would feel standing in front of the judge's desk four or five years from now, being told that B. B. Laster's boy had finished law school and was going to be put up for solicitor. What would Earl do on that day when the judge lowered his head and went back to his reading? I stayed with my reading, too, working back through the years of trials set down in the dusty binders, and I had to go back over twenty-five years to find a time when he had not been judge. As I read, listening to the judge's own page-turnings and grunts and pipe-stokings at my back, it struck me that most of those cases, at least in the fifteen years Earl Gordon had been solicitor, had been decided not in the courtroom but on the day the judge concluded it was necessary to have the suspected killer or land-line mover or knife fighter arrested.

"Well, I believe that's enough for today," the judge announced a few minutes after four o'clock. "We'll be keeping late hours enough these next few months, especially if the preachers and sheriff and solicitor have their way."

"Judge, about this plan of the sheriff's," I said. "You know Bluenose and I have been pretty good friends."

"I believe I've spoken of that in, shall we say, a roundabout way."

"Well, I was wondering if I could try my hand at talking Bluenose into coming in. I'm afraid somebody's going to get hurt if they go after him, Judge."

"I doubt it," the judge said. "The Trogdons are an independent lot, but they're not violent by habit."

"But you don't know Bluenose's mood, Judge."

"And you don't know my job, either," the judge said with a snap in his voice. "You're a smart boy. You catch the drift of things quickly, but I'm still the one man who decides these things in Pover County."

"That's a big load for one man," I said.

I wished immediately I hadn't said that, fearful that I had pushed the old man a little too hard. But the judge, of course, knew exactly how to handle it. He got up from his desk and walked over to me and put his hand on my shoulder.

"Ah, Brant, it's good to have a young man around," he said. "Herman, rest his soul, was too busy catnapping to ever examine things for what they are. You're right, in a way. Ideally we live under the rule of law, pure and simple, but up here in the country we have to swing in a little wider arc than the law professors might think proper. There's no harm to it if you have the right kind of men watching after things. I flatter myself that I've been that kind of man. I believe your father would tell you I have, don't you?"

"Yes, sir," I said. "I'm sure of it."

"Good, let's close things down for the day."

So we locked the office and went down the dim corridor and out onto the high portico of the courthouse. We stood together for a moment in the weak winter sun.

"Don't be troubled about Bluenose," the judge said. "I've known the Trogdons for a long time now, Bluenose and his father before him. Pover County whiskey made me a popular young fellow around my fraternity house at the University. I'm not going to let things get out of hand."

"Yes, sir," I said, "I appreciate that."

The judge turned and smiled at me. "I feel most at ease with you, Brant, even when you challenge me, which by the way, I don't commend to you as a standard practice. Good day now."

The judge went on down the long steps then, angling away from me. I stood watching him take each step carefully, as if he knew that his bones would break like schoolroom chalk should he fall. Watching him go carefully down, I noticed that his shoes were of soft leather and well shined. He was an old man who took care of himself.

After I left the judge, I drove back to Milo. Poppa had already closed the store and gone home, so I was able to leave my car behind Ozro's shack. It was flat dark by the time I had walked out to the trail leading down toward Bluenose's place. I hollered several times as I descended into the gorge to let Bluenose know it was me. There was a fire in the pit out front, but I found Bluenose back in the second room of his cave. The still was cooking and the smell of the hot mash was strong there under the rock.

"Well, I didn't look to see you down here no more after you joined up with the law," was the first thing he said to me.

"Just had to have one more look at a fellow that got four quail with one shot," I told him.

"Five," he said.

"All that counts is what's picked up."

"Well, I ought to have took the last one out of your hide for not helping me hunt it. How was the judge today?"

"That's what I came for. The judge told the sheriff to raid you tonight."

"That a fact?"

"Yeah, the Holy Rollers made 'em do it because you jumped on Pride Hatton. I wish you hadn't done that."

"Oh, smiting that bastard was worth whatever trouble it brings me. But listen, if I was a court clerk I'd be lighting out for home right this minute. You ain't got much time."

"How come?"

"I been hearing Elbert's boys sneaking around out there since dark. That double-dealing son of a bitch must have a dozen men spread out behind us and over across the river. They'll be coming on in to bust up the still in another hour or so."

"I didn't count on them getting down here so early," I said. "There's no use me hurrying now. They're bound to know I'm here, all the yelling I did coming in."

"Yeah, but you can lie out of it if'n you don't get caught with me."

"Listen, you can't sit down here and wait on them. We can slip out of here right past them, and I'll go get the car and drive you into Birmingham. You can lay up at the whorehouse for a few days."

"Brant, you know I think the world of you and there's not many fellows in your position that would stick by an old owl hoot like me, but I ain't running. I been knowing this was coming for longer than you. The sheriff told me two weeks ago it would take more money for him to keep the preachers off me, and I told him to let 'em come. That sealed it."

"It's him that's coming," I said.

"I don't believe he'll get me, though," Bluenose said, indicating with a jerk of his head the spot where a repeating rifle leaned against the wall of the cave.

"It's not worth it to get into that kind of trouble," I said, "or to get yourself killed."

"That's where you're wrong, Brant," he said. "There's been three generations of Trogdons made whiskey under this bluff, and I'm the last one that will. None of my boys'll ever set foot down here. Elmiry'll see to that. I'm the last, so it don't make no difference whether they get me tonight or two years from now or twenty years."

"Listen, the judge is not all that hot for this thing. He'll let it pass if he can. I heard him tell the sheriff . . ."

"Don't come down here talking judge-this and sheriff-that to me," Bluenose said. "I don't need them telling me what I can do and what I cain't do. I've always made good whiskey and never forced a drop on a man that wasn't thirsty for it. I've kept to myself and supported my family and paid these bastard sheriffs and snuck whiskey to the judges and you see what it's got me—a bunch of their cur dogs circled up around me like I was Geronimo."

"I wouldn't argue with any of that," I said, "but right or wrong doesn't matter just now, because they're coming. They're coming tonight and the main thing is for you not to shoot anybody. All that will get you is the rest of your life in jail."

"Brant, whether it goes rough or smooth is up to them, but I know one thing. I've laid down for my last night in a jail house. You can . . ." Bluenose stopped talking and threw his head back and listened, holding his mouth open. A loud crashing and rattling of brush had commenced on the side of the gorge above and behind us. The sound came to us down the natural chimney above the still. From time to time we could hear a man holler in a long, distressed whoop. The noise was getting closer, quite rapidly. Bluenose grabbed his rifle and we scrambled down the tunnel and out into the front room of the cave.

"Looks like they're coming," he said, "but I sure figured them to be a little quieter about it." He worked the lever action on the rifle, and in the firelight I saw the copper flash of a cartridge sliding into place. The crashing and hollering came faster and closer, gaining speed like a train. I went over and hid behind some boulders, in case they started shooting.

Now pebbles and big rocks were dropping off the lip of the bluff and raining down in front of us into the river. The hollering was so close that we could hear gasps and grunts in between the long yells. The debris rained harder into the water and then a dark shape, big and round like a boulder, sailed out from the roof of the bluff above and hit the river with a splash like you'd thrown a horse in. I glanced over at Bluenose. He was staring out toward where the light of his cook fire shone on the deep pool in front of the bluff.

"Goddam," said a voice from the middle of the river, and a head swam into the light, making its way toward the fire. We could hear the heavy breathing as the swimmer beached himself on the sand and heaved to his feet. There, dripping in the light of the fire, stood Ozro. Bluenose had the gun trained on him.

"Put that damn thing down, Bluenose," he said. "I wouldn't be here if I hadn't fallen off your damn steep-ass mountain."

It should have been funny, the very idea of Ozro losing his balance and, propelled by his great weight, careening down the side of the gorge. I could just see him, snatching at bushes and trees as he passed, his stubby legs churning harder and harder to keep up with the ever-faster downward plunge, until finally that huge heap of flesh tipped over for the scrambling, gravel-snatching, hooting slide down the last steep incline to the river.

The idea of Ozro falling out of his ambush should have been funny, and it would have been if Bluenose had ever wavered an inch with the gun. But he didn't. Ozro stood shivering in the cold, taking the measure of his old friend, and then made his first step away from the river and toward the fire.

"Don't move," Bluenose said.

"No shit, Bluenose," Ozro pleaded, "put that damn thing down. I'm about to freeze."

Ozro's eyes looked tiny in his fat cheeks, little pig eyes, and I thought he might cry.

"Old friend," Bluenose said, "you were up there with the sheriff and that means you ain't on my side. This is the day you betrayed me. Three hundred and sixty-five days from right now you'll be celebrating your first anniversary as a corpse."

"Ah, Bluenose," Ozro said. "You know this wasn't my idea."

"You're a grown man. I figure that means you're doing what you want to do."

Ozro did begin to cry then, shaking hard all over, and the tears shining in the firelight looked lost and hopeless on the expanse of his fat face.

"Just watch your belly, Ozro. I'll bet you can see the hole before you feel anything," Bluenose said.

Ozro kept crying soundlessly. I knew he must be remembering my telling him that Bluenose couldn't be pushed much further. I had walked up beside Bluenose by this time, trying to think of something to do. I stepped in front of him and took the end of his rifle barrel, holding the muzzle against my own stomach.

"You'll have to shoot through me to kill him, Bluenose," I said, "and I don't believe you'll do that."

Bluenose looked at me steadily and his eyes had that flat look that a dog's eyes get right before it bites.

"No, I don't reckon I could do that, and I don't reckon I can kill this fat son of a bitch, either." Ozro, still dripping, made a dive for the fire, allowing Bluenose a wide berth.

"I reckon you call yourself putting me under arrest," Bluenose said. "I mean you falling down the hill and landing in the river and taking advantage of my fire, that does constitute an arrest, don't it?"

"No, it don't," Ozro said. "But there's some fellows back up the hill there that's got their hearts set on it and you might have to shoot them to change their minds."

"That'd be all right, too," Bluenose said. "I don't much give a shit what happens. It's just a matter of time till they get me."

"Not if you do what I tell you," Ozro said. He was standing so close to the fire that steam was coming off his pants legs. "Do what I tell you and you might stay out from behind bars long enough for things to slide back to normal. But you let them catch you down here and you'll get two or three years easy."

"What you want me to do, Ozro?" Bluenose said. "Run?"

"Yeah, and you better do it quick, too. But before you go, you and Brant need to load that still up with sand and sink it right here in the river. Come spring, you can just dive in and pull it out and you're back in business. You'd be doing yourself a favor. You'd be doing Brant one, too, in case you ain't thought about the risk he's took for you. Course I know it's a insult to mention gratitude to a Trogdon. A free and independent lot, ain't that it, Bluenose?"

"Ozro," I said, "I stopped him from shooting you once tonight. Just shut up. Bluenose never asked me to come."

"Leave him be," said Bluenose. "Ozro's just trying to shame me into cooperating. It's one of his oldest tricks. Go along to get along, that's our man Ozro."

To my surprise, Bluenose propped his rifle against a rock and ambled over to the fire. As if he didn't have a care in the world, he squatted down beside Ozro and held his hands out to the fire.

"Tell me why you pushing this so hard, round man," he said.

"I just want you out of here. I'm scared of what's coming. I know you ain't playing, and neither is Elbert Willis."

"You got more'n my welfare on your mind," Bluenose said. "Let me hear it all."

"It's gonna be a mess with Brant down here," said Ozro. "That's the thing of it. B. B. ain't never done nothing to you, Bluenose."

"Goddam you, Ozro," I shouted. "I'm my own . . ."

"You're God's own fool is what you are," said Ozro, glaring at me. "Would you shut up for once? We ain't playing down here now."

"Both of you shut up so I can think," Bluenose said, mildly. "How you figure to explain letting me get away, Ozro?"

"I'll say this place was bare as a doorknob when I got here. Course Elbert won't believe me, but he ain't gonna dispute me much, all I know on him."

"I reckon I could slip down the river and climb out at the bridge," Bluenose said. "It ain't in my nature, but it might be the smart thing to do."

Bluenose looked over at me, but I gave no sign of approval or disapproval. Ozro was right. He did better when I kept my mouth shut.

"You got to move if you gwine to do it," Ozro said. "Elbert Willis'll be standing right here inside an hour."

"I reckon Brant will have to go out with me," Bluenose said.

"Unless he's got a hell of a fine story about why he happened to be going for a walk down this way tonight," Ozro said.

Bluenose studied the fire for a few moments more; then, without a word, he got up and started back through the boulders toward the entrance of the tunnel to the still room. I followed him. By the light of the lanterns hanging back there, he shoveled the coals from the fire box out onto the rock floor of the cave. Then I helped him drain the steaming mash out of the boiler. It gushed in a thick tide into the waste vat, filling the room with its sharp, sour odor. The thin metal cooled quickly, and we wrestled the conical copper boiler down through the little tunnel. Its larger end barely passed through the narrow opening that led to the river. Then we went back into the still room to gather up all the small items we could carry, including the condenser and the long copper worm and Bluenose's funnels and measuring scoops.

"I wish I could hide my kegs," Bluenose said, surveying the neat stacks of twenty-five-gallon barrels he used for aging the whiskey. "They'll bust them up, I reckon."

"Not the ones that are filled," I said.

Bluenose snorted. "I reckon old Willis will spare the axe, way he loves whiskey. Either way, I'll lose my fresh kegs. Old feller up on Sand Mountain made them for me. He used to have a regular business making kegs for quality whiskey. He died a while back. Come on, let's get out of here."

Out by the river, we tied the entire rig—boiler, worm and all—together with plowline and weighted it with rocks. Then Bluenose and I took off our clothes, so they'd be dry when we got ready to run for it. Carrying the still between us, we waded out until we could feel the place where the bottom shelved off sharply into the deep pool. We stood waist deep in the Sipsey's cold waters. I felt the current snatching at my legs. Bracing ourselves, we gave the copper still a shove that sent it surging out over the deep water before it lost momentum and started sinking. It went down with a last shuddering release of bubbles and then there was nothing. Bluenose and I hustled for the fire. Ozro had chunked the fire to a roar and he stood over it, flapping his shirt in the blast of heat to speed its drying. He was having a nervous fit now.

"Y'all hurry up. You ain't got no time to waste now," he fretted. "Just get your clothes on and get out of here."

"Goddammit, Ozro, I reckon I understand this situation about as good as anybody," Bluenose said. "You're just worried about your own hide, that's all."

But Bluenose and I didn't waste time getting dressed, for a fact. We jerked our clothes on before we were properly dry and then Bluenose gave Ozro a short farewell cussing about what was going to happen to him if he told where the still was hid.

"Wait a minute," Bluenose said. "There's one more thing. I may be running, but I ain't about to let you bastards have my good Winchester."

Bluenose reached out and snatched away the blue chambray shirt Ozro was drying over the fire. Using his teeth, Bluenose ripped two long strips of cloth out of the back of the shirt, rending it into two unjoined and useless halves. Ozro didn't say anything. Bluenose took the strips and tied them into a sling for the rifle and hung it across his back.

"That'll give you something to explain," Bluenose said, and we were off at last, leaving Ozro at the fire pondering his divided shirt.

We followed the little secret path that led from the bluff to the main trail running up and down the river. We moved east then, crossing back over the roof of the bluff and heading on toward where the steel bridge crossed the gorge. We walked without talking, always on the alert for the sheriff's party. The dim trail wound among trees and the big boulders that jutted from the sides of the gorge, and brought us finally to the place where the bridge arched out through the darkness above us. We were exactly under the bridge, and looking out across the river, I could see its spindly steel columns marching away from us in pairs. We stood between the first two columns on the north shore; they were anchored into the rock on which we stood. The gorge was narrow at this point, which was why the bridge was here, but steep also. It would be a hard, dangerous, knuckle-busting climb. Bluenose led us up a steep wooded slope to the base of a sheer cliff of gray rock about fifty feet high. We searched about until we found a tree growing hard against the face of the cliff. We climbed the tree, one at a time. From below, I watched Bluenose make the leap across a space of sky from the swaying treetop to the cliff. It scared the living shit out of me, but I did it, too, landing beside Bluenose in a situation even more terrifying. From the brink of the cliff, a giant face of smooth rock swept upward and away at an incline too steep to allow standing. We lay plastered to the cold rock.

"Goddam," I panted, "did you know it was this bad?"

"Bad, hell," Bluenose said. "When I was a kid, I used to come up here and climb these rocks just to kill time, while my old man was working whiskey. This is a goddam lark, Brant. That's what it is." Bluenose was smiling at me, a crooked ironic smile, like a man who could stand good fortune or bad, as long as it brought adventure. I was, not to exaggerate, frozen with the fear of sliding down the rock face and over the brink of the cliff.

"Now, when we start up this thing, your inclination is going to be to slither along on your belly like a snake," Bluenose said. "But you get up on hands and knees so you can get some traction with your feet and get you some momentum moving up. Keep your belly off the rock and you'll never fall."

Bluenose took off then, scrambling away on all fours, rising through the darkness with a high-backed, loping crawl like a racoon's. Having no choice, I followed, against all inclination pushing my body out from the rock and imitating Bluenose's coon crawl. I scrambled wildly away from the brink of the cliff and found myself moving upward steadily, heedless that the bare rock burned and bruised me, hand, shin, and knee. Soon I stood panting beside Bluenose in the trees that grew in a ragged line along the upper edge of the rock escarpment.

"Jesus," I said, looking back down the long slide of stone and out over the dizzy drop down to the river, shining silent and silver-black far below us.

"I believe a man could keep you out there on that rock just a little bit longer and convert you," Bluenose kidded. "Now you see why my trail is where it is. Ain't just anywhere you can walk out of this gorge standing up on two legs and carrying sixteen gallon of whiskey."

"Lasters just ain't much good on high places," I said. I looked up to the sharp, black outlines of the bridge passing over our heads. "Remember my cousin Elroy Laster?"

"The one fell off the bridge," Bluenose said. "Poor bastard thought he was a bridge-builder." He turned toward me a face that looked blasted and craggy in the moonlight; all joy of adventure had drained away and his features were lapsed into a look of blank despair. "Poor bastard done hisself in just by believing what there wasn't no reason to believe in. That poor dumb country peckerwood bastard thought he was a bridge-builder. You think the law ain't truly just a pile of shit. I believe times ain't changed. I say I know times have changed, but I don't believe it. I don't live like it."

Bluenose turned abruptly and began moving off through the trees. I followed. The last part of the climb was easier, a steep, thickly forested and pathless slope leading up to the road. When we reached the road, we turned south, walking out onto the bridge and looking down at the river far below. We were so far upstream now from Bluenose's bluff that we couldn't even see the glow from the fire. The gorge, silent, deep, and dim, hid all in its vast containment. We decided it would be too risky after all for me to drive Bluenose down to Jasper. By the time I walked up to Milo and came back with the car, the sheriff's people were likely to be patrolling the road. Ozro wouldn't be able to hold them down there long after they discovered we had slipped out. Bluenose would simply walk on down to Jasper, since the sheriff couldn't touch him once he got on the Walker County side of the gorge.

"Where you going to hide out?" I said.

"I might try to drift on down to Miss Lottie's and see if she'd put me up for a few days."

"Be careful down there," I said, remembering the rage the whore Polly had put him in. "You don't want that judge to get hold of you again."

"You know me," Bluenose said. "Here take this and throw it in your car till I get back. I cain't travel with it."

He was holding the rifle out to me. I didn't take it.

"I'm scared to walk all the way back to Milo with it," I said. "What if they catch me? How am I going to explain being down here in the middle of the night with a rifle?"

"How you going to explain being down here without one, Mr. Court Clerk?" Bluenose said.

"Just hide it in the woods somewhere," I said. I really did not want the rifle, and not merely for fear of being caught. As Bluenose thrust it toward me, I realized that it was the very image of the rifle I had carried in the deadly, lonesome country of my vision.

"I don't aim for it to get all rusted up," Bluenose said. "Take this goddam rifle. They ain't no point in turning chickenshit now, after all you done already tonight."

I took the rifle and slung it over my shoulder. "You're right," I said. "I'm in too deep to worry now."

"Fare thee well," said Bluenose.

He started for the Jasper side of the bridge, and I turned back toward Milo. The bridge held us high in the cold night as we started our separate ways. When I reached the end of the bridge, I turned and watched Bluenose out of sight on the other side, and he never looked back. The rifle, suspended by the rags of Ozro's shirt, pulled at my right shoulder with a steady, pleasant weight.

Anticipating the hullabaloo that was going to break out at the courthouse the next morning, I decided it wouldn't hurt for me to be seen somewhere else that night. So after I got back to the car, I started driving out toward Blake's house. It was still early enough to drop in, maybe take her for one more ride.

I killed the lights a couple of hundred yards below the house and let the car roll on slowly through the darkness until it came to a stop across the road from her house. I could see her framed in the lighted window as she sat at the living room table, working over her books. I sat in the car a long time and watched her, the proper teacher at her homework. The way she bent to her books, secure in her beauty and innocent of whatever danger there might be out in the wide night, reminded me of how lucky she was. Nothing—not all the strange weapons in the world, not the Dream of Atlanta a thousand times—could have made me harm her that night. For I had control. That's the thing that got me home.

CHAPTER SIXTEEN

First thing the next morning, the sheriff dropped by Judge Coxwell's office. He wanted permission to—as he put it—"kick this little bastard's ass." He accused me of helping Bluenose get away. The judge asked him how he knew that.

"Brant Laster was in the woods soon as dark fell, hollering to let Bluenose know we was coming," Elbert Willis said. "Every man with me heard him. Then when we get down to the bluff, there sits Ozro Jenkins, saying he ain't seen Laster or Bluenose— and Ozro supposed to be helping us."

"Sounds to me like you just got outsmarted by Bluenose," the judge said.

"I ain't so stupid that I cain't figure out this Milo bunch—thick as thieves," Willis said. "I got betrayed, that's what I got. This boy tipped Bluenose off and Ozro let 'em both go, because he's scared to cross B. B. Laster. Well, Judge, I ain't scared and I ain't so dumb that I don't know this new clerk of your'n is working both sides of the street."

"You've made your suspicions clear enough, Elbert," the judge said mildly. "You saw Brant down there, did you?" "Didn't have to see him. I heard him hollering. I recognized his goddam voice."

The judge paused to light his pipe, inclining his head downward to show all that fine white hair. "Well, Elbert," he said finally, "you've been at this business long enough to know you've got to have more than your suspicions about who owned a voice you heard hollering in the woods in the middle of the night."

"Why are you protecting this little pissant, Judge?" the sheriff demanded, made brave, I sensed, by his giant puzzlement. "Just tell me that. Ever since you hired him, it's been all the talk how thick him and Bluenose is. Now dammit, what truck you got with them?"

The judge lurched forward in his chair, hurling his pipe with a clatter into a glass bowl on his desk. "You hear this, my man," he said. "You best mind who you're speaking to. You're putting out a lot of loose talk because you let Bluenose get away. Well, I've heard loose talk from time to time about you, Elbert. What if I believed that talk with no more proof than you've got on Brant here?"

Elbert Willis didn't say anything. The judge had canceled his ticket, all right, and that puzzled me as much as it did Elbert Willis.

"The thing to do is just ask the man himself," the judge went on. "Brant, were you down on the river last night? Was it you Elbert heard?"

"No, sir," I said.

"Did anyone see you elsewhere last evening?"

"No, sir," I said. "I was by myself. I don't guess there's anybody could vouch for me. Poppa turns in right after supper."

There was really nothing more I could say, for I had abandoned my plan to take Blake for a ride. I had been satisfied finally to leave Blake as I had found her, departing with no dark alibi.

The sheriff snorted and said, "Well, I figured he'd just 'fess right up." Then he stomped out of the room, casting at me one last knowing look.

The judge sat there for a long time, rubbing his chin with his hand and staring at the door the sheriff had just slammed.

"Brant," he said finally, "you violated my confidence, didn't you?"

"Yes, sir," I said.

"I've made myself look a fool for you just now," he said in a voice that betrayed neither anger nor concern. "I'll not do that again. Do you understand? I'll not be embarrassed or betrayed ever again."

"Yes, sir," I said. "I believe I ought to just quit before I cause you any more trouble." I was thinking the judge wanted that, and was holding back from firing me outright out of respect for my father.

"No, no, no," he said, shaking his head quickly. "That's not my meaning. There's an advantage to your staying. I just want you to understand your situation, the fact that you have no more leeway." He swung his eyes into contact with my own and held my gaze. "You see, you owe me a repayment now, don't you?"

"Yes, sir," I said, "that seems the way of things."

"Indeed." He smiled. "The dawn of understanding, shall we say."

I didn't respond to that.

"I mean no insult, Brant," the judge added quickly. "I might just as easily be referring to my own understanding. I've decided you were right in the way you handled this, rather clumsily so, but right nonetheless. We do need to get word of warning to Bluenose. Elbert won't rest until he's nailed Bluenose now, because the preachers won't give him any rest. I believe the best thing all around would be for Bluenose to just move on and set up his operation somewhere else. I know it'll be hard on him to leave, but I think he might like a new location better than jail."

"I may run into someone who can get word to him," I said.

Judge Coxwell leaned over his desk at me. "Don't be coy," he snapped. "You tell him. Don't send word. Don't go to him, wherever he's hiding, if he's out of the county. You simply wait and tell him my decision on the day he sets foot back in Pover County. You check his house every morning on your way to work and every evening on your way home. When you see him, tell him I said his time was up. You tell him straight that I said to get out of my county forever. That's the way I want it handled. It's your job to do it that way. Don't cross me again."

The judge could make a point when he tried. The words bored into me. "Yes, sir," I said, feeling truly hired by him for the first time.

I did what the judge said every day for a week. Finally, one cold afternoon, just before dark, I found Bluenose, but the timing was no good. Just as I got to the Trogdon place, I saw him coming up the road on foot. I stopped the car in the road opposite the house, opened the car window, and waited for him.

"How long you been back?" I said, still sitting at the wheel.

"Just this minute walked up. Ain't even been in the house yet," he said. "How's the law business these days?"

"Not so good. The judge says you got to get out of his county for good. I'm sorry."

"No need to be. The judge ain't gonna cause me no discontent. I learned something about this running I let you and Ozro talk me into. It ain't no good. A man like me's got to stay on his ground. So I'll be living in my house here and I'll be down at my bluff, when I take a mind to work, doing my work, and I'll molest no man that don't molest me. Lawmen like you and the judge ought to see the justice in that."

"It won't work, Bluenose. I'm sorry. But the judge will have you in prison . . ."

"Oh, it'll work all right," Bluenose broke in. He spoke with neither friendliness nor anger, with no more feeling than if I had been a rank stranger. "It'll work as long as it works, be that long or short. Elmiry's been saying that I was living in my End Time anyhow. Who knows how long that might be? You'll be bound to tell Elbert and the judge that I'm back, I reckon. So you tell 'em that I'm home till the End Time."

"I don't know that I'll tell them anything."

"Oh, you best, Brant, and you will." He stood looking at me for a moment, his arms crossed against the cold since he had only a denim jumper for a coat. "See you later," he said.

I watched him walk across the yard toward his steps. He turned back toward me. "I'll be needing my rifle," he called. "You got it with you by chance?"

"No," I lied. "It's at the house."

"Drop it off in the morning," he said, again without the affection I had deserved in the old days or the rancor I might have expected in these new ones.

He mounted the steps and struggled briefly with the door, which would not open. He knocked. In half a minute, the door opened inward, and I saw Bluenose raise his hand in what looked to be a greeting.

Then there was a loud roar and Bluenose came off the porch backwards. He came off very fast as if he'd been snatched with a rope, never touching the steps, and landed flat on his back in the bare yard. He never moved. Elmira stepped out on the porch. She had Bluenose's shotgun in her hands, and she broke the gun and pulled out two shells and threw them on the ground beside Bluenose. She closed the gun again without reloading, and then she looked straight at me and never moved nor took her eyes off me as I left the car idling in the road right in front of the house and walked up in the yard. It was hard for me to breathe and I kept rubbing both hands on my trouser legs as I walked. It is that helpless motion so many people have when they come up against something that is utterly beyond their power. I have it. You rub your hands over and over on your thighs like you are wiping the sweat off and getting ready to grab hold and straighten everything out, but there is nothing to grab. I was doing that and breathing funny and I could feel the tears in my eyes, but I wasn't actually crying, I don't think. There was no question he was dead. She had given him both barrels very close so the hole in the front of his chest wasn't too big. I knew his back would be bad. I had seen the stuff fly when the pellets came through, and a big circle of blood was spreading out in the dirt around his upper body. Elmira clutched a long piece of paper. It dangled from the hand that held the forearm piece of the shotgun.

"He's dead," she said.

"Oh shit," I said. "Oh goddammit." Bluenose's face was peaceful and pale, the pits and veins prominent in his nose, his skin as wasted and rough looking as a field that's plowed and never planted, rough and dead looking as such ground is after a drenching rain.

"I had to do it," she said.

I couldn't bear to bend down to touch him. His eyes were open. The circle of blood was spreading.

"I told him over and over I'd do it if he didn't quit." Elmira's voice was very calm. I was looking at the body and her voice droned on above me. "He had warning, plenty of it. I promised him and I had to do it. He has been washed in the Blood of the Lamb."

"Pride Hatton told you to do this," I said.

"He ain't told me nothing," she said. "I know what you think, you little heathen bastard, but I had my dream afore I ever heard of Pride Hatton."

"But he told you what it meant. Blood flowing like a river, each angel holding a sword, all that Holy Roller shit."

We stood wailing at one another, two damned crazies locked in theological debate over Bluenose's body, the blood of lamb slaughter spreading a halo in the dirt beneath him. I stood outside myself, watching it, like a lawyer.

"You think you're smart," she said, lapsing into a dull, distant voice. "You think you're smarter than God, just like he did. I had my dream for all these years. I ain't hiding nothing. All Pride Hatton did was tell me my dream was an anointment. He done that when I testified about it in the church. All Pride Hatton did was make me a new woman. I got the proof I had my dream for all these years, all them lonely whiskey-suffering years. Well, you get this, you whiskey-sucker, I am a new woman born today."

The new woman's steady, factual voice stopped, and I studied her face, which held eyes as bright and enigmatic as crystal marbles. I let my gaze drop down to Bluenose's old shotgun and then to the paper dangling from her hand.

"What you got there?" I said.

"Nothing."

"Your proof," I said, or actually the lawyer who was a part of me and outside me as well said it, said it in his understanding of such things.

"It's nothing of yours," she said. "It's just something I was holding when he came in."

It was the Clabber Girl calendar. The way it hung from her hand I could see the girl smiling vacantly and upside down toward Bluenose's body.

"He was just standing there. He wasn't making a move when you shot him." I started up the stairs toward her, my eyes still on the hand that held the gun and calendar.

"Give me that."

She held the gun out to me without protest.

"No, the other."

She drew back and I grabbed the calendar as she tried to get it behind her back. We both had hold of it.

"Don't tear it," she shrieked. "It's mine. Let go."

The shotgun fell to the floor as we struggled over the calendar. No longer calm, she was screaming for fair now, a high, piercing, mad scream that sounded like it had been locked up inside her for a long time. It went on and on while we fought for the calendar. "Don't tear it. Don't tear it," she wailed.

I had a good hold on it, with the bottom half twisted up in my hand. I could see the Clabber Girl's face and torso crumpling up.

Whiskey Man

Elmira was trying to get her body between me and the calendar and hold it away from me at arm's length, the way you would turn away from a player who was trying to steal a basketball from you. With my free hand I grabbed her wrist and started squeezing. Her fingers went white and she started crying instead of screaming. I put everything I had on her wrist. It was thin and I could feel the bones shifting, going together, and I was sure something would break. Finally I saw her fingers move and her hand started coming open, slowly, like an arthritic claw. I took the calendar and jumped down in the yard.

"Give it back, oh, give it back," she sobbed. "It's mine."

I could see children moving in the darkness of the house. She went slowly to the floor beside the shotgun, collapsing downward into her own lap. She held her head and wept for the loss of her calendar.

"What are you going to do with him?" I said, nodding toward Bluenose.

"Nothing, I'm through with him. Just give me back my calendar." She went back to her crying, but her tears were not for the dead man.

The children were creeping forward out of the darkness. I could see them coming. What could I do? I took the calendar and went back to my car. Then I went down to the store. I got there just as Poppa was closing up. He was running late. I went into the store and stopped just inside the front door and examined the calendar's back, where I had seen writing. This is what it said, in a tiny hand: "18 Matt. 21–22." Then after that came rank on rank of tiny counting marks in groups of five, four vertical and one slashing across the four. They filled the back of the old calendar. My father called to me from the back of the store when he came out of the stockroom and saw me standing there.

"Poppa," I said, "quote me the eighteenth chapter of Matthew, the twenty-first and twenty-second verses."

"That's an easy one," he said. " 'Then came Peter to him, and said, Lord, how oft shall my brother sin against me and I forgive him? Till seven times?

"'Jesus saith unto him, I say not unto thee, until seven times; but, until seventy times seven.'"

I didn't need to count the marks on Elmira's calendar. I knew there would be four hundred and ninety. Bluenose had finally run his string out, never knowing why she had kept that calendar all the years, marking off his every offense from the first night he slipped from their bed to run his fish trap.

"Why did you want to know that verse, son?" my father said. "What's that in your hand?"

"An old account," I said.

CHAPTER SEVENTEEN

Whem I got back to the Trogdon place, Bluenose's body was still in the yard, exactly where it had fallen. I had told Poppa what happened and sent him to tell Ozro to meet me back at his shack. I had fetched a big pile of clean burlap bags and one blanket from the store. I took Elmira at her word and I figured it was up to me to take care of the body.

Pride Hatton came out of the house when I pulled up in the yard. I stopped with my lights across the body. The shotgun shells still lay beside Bluenose and they cast small shadows. One stood on end like a silo. I thought: You could toss shells off that porch all day without getting one to land like that. I got out of the car, leaving it running and the lights on. I walked up to the porch.

"Brother Laster, we meet on a sad day," the preacher said. "Now perhaps you can see the evil that liquor brings."

"I didn't know she drank," I said.

"Evil is visited on him who spawned it."

"Maybe you're right, Hatton." I looked up at him. The harsh lights of the car made his face look angular and fanatical. I thought of Bluenose's repeating rifle, which was stored in the luggage trunk of my car. "Maybe I ought to visit some on you, you murdering son of a bitch. Maybe I ought to blow your goddam lying Holy Roller head off."

Hatton came down the steps and stood very close to me. His

hair was slicked down and it shone greasily in the car light. The night had gotten mortal cold.

"That's twice you've called me those names," he said, very softly. "You don't want to make the mistake of thinking you can go on doing that just because I'm a man of God. I have my limits."

"It's a shame one of your limits ain't that commandment about not killing other folks," I said. "I know you put her up to this."

"Judgment belongs to the Lord," Hatton said, not in the least shaken by my accusation.

"So does vengeance, I thought."

"Self-defense is not vengeance," Hatton said. "I figure in your new capacity with the court you'd have to agree that this was clearly self-defense, even given your friendship for this dead man here."

"My capacity consists of doing what I'm told," I said, "but I figure this is premeditated murder in the first degree, and I aim to get a warrant sworn out in the morning. I'm going to get one for you too, Hatton, as an accessory. I'll see you in jail for this."

"First you got to find a jury somewhere in this county that will believe this woman didn't have to defend herself from this drunk, this notorious drunk of reprobate mind. Not even a smart lawyer-boy like you can hide what he was." Hatton, I could tell, was taking my measure, testing to see how much I knew and how much pull I had at the courthouse.

"Pride Hatton," I said, "if all preachers were smart as you, no telling how far Jesus could have gone. But you'll have a hard time praying away the proof I've got."

"What would that be, this proof of yours, Brother Laster?"

"You know the eighteenth chapter of Matthew, the twenty-first and twenty-second verses, I guess."

"Yes, indeed, forgive 'seven times seventy' is the word of the Lord in that passage."

"Ask Elmira about that. Just quote her that scripture and tell her I've got her tally sheet. She'll know what you're talking about. You just ask her, Hatton."

"Maybe I will. But first let me give you some good advice. You don't deserve it, but you've got a good future around here, just because you're your father's son. I wouldn't ruin myself by persecuting this woman, if I was you."

"You better worry about your ass, not hers," I said. "I think that's what got you into this—a fine bachelor preacher like you worrying about her ass all the time. I'll tell you the truth, she ain't no bad-looking woman, you fix her up a little."

I could tell I had finally jolted him. His face got rigid and hot looking, and I thought he was ready to jump on me. "I ought to stomp your guts out," he said.

"I wish you would, you butt-suck Holy Roller bastard. You just raise your hand and I'll show you some goddam self-defense that won't quit."

I wanted it, too. I actually wanted it, no bluff talk. I felt the pull of Bluenose's gun, lying in the trunk like Judgment, oily and smooth and full of shells. All I needed was to get started, and I might just settle everything, clean out everybody that needed it in one dreamy rampage.

"I wouldn't give you the satisfaction," Hatton was saying, a little scared at last.

"You're not a dumb man, Preacher. I guess that's enough talk, isn't it? I've got a dead man here to do something with, unless Elmira is just planning to let him go back to the soil right here. You asked her what she plans to do with him?"

"I think she'd be satisfied to let you handle it," Hatton said. He was calm again, I had to give him that. I'm not sure he would have been so calm if he had known what I had in the trunk and how careless I was feeling. The preacher looked down at the long corpse, ashen in the bright lights. It was the first dead body I'd ever had any close contact with, and I was stricken by its utter stonelike stillness. Shakespeare notwithstanding, death is not but a sleep. I stepped over to the car and started arranging the burlap bags on the back seat and floor board. It didn't look like Bluenose was bleeding any more, but I didn't want to take any chances of ruining the car.

"I guess y'all will insist on what's called a Christian burial," I said, coming back to face Hatton across the body.

"Whatever you like. Naturally, as a minister of the gospel, I recommend it."

"Bullshit, Hatton, you're a preacher only because the circus didn't pass by the day you were ready to leave the farm. You're such a big Christian, I'll let you preach the service."

"You think you're a hard young man," he said, "but you're going to get broke—broke open like a shotgun."

"Well, the least you can do is help me load the body," I said, ignoring his prediction.

Hatton, still giving me a furious, rabid-fox grin, said, "Let every man bury his own dead. All my people are living." Then he went inside.

There was no way of putting it off any longer. For the first time, I touched the body. It was cold and stiff, as I expected, and its absolute deadness reminded me again of the cold of the night. The temperature had dropped steadily since dark. I grabbed the body around the chest from the rear and backed into the open door of the car. It came in hard and uncooperatively and while I worked positioning it on the bags, I was careful not to look at the big hole I knew must be in his back. But when I got through I saw that my shirt front was smeared with blood and bits of Bluenose, and standing beside the automobile, I was sick there in the yard.

By the time I got back to Milo, light was showing from the constable's shack. Ozro was sitting in there all bundled up.

"Well, your daddy says he's gone," Ozro said when I came in. "Elmira shot him."

"What for?"

"For pissing her off one time too many, it looks like."

"Goddam, I loved him like a brother," Ozro said.

I didn't say anything.

"You know I did, Brant, even if we did have our differences these last few months. If I hadn't liked him, I wouldn't have come down and warned him the other night."

"You warned him because you lost your footing and fell in the river," I said, "but it don't make a shit any more to me and for sure not to him."

"I just don't want you to think hard of me, Brant, him being gone and all."

"I don't think about it," I said.

"Where's the body?" Ozro said.

"In the car," I said.

He didn't say anything, just followed me out of the shack, kept following me when I went to the store without stopping at the car. We got a couple of crates and some long planks from the back and returned to the shack. We made a table with them.

"One thing for sure," Ozro said. "There ain't no danger of the body getting high, cold as it is in this goddam shack."

We went out to the car and brought the body in and laid it on the planks. Ozro looked at the holes in the chest.

"His back must be a mess," he said.

"I've not looked," I said.

We rolled the body over and looked. "Oh shit," Ozro said. There was no more bleeding. It was bad. We put the body back, resting face up.

"It's a shame he doesn't have anybody to sit up with him," Ozro said.

"He does. You're staying," I said and I got in my car without another word. As I drove away, I could see Ozro look out the window after me and then he disappeared, and I knew that Ozro's sense of the proprieties of death would keep him at his desk in the heatless shack throughout the night. Sitting up with the dead was an important custom in the hills, sort of a wake without whiskey. Usually it was done by the dead person's family in his own home. Bluenose's case presented problems in this regard, as it did in that even more important custom of getting the deceased "preached into heaven." Being preached into heaven meant having a preacher declare at your funeral that you had lived in such a way that God was bound to let you into heaven. Of course, none of the Milo preachers would dare preach Bluenose Trogdon into heaven, but I figured to get it done despite them.

"I'm going to get Bluenose buried and Elmira put in jail," I told Poppa the next morning when he asked my plan.

"It's not good to mess with other folks' grief," he said, "especially when the law's involved."

"Well, in this case, I'm a witness and I aim to see her pay for it." I was eating my breakfast hurriedly, anxious to get away from him.

" 'Judge not, that ye be not judged,' " my father said.

"Seems like Elmira missed all those judgment and vengeance verses," I said.

"Where are you going to bury him, son?"

"Right beside his mother and daddy in the Pover Cemetery," I said.

"Well, you know our cemetery stewards committee is supposed to meet on any new burials, Brant. I don't think you can bury him that fast."

I looked at my father closely. He seemed worried.

"Aren't you on that committee, Poppa?"

"That's right. Me for the Baptists and Mr. Hibbert from the Methodists and a couple of others from both churches."

"You better get them together quick then if y'all want to approve Bluenose before he goes in the ground."

"That's just my thinking, Brant. They may not approve it. There are no more Trogdons in either the Methodist or the Baptist church and Bluenose hasn't been in any church for years. Maybe Brother Hatton's church could find a place to bury him as a favor to Elmira."

"They won't help," I said, "but it doesn't matter what your committee does, Poppa. Bluenose is going into the ground right there beside his folks." I got up from the table. "I'll see you after a while. I've got to find a gravedigger and a preacher."

The gravedigger I found had been sitting up all night with a body and he was not too happy to find out that he was a gravedigger.

"Listen," Ozro said, "if I get all involved in this business, I'll never get elected to anything again. Besides I'm tired and near froze."

"Digging will warm you up," I said, "and four years from now folks will have decided you did the Christian thing. Besides nobody else would have your half-ass job."

"Those things you say ain't funny any more," Ozro said. "You don't like me now, do you, Brant, because of all this, I mean?"

"I like you, Ozro," I said. "This is just a bad time and I need your help. There's no one else."

"Well, maybe it'll make me feel a little better about Bluenose, even if it does lose my job for me," he said. "You want to look at him this morning? He looks pretty rough."

"No," I said, and we went over to the store. I opened it up and got Ozro a new pick and shovel. Then we went across the big, empty intersection to the church and I marked off the grave in the hard, grassless clay next to old man Trogdon's grave.

"It don't look like easy digging," Ozro said.

"It won't be," I said, but I didn't tell him about Poppa's committee. I figured he'd find out about them soon enough.

"You know, Brant, it was pretty rough sitting up with Bluenose. I mean, I got to feeling bad and low about these last few months. And him just laying there stiff and blue, nothing like he was when he was alive. It was rough, I'll tell you." He scratched at the ground inside the markings with his shovel for a moment.

"I guess you know I feel deep down like it was my fault, at least a part mine."

"No," I said, "it was all decided a long time ago. Now I know there was nothing in the world that any of us could have done to stop it."

"Thanks," he said. As I walked back to the car, I could hear behind me the regular fall of his pick on the reluctant clay, pancaked by time and rain and the footfalls of mourners now dead and mourned into the ground themselves. I swung the car onto the road and went on to Fever Springs and beyond it, to the home of one of Bluenose's old-time friends.

Carther Rooks came out on his porch, hitching at his pants. He looked at me, then out at the creek where the mist was rising. He rubbed his eyes and his forehead and what hair he had for a long time with his left hand; he walked to the edge of the porch, hacked and spit. He opened his fly and commenced urinating and the urine brought steam from the ground. Carther lived in some bottomland out west of Fever Springs on a winding, deep creek that eventually ran into the Sipsey.

"What you want?" he said while he was pissing. He hacked and spit again, white phlegm.

"You don't remember me, do you?"

"No. If'n I had remembered you, I would have said, What you want, Buck, or Jim, or whatever your name might be."

"I'm Brant Laster."

"B. B.'s boy?"

"That's right."

"I used to know B. B. well, back in the old days. Good man."

"Yes, sir."

"Well, you can go ahead and hunt on my place if'n you want, Laster. I don't care."

"That's not what I came for."

"No, on second thought, I reckon not, judging from them clothes."

"I need a preacher," I said.

"Well, son, I am not a preacher. I am what you would call a failed preacher, a back-slid preacher, one that has slid as far back as you can go."

"Are you still ordained?"

"Far as I know I ain't never been unordained," he said. "But that don't matter. Fellow your age usually needs a preacher for just one thing, and I'd hate for you to try being married with the kind of spell I could throw."

"I need a funeral," I said.

"Whose?"

"Bluenose Trogdon."

"Dead or dying?"

"Dead."

Carther breathed three long heavy breaths and ran his hands back and forth across the roll of belly fat just above his belt.

"How?"

"Wife shot him."

"She sure was a pretty thing when she was young. And a mean one nowadays, according to what you just told." He tilted his head to the left and rubbed his chin a while, then he rubbed the back of his head and his neck, rubbing himself the way a man will after a heavy sleep.

"Why do you want me?"

"I didn't figure any of the preachers around home would bury him and if they did, they wouldn't preach him into heaven."

"Well, I'll do that for you, Laster," he said. "Know why?"

I didn't.

"Because I don't believe in that stuff any more and I'll preach him any damn where you want him."

"That's all right," I said, "Bluenose didn't believe in it either. Neither do I."

"Still," Carther said, "it don't hurt to say the words over a man. There's a chance all three of us could be wrong, you know."

"Yes, sir, I've thought of that."

"Like as not I'll even repent again when my time comes. It's hard to go out into the dark with nothing at all to bear you up. When we going to do it?"

"This afternoon over in Milo. I want you to come on with me now."

"You got the grave dug yet?"

"Don't know. I left a fellow to do it, but I don't know if he'll finish."

"Well, the preaching will cost you two dollars; for three dollars I'll bring my boy and he'll handle what digging there is left. I sure hate it about Bluenose. He was over to the rooster fights just last summer. I give him a bird."

"How about a gallon of whiskey instead of the money? I got it in the trunk."

"That's good," Carther said. "Get it now."

I went to get the whiskey and he went back inside. I could hear him yelling for somebody named Luke to get up. In a bit he came out with a strong, stupid-looking boy of about eighteen.

"Here's Luke," he said, jerking his head toward the boy. I handed Carther the whiskey. He held the jug high and looked at it and then uncapped the jug and took a short drink, ignoring Luke's request to pass it around. Carther climbed in the front seat, cradling the jug carefully in his lap.

"Case you don't know, boy, this stuff, along with certain scriptural doubts, is the main reason I am a failed preacher. Preaching is how I knew your daddy. Whiskey is how I got to know Bluenose."

I cranked the car and swung it around in the yard. We started up a rutted wagon trail away from the creek toward the Fever Springs Road.

At the courthouse, I left them in the car. It was nine o'clock, about time for the judge to be in. He was at his desk when I got to the office.

"Good morning, Brant," he said. "When I didn't see you I was afraid this cold weather might have made you sick."

"No, sir, reason I'm late is something come up—a killing."

The old man came forward in his desk chair just a little. "How's that?" he said.

"Bluenose Trogdon's wife shot him off their front porch yesterday. I was passing by on my way home and saw it happen."

The judge looked a little pissed off, but not really concerned, like you might figure a doctor would look when he's lost a patient he didn't expect to lose. "I thought Bluenose was going to change territories."

"I don't reckon he really had a chance to, sir. He was just getting back home himself when I got there. I never got to deliver your message."

"You say you saw it?"

"Well, I saw it from my car. Then I walked up to the house. Bluenose was dead when he hit the ground. Both barrels in the chest. Elmira said she warned him she was going to do it."

The judge didn't say anything.

"She murdered him with clear premeditation, sir." I pulled the calendar from my inside coat pocket and handed it to the judge. "Are you familiar with the Bible verses named on the back of this, sir?"

The judge took the calendar and laid it face down on his desk. Then he took some gold-rimmed glasses from a black case and put them on.

"Eighteen Matthew, the twenty-first and twenty-second verses. I confess my Bible knowledge is not up to that challenge. What passage is it, Brant?"

I told him. He held the calendar like a legal document, left hand at the top, right hand at the bottom, looking it over up and down. Once he turned it over and remarked on the date.

"And these tally marks, here, are for keeping count of something, I take it. What is the significance of this, Brant?"

"To make a long story short, from the time they were married Elmira marked down on that calendar every time Bluenose did something she didn't like. Yesterday, she had it in her hand when she shot him."

"You're saying she allowed him four hundred and ninety sins, then killed him." The judge put the calendar down flat on his desk and smoothed it out with his hands. "That was not exactly the interpretation the Master intended if I take the scripture correctly."

"But it is premeditation, Judge."

"Perhaps," he said, "but there is usually an element of self-defense in these family shootings."

"Not in this one," I said. "There's more. Pride Hatton, the preacher, put her up to it. All the time she's been keeping this count, she's been having a dream about the Blood of the Lamb and angels of vengeance and such like. Then Hatton interpreted the dream for her, told her it was an anointment from the Lord. He convinced her the Lord meant for her to kill Bluenose. She told me that, Judge. I can testify to it. He's a party to it as sure as if he handed her the gun."

"I'd hate to have to try to sell that testimony to a jury, especially coming from you, Brant," the judge said.

"She said she told about the dream in church and that's where he told her it was an anointment. We'll find somebody in that bunch who'll testify about it, too. I'll find them myself, Judge."

"I'll just have the sheriff go out and look into it," the judge said. "Meanwhile you stay clear of Elmira and Hatton and everybody else."

"You'll send Elbert out with warrants for them, won't you, Judge?"

"Plenty of time for that later, if it's called for. A woman with a house full of children isn't going to run off. Nor this preacher for that matter, if he's got any sense."

"Yes, sir, but I saw this man killed with a shotgun, and this woman met him at the door of his house with that gun and her calendar and plenty of malice aforethought. I don't see why you can't send warrants out with the sheriff, at least for her."

"Brant, it's an upsetting thing to see a man killed, any man, much less one you knew. Now trust me in this. It's always best to go slowly in these family matters."

"Yes, sir, I know, but . . ."

"I'll handle it, Brant. Don't be tiresome. I'm sending Elbert out right away. Now you take the day off and try to calm down. I know you're upset."

"Yes, sir. Thank you. I'll see you in the morning."

I left to go take care of the burying. The back-slid preacher and his son and I worked on the whiskey while we waited for a carpenter there in Fever Springs to make us a rough pine coffin. Then we tied the coffin on top of the car and headed for Milo. Back at the courthouse, I knew, the judge would be handling it. He had said he would take care of it and somehow I knew he would.

I have noticed that when a man has been laying with the bottle for years and the juice has really got him, it doesn't take much at any one sitting to get him drunk. Carther was like that. Three or four pulls on the new jug and he was plenty loose, carrying on about what a fine fellow Bluenose was and what all they had done together after Carther fell out of the church. When we pulled under the big tree at the graveyard, Carther was blowing and going on, and there was a little group of men gathered around the Trogdon plot. Ozro was sitting on a pile of dirt and four men were standing in front of him. One of them was my father; another was Mr. Hibbert. The others were two farmers of no consequence except they were on the cemetery committee.

Carther got down out of the car and stumbled back against it, bracing himself by throwing both arms out. He was oiled nicely. "Well, I'll swan," he said, looking at the committee. They looked at him and I saw Mr. Hibbert say something, but we couldn't hear. Carther righted himself after surveying the group for a moment. He produced a small, worn Testament from his hip pocket and headed toward them, stepping vigorously and swinging his free hand in time with his walking, like a man comes across a field when he is about to run you off his property. Luke and I followed him.

"Carther Rooks," my father said. "I thought that was you. I haven't seen you in a long time."

"It is been a sight of years," Carther said. He wiped his face, which was sweating despite the cool air, with the sleeve of his dingy, longjohn shirt. "This here the grave we going to use? It ain't finished yet." Carther leaned out over the grave, swaying dangerously above the hole, and said, "Needs about three more feet. Let my boy have the shovel, Ozro." He addressed my father, Mr. Hibbert and the other men: "Now you fellows don't mind the wait. Luke here will have the grave dug by the time Brant runs and loads up the body. Then we'll get the service under way before you know it."

Luke started to take the shovel from where it had been stuck up in the pile of dirt Ozro had shoveled up, but Mr. Hibbert grabbed it first. "Luke don't have any need of this," Hibbert said, "because this grave is deep as it's ever going. What you don't understand, Carther, is we ain't here to attend Bluenose's funeral. We aim to stop it."

"The man's dead, Bealey," Carther said. "He cain't hurt your dirt. Besides a man has a right to be laid down beside his folks."

"He might have a right if he'd been coming to one of our churches and helping keep the weeds off his folks' graves all these years," Hibbert said. "But he didn't. Bury him down there on the river where he wasted his life."

"It's a hard thing to deny a man a hole in the ground," Carther said. "What the hell, his daddy was a whiskey man. You aim to dig him up, Bealey?"

"I ain't looking for no advice from you, Carther. I'll say this though. You're the right man to handle the service. A drunk preacher to bury a drunk."

Hibbert was standing across the grave from me. He held the shovel like a staff, with his hand just below the blade.

"How about it, Poppa," I said. "Are all y'all agreed with Mr. Bealey?"

"There's four on the committee, son. That's the way we voted."

"I'm sorry to hear that," I said. I walked around the grave to stand in front of Mr. Hibbert.

"Mr. Bealey," I said, "how about you letting Luke have that shovel?"

"What's he need it for?"

"To finish this grave."

"We've done told you our decision. Your own daddy told you how the vote went."

"I know that," I said. "And I'll tell you the same thing I'd tell him if he was holding the shovel. You're an old man and you're standing in the way of something that's going to happen whether you want it to or not. Bluenose is going in the ground beside his daddy, because it's his right. With Bluenose gone, the Trogdons are through. They'll never trouble you again."

Hibbert wouldn't look at me. He did seem very old and tired.

"Now the thing for you to do is to let Luke have that shovel, so we can bury Bluenose and so Carther can preach him into heaven."

"I ain't going to do it," Mr. Hibbert said.

"Yes, sir, you are," I said.

"Brant, you wasn't raised to force your way like this," my father said.

"I wasn't raised with folks getting shot open on their front porches either, Poppa. Now you know I'm right."

I took hold of the neck of the shovel, just below Mr. Hibbert's hand.

"Let go, Mr. Bealey," I said. "Let go and get on back to your store."

"No," the old man said.

"You let go or I'm going to break your arm," I said, reaching the last word just as my voice started shaking. Mr. Hibbert didn't say anything. He just stood there with his hand on the shovel, looking over my shoulder out toward where Bluenose's casket lay on top of the car.

I figured one of the farmers, who were younger men, would step up and call my hand, but after a long silence, one of them said, "It ain't worth fighting with this kind of folks over a dead drunk, Mr. Bealey."

I pulled gently on the shovel and he let his hand fall away. Luke took the shovel and stepped down into the grave. I watched him start to dig and when I turned back around, I saw that my father and the other three men had already reached the road. They started on toward Milo without ever looking back. I left Luke digging and Carther in charge of the jug, and Ozro and I went in the car to fetch the body. Just as we entered the Y, we passed the four cemetery men walking, but none of them looked at us, not even my father. Ozro and I parked in front of his shack and undid the plowline I had used to tie the casket atop the car, and took it inside. Both of us kept our eyes off Bluenose as much as possible while we put him in the casket. Then Ozro got a hammer from the drawer of his desk and some nails and we nailed the lid on. It was hard to lift the loaded casket on top of the car, but we struggled it up there and Ozro stood on the back bumper to hold it in place while I drove slowly back across to the graveyard. What few people there were circulating around the two stores and the post office stopped to watch us pass. I saw my father watching from the window of his store, and Miss Sarahgrace had come out on the steps of the post office. As we passed in front of her, I saw that she was crying, and I thought it was a shame she didn't have Uncle General there to comfort her. It was the one place in the world where he could do some good, comforting her and maybe playing "Blind Mule in Flat Top Mine" at the funeral for us. Yes, I thought, if General were here, that's what I would do, make him play "Blind Mule" for free.

Whiskey Man

By the time Luke finished the grave, Carther had gotten so drunk he was blubbery. He kept going on about all the good times he and Bluenose had had and how Bluenose hadn't ever hurt anybody, while Luke, Ozro and I lowered the casket. We were still working at that when Carther kind of straightened himself out and announced he was starting the service. I let him go. He went to preaching about how there was no high nor low in Jesus and that if the Bible was true, then Bluenose would be in heaven as surely as any preacher. By that time, we were all standing around, having finished with the casket. All day it had been overcast and sunless with the sky the color of old dishwater. Finally a misty rain had started, the kind that is sometimes good to hunt in. Carther was blubbering and preaching hard as he could go, leaving no doubt that Bluenose was bound for heaven. I looked down the road toward Milo and saw my father coming. He came on steadily up the road through the mist, past the big tree and across the graveyard and finally stopped between me and Carther. Carther shut up and looked at him. My father nodded his head toward the grave and Carther opened his Bible.

"Now's the time for the scripture," Carther said. "I always used to close every service with a special scripture back when I was given to preaching regular, and this is the one I picked special for Bluenose. I know this book from cover to cover and this here is ideal for a man that's been turned against like Bluenose has. This is the first eleven verses of the hunnerd and second Psalm.

" 'Hear my prayer, O Lord, and let my cry come unto thee.

" 'Hide not thy face from me in the day when I am in trouble; incline thine ear unto me; in the day when I call answer me speedily.

" 'For my days are consumed like smoke, and my bones are burned as an hearth.

" 'My heart is smitten, and withered like grass; so that I forget to eat my bread.

" 'By reason of the voice of my groaning my bones cleave to my skin.

" 'I am like a pelican of the wilderness; I am like an owl of the desert.

" 'I watch, and am as a sparrow alone upon the house top.

" 'Mine enemies reproach me all the day; and they that are mad against me are sworn against me.

" 'For I have eaten ashes like bread and mingled my drink with weeping.

" 'Because of thine indignation and thy wrath; for thou hast lifted me up, and cast me down.

" 'My days are like a shadow that declineth; and I am withered like grass.' "

"Amen."

"Amen," said my father, and the rest of us, too.

Carther picked up the half-empty jug that was by his right foot and took a drink. He handed it to Luke who drank and passed it to Ozro. After him, it came to me and I drank, without hesitating or looking at my father.

Of course, I knew Poppa wouldn't drink, so I just lowered the jug, holding it by the little circle of glass on its neck. We all stood there looking into the grave at the wet yellow pine of the casket. A few clods of dirt had slipped in and broken on the clean wood. I could hear Carther crying like a woman. He was really sloppy.

My father reached over and took the jug. "This is from the same Psalm that Carther read us," he said. "It's the twenty-third through the twenty-seventh verses."

" 'He weakened my strength in the way; he shortened my days.' " As he recited, he tipped the jug up and began pouring Carther's whiskey down onto Bluenose's casket. Poppa was so solemn that not even Carther protested, although he fairly danced in his despair. We watched as the whiskey washed the dirt from the new yellow lumber, and the whiskey smell rose to us from the grave, rose heavily on the wet, still air.

" 'I said, O my God, take me not away in the midst of my days; thy years are throughout all generations.

" 'Of old hast thou laid the foundation of the earth; and the heavens are the work of thy hands.

" 'They shall perish, but thou shalt endure; yea, all of them shall wax old like a garment; as a vesture shalt thou change them, and they shall be changed.

" 'But thou art the same, and thy years shall have no end.' "

The jug was empty when he finished and he tossed it in, too. It thudded on the lid of the casket but didn't break. "Whether we like it or not, God will judge Bluenose Trogdon like he judges any man and not one whit more stern. His ways are not our ways. The God of vengeance is the God of love. His mercy, which is bigger than the sky, is just as wide for the drunkard as for the saint. And I pray that Bluenose Trogdon finds a home in the arms of God and rocks there forever in the years that have no end. Amen."

"Amen," said Carther and then the rest of us.

"Have them fill it up, son," my father said, and he turned for the second time that day and walked back to his store from the grave of Bluenose Trogdon.

I left, too, by and by, hauling my load of drunks, and much later I realized that I had forgotten to tell them that say what they liked, we had just buried a man who had killed five quail with one shot.

CHAPTER EIGHTEEN

Premeditation and the element of self-defense are important factors in any murder case, Brant, you must appreciate that," the judge said the next morning. He sat at his desk with the air of a man who, after a fine night's sleep, is making short work of the first of many problems he intends to handle that day.

"Yes, sir, I'm aware of that," I said. I felt fuzzy and haggard. It had been late when I had gotten home from taking Carther and Luke back to their house, and when I finally slept, I dreamed of everything I did not want to dream of. "But it seems to me that neither of those things presents a problem in this case."

"I ain't so sure about that," the sheriff said. As usual he was standing between my little worktable and the judge's desk. "Leastways, it looks to me like a clear case of self-defense. The woman said he came in drunk off a long bender—first time he'd been home since that night we chased him—and she had to shoot him to protect herself and the children. The man's a known drunk, been in jail for fighting in Birmingham, wanted for whipping a preacher here. The woman don't let the doors of the church open without she's there, according to her preacher. Whose side is any sane man going to take?"

"Her preacher?" I said. "Was Hatton there when you talked to her?"

"Yeah, he said he'd heard Trogdon threaten her plenty of times."

It is a mistake to think that just because you do not like a man, he must be stupid. Neither Elbert Willis, the sheriff, nor Pride Hatton was stupid. I knew, too, that they must have gotten on well, and that when the sheriff had left, they were both aware of the trade they had made to assure order in the affairs of God and the state of Alabama: Elmira Trogdon had clearly acted to save her life and her children, and Sheriff Elbert Willis could count on support from Pride Hatton's pulpit. As we talked, the judge had turned his chair so that he could look out the window behind his desk. His left elbow rested on the arm of his chair, his chin supported in his hand.

"Your Honor," I said, "self-defense just won't hold up in light of what she told me. She said she had warned him that his string was running out, that she wasn't going to put up with his staying gone any more. She said this, in these words, to me while his body was still warm: She said, 'I told him over and over I'd do it if he didn't quit.' In other words, she shot him for drinking whiskey and that's murder, no matter what the preachers say."

The judge didn't say anything.

"And besides, what about the calendar?" I said. "That shows premeditation over the years. She'd been planning it ever since they were married. Then, this peckerwood preacher tells her to go ahead with it. What the hell does it take to make a case? If they're not guilty, nobody ever will be."

Then the judge said something that let me know I had been had, and I'm sure that's exactly why he said it—to let me know it was no use. He said it very calmly, still looking out the window. "By the way, Brant, what did you do with that calendar?"

"I left it with you, sir, on your desk."

The judge swung slowly around to face me, and said, very evenly, "No, surely you're mistaken. I remember handing it back to you. Perhaps you left it at home or gave it to Elbert."

"He ain't given me no calendar," the sheriff said. "I don't know anything about any calendars in this case."

"I left it with you, sir. In your hands."

"No, of course you didn't," the judge said. "I never neglect things left in my care. But I hardly see how you can ask the district attorney to prosecute this case when you predicate your whole testimony on this theory that she had planned the murder for years, especially when you've lost what is supposed to be the main piece of physical evidence."

The judge never took his eyes off of me and in those eyes was exact knowledge of everything he was doing. He did not try to hide that from me. His eyes said he would never veer from his course nor delude himself about the nature of it. Finally I looked down at my desk to break our contact, and the sheriff spoke up.

"Well, like I said, I ain't heard nothing about a calendar, but I know this. I've seen enough trials to know that no jury in the world will convict a woman with five kids on the testimony of her husband's drinking partner and running mate. And that's just what you are, Laster, his main buddy. Far as I'm concerned, Judge, the county ain't got no case or any call to bother Miz Trogdon any more."

"Yes, thank you for coming in, Elbert," the judge said. "I'll let you know if we need to do anything further. You seem to have covered it pretty well."

The sheriff left us there in our silent knowledge of each other. I had an urge to tell the judge: "All right, I should have known better, did know from the start that you would handle it this way, even if she had shot him in church, as he prayed, in front of the whole congregation." But I didn't even confront him for the theft of my evidence, the calendar, and the judge, in this as in all things, was circumspect, gentlemanly, assured both of himself and of the relative nature of truth.

"Brant, it is a mistake to let yourself get too close to a given case," he said. "Of course, I will take part of the blame for this. I was too lenient, letting you carry on with questionable people when I should have tightened down more." The pipe came out and he worked on it, talking to it as much as to me in that easy way he had, stroking me with his voice, much as I have seen some men gentle a horse by talking to it. "But, perhaps I'm not unlike an overindulgent father in this. I let my high hopes get the better of my judgment." He gave me that winning smile through the cloud of smoke he sent up around his head. Somehow that has remained my central image of him, the handsome, aged face smiling through the fragrance and smoke of his pipe. "But all this is behind us now. Nothing need have changed."

"Sir," I said, "I believe I've read of private citizens swearing out warrants and hiring special prosecutors when they were dissatisfied with the elected officials' handling of a case."

"There are provisions in the code which allow that, under certain circumstances. But I'm sure it's only happened—" there was a faint change in his voice—"in much larger places." Still the smile, still the tinkering with the pipe, but I could sense at work that same intelligence which had foiled me before.

"What if I did that, sir, or tried to?"

"Well, you're a grown man. You must do as you think best." Very shortly, this. "I shouldn't think it would make you very well liked hereabouts."

"If I chose to do that, would you give me a warrant?"

"I'm afraid that's beyond my province entirely," he said. "The granting of warrants, I mean."

"But you control it," I said.

"Really?"

"So you said."

"Did I? Perhaps you're right." I could see it coming, the mind at work ceaselessly on the very relativity of things, the same smile that accompanied praise or rebuttal. "It is a trait of old men that they indulge themselves with exaggerations of their own power. If I indicated that, you must forgive me. Warrants really should be the province of our circuit solicitor, as you surely must know by now."

"But you said he was incompetent to handle it, so you did it by mutual consent. You called him a fool."

"You embarrass me, Brant. I may joke occasionally about some of Earl's shortcomings, but not so unflatteringly as that, I hope."

Again silence. The old man opened a book, began reading. He sat there in his lawyer's suit, pipe ash lying in a fine lace on the black lapels. I watched him until he looked up again and caught me.

"One of the things you must learn in the law, Brant, is to be content with the disposition of things, even if that disposition does not fit some ideal conception you may have. That is the entirety of our profession and what I might call our art—to make the most serviceable arrangement possible under the circumstances that prevail. Come now, drop this. Let's end this strain between us."

I nodded that I would, for it no longer mattered. The judge, as usual, was quite late returning from the noon meal which he always took at home. While he was gone, I stepped down the hall to the district attorney's office. When I opened his door, Earl Gordon looked up at me without affection.

"I'm not here in line with my work," I said. "I'm here as a citizen of this county. I formally request you to swear out a warrant for Elmira Trogdon for shooting her husband. I hereby bring the charge that she committed the crime of murder in the first degree."

He said nothing, watched the lintel above my head.

"Will you do it?" I said after a moment.

The big gray man dropped his eyes to meet mine and still said nothing. I stood there for at least two more minutes. He stared at me in silence until I left and closed the door behind me.

The judge and I worked in a friendly mood until five o'clock. He thought everything was fine between us now and we worked together in a silence as close and friendly as you might find at some family fireside. I found that I felt no anger at all, felt none and could summon up none, not even by reminding myself how the judge had stolen the calendar and lied about the warrant. He had blocked me cleanly and without malice, and I couldn't be mad because none of it had surprised me. I had been forewarned by Bluenose, by the judge himself—forewarned that things must be handled, that the people will get what they want, that life for all of us, for the living, must go on.

When I left, Judge Coxwell gave me a smile and a good evening so cordial that I could tell he was sure I had come across, that this little episode which he had handled so well had knocked the bullshit out of me and that, because I was a bright boy, I had seen how things were. I could tell that the judge felt certain when I left him that day that he had gotten himself a good man, a grown and practical man.

CHAPTER NINETEEN

I left the judge and in the last light of day started the familiar drive home to Milo. The road carried me through country I had hunted with Bluenose and on down to Bluenose's house. Or rather Elmira's house now, the law of Alabama holding that in the absence of children who have attained the majority the widow is sole heir, even if she is, as in this peculiar case, the agent of her own widowhood. Hatton's wagon was drawn up to the porch and I thought of them in there, the preacher and the widow, together in Jesus. Soon they would be together in something more substantial than His name.

Full darkness fell and I drove on without bothering to switch on the headlights. A hundred yards or so above Blake's house, I killed the motor and once again let the car coast to a stop across from her front yard. I worked the latch of the car door very quietly and stepped out on the hard claypan of the road. For some reason, a pure and untainted passion stirred in me. I felt that familiar, rising tightness in my chest, the quick, slivering movement of blood toward the front of my body. I thought of Blake's body under my hands and her hands light in the small of my back. I went around to the rear of the car and quietly raised the lid on the baggage trunk. From the blanket in which it was bedded, I pulled Bluenose's rifle, clean and faintly oily and cold as the night air. I studied the lighted windows. Blake was not to be seen, but I could wait. I propped the rifle on the running board and stood shivering in my shirtsleeves, a patient man. With neither jealousy nor remorse, I thought of Blake and me as we had been in the old times before we ever left Milo. Maybe Elmira had gotten just that kind of purification of memory from what she had done, reclaiming with death her first fine, musky nights with Bluenose from all the drift and debris washed down upon them by the flood of time. Well, if I was joined to Blake by all our years together, I was joined to Elmira, too, had been since that day in the store when I read in her eyes the secret of her dream of the Lamb. Since that day we had been bound together in that old washed-in-the-Blood sister-and-brotherhood of blunted expectation. The signs all pointed to that; no serious student of our literature could miss the signs.

I was shaking harder now from the cold, from the force of memory, from anticipation of my hillbilly solution. I reached over and slammed the car door as hard as I could. Blake came to the window. She brought her hands up around her eyes so she could see into the darkness. She left the window; the door opened. I saw her standing in the block of light, her silhouette stark and familiar. Again I remembered my hands on her, but this time there were other memories, too, other hands. The Dream of Atlanta, the original and true one, descended on me.

"Brant," she called.

I made no response. As she came toward me across the yard, I picked up the rifle.

"Brant, is that you?" Blake said as she reached the edge of the road. She was hugging her arms against the cold.

I stood there, feeling her suspense, holding the Dream of Atlanta whole and complete in my head. I was in the dream and outside it, too, both audience and actor. Blake's voice seemed far away and her words did not matter. I was pulled into the dream, remembering most vividly that part which I had trained myself never to think about, the part which had changed my life.

"I'm sorry about Bluenose," Blake said as she drew near. "Why didn't you come get me . . ."

Her voice trailed off as I raised the rifle, rested it aslant across my stomach.

"I wasn't thinking about you," I said. "Now, I'm thinking about you."

"Why are you doing this, Brant?"

"To let you go," I said. "To be rid of you."

I told her then how I had received the Dream of Atlanta. That secret trip to Atlanta was the one thing I had wanted her never to know about me, but it would not matter for long now. So I told of following her and the blond-haired young man throughout that night, trailing close behind when they left the dance and strolled over to a big house at the edge of the campus. I watched as he fetched the small discreet suitcase from his car, which was parked at the curb in front of the house. I saw him take her up the outside stairs which I, being a college lad myself, knew led to the young man's rooms. I waited for them to reappear and sure enough on the next morning they did. From my hiding place, I saw that Blake looked brave and satisfied and beautiful, and like the blond-haired young man, she was dressed for church on that fine Sunday morning in the early spring in the city of Atlanta in the kingdom of that other South. I let the whole story out in one lump and afterward I felt drained and distanced far beyond shame.

"So that's the blond-haired man you kept going on about. You actually saw him?"

"Yes."

"I had almost forgotten him," she said. "He wasn't a very important person in my life. He wasn't the one I was going to marry. We had had a fight. We didn't see each other for a month or so. I started going out with this other person, the one you saw."

"So to pass the time you screwed him. You screwed him and now you think I could take you back after all that."

"After all what?" she said. "I lived the life you taught me. That's what you can't stand, me living for myself while you crept around in the darkness. You were right all along, Brant. You could not pay the price. Why did it take me so long to give you up?"

"Because I wouldn't let go," I said, "but now I can. I leave you to whoever will have you. I leave you to your Black Belt friend," I shouted. I felt giddy with outrage and ready once more for what I had planned.

Leaning back against the car, I held the rifle vertically in front of me and hugged it to my body. I felt the hammer dig into my belly. The barrel lay rigid against my chest. With my left hand, I guided the end of the barrel inside the V of bone under the point of my chin. I felt the cold circle of metal press into my flesh as I spoke.

"Maybe MacShan Satterfield can take you to the New Year's ball they have down in Montgomery. All the gentry will be there, and the politicians. You'll both love it, I know. Sooner or later, every whore and crook in Alabama winds up in Montgomery."

I tilted the rifle butt away from my body so that the bullet would range cleanly upward and back, range into my mind like some punishing explorer of memory and time. The end of the barrel had warmed to the temperature of my body. The thumb of my right hand was on the hammer, my index finger moved in weary measure toward the trigger. I was filled with an indifference which felt like religion.

Blake lunged against me with surprising force, snatching the rifle barrel aside so that it pointed aimlessly into the sky. Her arms were tight around my neck, and I could feel her tears.

"I love you, Brant," she sobbed. "Why can't that matter?"

"You better get away from me," I said, but she kept holding on. "Please love me again, Brant. Please try."

I got a hand between us, against her chest, and pushed. She stumbled back, falling. The rifle, which had been pinned between us, clattered to the ground. Blake went down on the cold hard clay and huddled there weeping. I rocked my head against the car, shutting my eyes. I was afraid to move, afraid I would find the gun in my hands again, but for another purpose.

"Get away from me before I do what Elmira did," I said.

"That's what you would like, isn't it?" she said, her crying stopped. "You two make a real pair, you and Elmira."

"How many were there, Blake? Just tell me that."

"One was enough for you," she said. "Just one snapped you like a matchstick." She made no effort to rise, but rather hung her head so that her hair fell forward, baring the back of her neck.

"Do what you came for," she said. "Do it now."

"Get up, Blake. Please stop."

"Do it," she said. She reached out and swatted the rifle with her hand. It spun on the ground, striking my foot. "Pick it up, goddammit. Do it if you can."

Blake's neck shone like a target in the night, white and vulnerable. I picked up the rifle, armed myself as I had been armed in the vision of Blake's death. Her voice rang down the long tunnel of my dreams. I took the forearm piece in my left hand and braced the butt of the gun against my hip, so that I could point the weapon steadily as I levered the shells one after another into the chamber. I jerked furiously at the lever, heard the metallic snick-snick-snick of the weapon's action. One after another, the bright copper cartridges spun into the air before me and clattered to the road, landing unspent between Blake and me.

"All that talk," Blake said, "but I knew you couldn't do it. It was no gamble at all." Blake got up and stood for a long time, looking me full in the face. "We were never in any danger, Brant. It's over. Nothing can hurt you now."

The expression on her face betrayed neither compassion nor contempt nor regret. I knew I would see it forever. I took the gun by its barrel, holding the weapon like a baseball bat. I took one quick step to the side to give myself swinging room and threw the gun high and whistling through the darkness. I heard it crash into the forest. I turned back to see Blake walking slowly toward her house, going a little shakily perhaps, in the manner of someone who has been in a fight in which the injury of victory was so little less than the injury of defeat as not to matter. But going for all that, going nonetheless toward the figure which stood in the lighted doorway now.

"Blake, what's happening out there?" Riley King called.

"It's all right, Daddy," she answered, her voice strong.

"Who's that out in the road?" he asked. But she didn't answer. She just kept moving on across the yard, toward the steps, her father, their home.

Then I was back in the car and the car was rolling for home again, down past the church looming skull-like in the darkness, past the graveyard where Bluenose lay in the absolute silence and darkness and time-without-end of that pine box, the smell of the whiskey poured on it already smothered and absorbed by the compact earth. It was not lost on me that over and over that day I had passed the grave of my grandfather, too, and that night when I lay down in the house he had built, there in the room and bed in which I had spent my life, I thought this: "Well, old man, you have revealed yourself at last. I know your secret and my legacy." For I knew as a certainty what none of them had ever guessed through all the years. In dying, my grandfather was simply leaving our high, hard place in the hills for reasons known to him alone, and in that leaving, he had forged our infidels' salvation, which is the denial of expectation, the abandonment of hope. What I had from him at last was the talent for sudden leaving.

CHAPTER TWENTY

I slept well into the morning, claiming sickness when my father
came to wake me for work. When I got out of bed I started
packing straight off. It was almost like packing for college again,
except I would carry no books, for lightness' sake and because I
sought no new knowledge. What knowledge I had would suffice,
perhaps too well. Hadn't Ozro said I was educated beyond my
capacity?

I took the car and went on down to the store, parking it out
front and leaving my suitcase at the foot of the steps. My father
was sitting behind the counter (a sign of age? I can remember
when he always stood) and the store was empty of people and
damn near stripped of merchandise, a circumstance my father
could blame on the fact that Hoover still sat (One of his jokes:
Mr. Hoover took his seat in the White House and told the rest of
the country to have a seat, too.) in the capital. In the President-
elect, at least, his faith was unshaken.

I walked up to the counter. My father sensed what I had come
to say.

"Is there nothing I can do to stop you?"

"No," I said, "it's necessary. There's one thing you can do to
make my journey easier."

"What's that?"

"Ask the judge to arrest Elmira and Hatton. That would give
me a lot of peace of mind."

"I've got no control over the law."

"You could ask him. The judge said he always tries to do what you want."

"It's none of my concern," he said. " 'Render unto Caesar that which is Caesar's and unto the Lord that which is the Lord's.' I am about the Lord's business."

"Yes, Poppa," I said. "I was wrong to ask." I was too near gone to remind him that he hadn't minded meddling with Caesar when it came to getting me Herman Giles's job. Instead I let him block me with that favorite Baptist scripture, the one that lets them disclaim responsibility for anything they don't want to think about. Well, he was an old man and my father, and if I had really wanted Elmira and Hatton punished I could have done it myself. I had had both the instrument and plenty of opportunity. I understood the man my father was, a man who accepted the dispensation of things. It was a wise way to be.

The old man stood up and pulled out that long wallet of his, worn and smooth as a saddle. "Here," he said, "you'll be needing some money." It was two hundred dollars. I took it.

"I appreciate that, but you don't have to."

"What's a man got to spend it on who has but one son," he said. "You going to look for work? I doubt you'll find any."

"I don't know."

"It's not long until Christmas, why don't you make the winter here? Strike out in the spring, when the weather breaks. Maybe you can wander around and wind up in Tuscaloosa in time for school to start. The judge would still get you in law school, I know. I'll get the money together."

"No, Poppa," I said. "Forget the law school. For good." How futile, I thought, to spend three years stumbling around through all those books to find out what I have discovered in as many months, to invest three years of your time and money and be so deep into it that you must pretend to believe that there is a law and that it matters, to try to convince yourself that Bluenose was a country fool who did not have it figured out.

The old man didn't say anything. He put his billfold up.

"Poppa," I said, "why are you so good to me when you can't approve of what I do?"

"In the book of Proverbs it says: 'For whom the Lord loveth he correcteth; even as a father the son in whom he delighteth.' That's what the Bible says, Brant, and you have been all my delight from the day you were born." Then he was crying, an odd snuffling sound, and he was greatly ashamed. "I'm sorry," he said when he got hold of himself. "You've got to understand. I am getting old. It's hard to take things, to adjust. The way you've been living has nearly killed me, Brant."

"Yes, sir, I know that. That's one reason I'm leaving."

"It doesn't make any difference where you go, son. If you keep on the way you're going, wherever you are, I have to live with the knowledge that if you die, you will go to hell. All my delight in hell."

"I'll try, Poppa," I said, "I'll think about things." I didn't mean that, but I had to try to give him something. I had thought about it all, though, permanently.

The old man had managed to quit crying. He smiled. "Maybe I'm a little selfish, too, Brant. You know in the Old Testament Samuel was condemned of God for the sins of his sons. God said, 'For I have told him that I will judge his house forever for the iniquity which he knoweth; because his sons made themselves vile, and he restraineth them not.'"

"Surely you don't believe God would blame you for my sins?"

"It's in the Book," he said, "and I believe the Book from cover to cover, from the first word to the last."

What of the wide and random mercy he had prayed for Bluenose? I might have asked. But I did not, for he was my father and knew his Bible. Instead I said, "Well, I best be on my way, Poppa."

The old man reached across the counter behind which he had spent his life, across which he had quoted from cover to cover the book he believed, and hugged me for a long time. I felt his tears on my neck. I could never get away from the Bible. A passage floated up in my memory about someone falling on a friend's neck and weeping.

Soon enough I took to the Jasper road, not looking down the road toward Fever Springs where I was to have been trained to perform in my turn what the judge did so well, toward my grandfather's grave and Bluenose's, most certainly not looking toward the high school where the students were in session before the teacher whose secrets I knew and could not forget. I left the car at the store and walked down the long incline of the land toward the river, crossing the bridge from which Elroy Laster, no bridge-builder, had fallen into history, and the river flowed over rock and sand and over the beaten-copper machine in which no mash would ever boil again.

Deep South Books

The University of Alabama Press
